D1740264

WITHDRAWN
FOR SALE

AD 02909371

The Dried-Up Man

The Dried-Up Man

Norman Russell

ROBERT HALE · LONDON

© Norman Russell 1999
First published in Great Britain 1999

ISBN 0 7090 6376 8

Robert Hale Limited
Clerkenwell House
Clerkenwell Green
London EC1R 0HT

The right of Norman Russell to be identified as
author of this work has been asserted by him
in accordance with the Copyright, Designs and
Patents Act 1988.

2 4 6 8 10 9 7 5 3 1

LINCOLNSHIRE
COUNTY COUNCIL

Typeset in North Wales by
Derek Doyle & Associates, Mold, Flintshire.
Printed in Great Britain by
St Edmundsbury Press, Bury St Edmunds, Suffolk.
Bound by WBC Book Manufacturers Limited, Bridgend.

Contents

1
The Dried-Up Man

Old Thomas Eves and young Jacob Bagnall, grave-diggers, pushed their barrow along the shale path at the bottom of the long, narrow garden. The grey bulk of Dovercourt House rose up rather menacingly from the top lawn to their left. On their right were some weathered iron railings and, in a moment or two, they would reach the creaking gate that led directly into the old parish churchyard. It was good of Mr Dovercourt to let them take this short cut through his grounds, rather than drag along the length of Ashgate Street.

It was a mild day, with a weak sun shining, though there were some ragged grey clouds moving uneasily across the sky. Young Bagnall carefully edged the barrow through the narrow gate leading from Mr Dovercourt's garden into the long grass of the town's burial-place. The graves of the humble seemed to be as self-effacing as their occupants had been in life, hiding demurely in the overgrown vegetation. Here and there, though, the proud but crumbling monuments of the well-to-do rose up to sing the virtues of the brewer and draper, the railway director and the banker.

It was towards one of these tombs that the older man led the younger. It consisted of a wide plinth of weathered stone upon which stood a rectangular stone chest. It was chipped and neglected, and covered in yellow lichen. A lengthy and unintelligible Latin inscription had been cut deep into the covering slab of granite.

'Now then, young Jacob, the first thing we'll have to do is clear away all this grass and these weeds from the end of the tomb – this end here, where you see the urn carved – and then dig down about a foot. That'll bring us to the vault-slab. Then we'll have to prise out that panel with the urn carved on it, because the vault-slab goes under it for about a foot. It's a kind of stone lock, so to speak.'

'I reckon you must have opened this tomb before then, Tom?'

Thomas Eves sat down on the end of the tomb. He was a firm believer in the adage 'steady is as steady does'. There was no need to be hurrying all the time. Jacob Bagnall sat down in the grass.

'Aye. Years ago it were. I've always been in this line of business, Jacob. All my life, and all over Warwickshire.'

For a moment he became lost in thought, unconsciously shading a vivid purple birthmark that crossed his brow. It had embarrassed him in his youth, and in moments of absence he would still try to hide it.

'You see all that writing, Jacob? That's Latin, that is. No one knows what it means except the gentry, and sometimes I wonder about *them*! But if you look carefully you'll see the name in plain English: "Josiah Anderson". And then you'll see some letters at the end: "MDCCCLXIV". That means 1864 – twenty-eight years ago. That's when we put Mr Anderson in here.'

'What kind of a man was he, Tom, this Mr Anderson?'

'Josiah? Well, he was a stern man, as they all were in them days, but very generous to poor folk. He'd lost a leg in his youth at one of them German battles.'

Old Tom's mild grey eyes looked over Jacob's head towards the west. In his mind's eye he saw a great Tudor mansion set in a swathe of mature woodland. He added, 'He was the grandfather of Mr Loxley Anderson over at King's Leyland. It's a cousin of Mr

Loxley Anderson who's being buried here on Thursday. One of the Greggs. Cousins, they are.'

Young Jacob looked with interest at the carved letters on the weather-worn tomb. Somehow the jumble of real names brought the unknown lettering to life for him. He was new to the town, a cautious immigrant from far-off Coventry. He was just twenty years old. Thomas Eves was well past seventy.

As they sat there, the clouds parted, and the big yellow April sun bathed the monument in radiant light. Thomas Eves laughed.

'That's a sign, that is, Jacob! Come on, let's get to work.'

It took them half an hour to clear the grass and weeds and to dig down to the stone slab that covered the entrance to the vault. That would be lifted on Wednesday evening. But they would have to free its inner edge now.

'Now be careful with this end panel, Jacob. There's no mortar holding it, just these two lead brackets. Just pull them back with the claw of your hammer – that's right. Now then, let's both pull it forward. That's it – pull – now lower it gently down.'

They lowered the heavy panel to the freshly dug earth and rested for a moment. There were festoons of cobwebs draped on the inner surface of the stone.

'That's just about it, Jacob, I think. We'll drag the panel round to the back and lay it flat on the grass. Then we'll tidy up a bit and go to the Royal William. It's thirsty work, this digging.'

Young Jacob Bagnall peered into the opened rectangular box of stone. He knew that they were always hollow, because he'd done this kind of work before at Holy Trinity church in Coventry. Little boys always thought there were bodies in these flat box tombs, but there never were.

Except for this one.

Jacob Bagnall's voice came small and high, as though from a distance.

'Tom, there's a shoe in there. With a foot in it. A mildewed shoe. There's . . . there's a dried-up man . . . Tom!'

*

During the course of the following morning Detective Inspector Jackson of the Warwickshire Constabulary received a telegram from the police sergeant at Ashgate St Lawrence. It was terse and to the point.

Dried body of man found in tomb here. Suspect murder –
Joseph Bramble, sergeant.

'. . . Which means,' said Inspector Jackson, turning to a morose, elderly man in a baize apron, 'that someone has illegally concealed a death. It happens, you know. Or maybe this Sergeant Bramble is right, and it's a murder. He must have had a reason for calling it that. Murder, I mean. Have you heard of him, Alf?'

Alf leaned heavily on the brush he was holding and sighed. He had work to do.

'Sergeant Bramble, did you say? No, Mr Jackson, I've not heard of him. But then, it's halfway across the county, is Ashgate. It's one of those tight little towns where everyone knows everything and says nothing. Not like Warwick at all.'

'There's nowhere like Warwick, Alf,' said Inspector Jackson.

Alf sighed and shook his head, and shuffled out of the office before Jackson could ask him anything else. It wasn't his place to be answering questions.

At first sight, Inspector Jackson gave the impression of being a comfortable countryman nearing middle age, a big man whose taste for amply cut brown serge suits made him seem stout. He had, at different times in the past, been mistaken for a kindly seed merchant by a man who went to Dartmoor, and for the steward of a smallish estate approaching retirement by a man who went to the gallows. But the bright keen eyes in the round, clean-shaven face revealed a waiting alertness that could be very dangerous to the unwary.

10

A dried body ... he would have to go over to Ashgate St Lawrence and investigate this case himself. Strange, that although he had known the name of Ashgate since childhood, life or fate had never called him there until that moment. Ashgate had always been ignored by railways, so he'd have to book a seat on the coach leaving the Volunteer at Thornton Heath. He'd need to summon the police surgeon, Dr Venner, which would mean securing a seat in the coach for him as well.

So Ashgate was 'a close little town', according to Alf. Better send Sergeant Bottomley ahead to spy out the land. He sat a horse well when he was sober, and would be there in under an hour. Bottomley had a famous knack of worming things out of unwilling people.

Jackson glanced up at the big railway clock above the fire grate in his back office. Half past nine. He left the room and walked down a brown-painted passage to the charge room, where an elderly constable with old-fashioned white whiskers sat at a table poring over a stack of charge sheets.

'Where's Detective Sergeant Bottomley, Constable?'

'I don't know, sir. He was around earlier. Alf was talking to him. Sergeant Cobbold's just stepped out to see Mr Rogers at the livery stable. He'll be back in a trice.'

'I'll have to get the midday coach to Ashgate, Constable. Tell Sergeant Cobbold that I may be away for a few days. And so will Sergeant Bottomley, if I can find him.'

'Very good, sir.'

Jackson returned to his office and picked up his brown beaver hat from the table. They could manage here without detectives for a few days. He'd need to telegraph a reply to this Sergeant Bramble, and walk up to Dr Venner's house. Then he'd go home and pack a few things. The Ashgate coach left the Volunteer at half-past eleven. He stepped out into the yard behind the police station.

Alf, the civilian helper, was fairly busy swilling down the cobbles.

11

'Where's Sergeant Bottomley, Alf?' asked Jackson.

'He's in the Crown, Inspector. Been there for the last hour.'

'Well, go and get him out of the Crown. Tell him to come here and see me. There's a steady canter in store for him. That should blow the fumes away.'

A steep walk uphill from the police station took Jackson very quickly into the green countryside. The cobbled road changed into an unmade winding track, along which several hundred years' worth of sparse buildings had sinuously arranged themselves into a hamlet. The April sun flooded the quiet enclave of Meadow Cross Lane, as the winding track from Warwick was called, bathing the cottage walls in golden light.

Jackson stooped a little as he entered the dim living-room of his cottage, as though the room were too small for a man of his girth. He would have to throw a few things together in a valise. This case would mean staying away from home for a few days.

As he made for the winding stair, he heard a light knock at the back door from the orchard. Then the latch was lifted and a woman stood, silhouetted for a moment, in the strong light.

'Sarah!' Was it right to sound so obviously pleased to see her? Especially today, of all days. . . .

She would always knock like that, though if he was out she would come in to do little favours about the house or leave him some fresh produce from her garden. The woman closed the door softly and walked into the room. She seemed to bring a kind of ordered calm with her.

'Hello, Saul,' she said, smiling rather timidly. 'I saw you coming up the lane. Is anything amiss?'

'It's a case, Sarah. I've got to go over to Ashgate St Lawrence with Dr Venner. It'll mean staying there for a few days. I'm just going to pack a few things. The coach leaves the Volunteer in an hour's time.'

'It must be something special to take you away from Warwick for so long.'

Jackson smiled to himself. She was always curious about his work, and always too shy to ask him outright. Well, why shouldn't she ask? Sarah Brown was his next-door neighbour, a widow of thirty-eight. He was a widower of forty-six. Why shouldn't she ask?

He watched her as she stood on his hearth. Was it right to feel so strongly that she belonged there?

'It *is* rather special, Sarah, and as you're so interested, I'll tell you. They've found a dead body in a tomb over at Ashgate St Lawrence. The local sergeant there thinks it's murder.'

Sarah Brown made a brief pout of distaste.

'A dead body in a tomb, Saul? What else did he expect to find, for goodness sake? But if you're going to be away, you'd better let me have a look at what's in your cold-larder. A body in a tomb? Whatever next?'

She moved in her quiet way into the next room. She had always had the gift of unobtrusive friendship and neighbourliness. She'll be casting an expert eye over what's in stock, he thought. What to leave and what to take in charge. There were times when he'd been away for days, and returned to curdled milk and rancid butter.

During the last few months he had begun to be mildly and illogically surprised to find that she was not a permanent presence in his house. Was it right to feel that way? Sarah Brown had her own life to live in Brown's Croft, the dun-coloured ancient cottage behind the orchard further up Meadow Cross Lane.

A wheezing grandfather clock in the corner suddenly asserted itself and chimed ten-thirty. Jackson went upstairs to his bedroom, and packed a small leather valise with some necessities. He glanced out of the latticed window into the lane. It was deserted, except for a few hens running in purposeful phalanx towards some domestic goal. He could hear Sarah moving quietly in the kitchen below. The longer she stays, thought Jackson, the more this house feels like a home again.

When he came downstairs, Sarah had emerged from the larder carrying a covered dish, which she put on the table. There was time to spare, as it was only fifteen minutes' walk to Thornton Heath. He sat down in his old cane-backed chair near the fire, and Sarah took a seat opposite him, something she did when she wanted to talk. She smoothed her white linen apron and placed her hands in her lap. She spoke to Jackson, but directed her eyes to the fitful flames of the small fire burning in the grate.

'I'm sorry it had to be today, of all days, Saul. I saw you setting out for Coldeaton just as the sun came up. At least, you've been able to go there first.'

'Yes, I've been there to Coldeaton Churchyard. Imagine, Sarah, today, of all days!'

It was Tuesday, 5 April 1892. In just under a fortnight it would be Easter. Fifteen years ago, Easter was past by 5 April.

He recalled the dew-soaked grass of the quiet graveyard as he had seen it that very morning, and the grave where he had placed his swathe of spring flowers, as he had done on this April day every year since 1877.

What was the lurking sensation that always accompanied him there, and came back with him to this cottage? Was it a still unassuaged anger that so much could have been lost through an overturned lamp? No . . . it was more like resentment, but of what, he was never quite certain.

The small fire burning in the cast-iron grate lit up the broad, confident initials cast into the iron back-plate:

E.M. 1676 J.M.

He sometimes wondered about E.M. and J.M. Husband and wife, he supposed, who had sat beside this grate in 1676 and the years following. This cottage had not belonged to his own family, the Jacksons, though he had lived here – what? – oh, twelve years.

Sarah had fallen silent, her thoughts evidently elsewhere. Jackson found himself glancing almost against his will at the stout, gnarled black beam that served as a mantelpiece. In the centre of it stood a sepia photograph of a woman in her late twenties, with an oval face framed by curling black hair. The rather formal set of the mouth contrasted with the large frank eyes looking out of the portrait with fearless confidence. The photographer had vignetted the image, so that the woman seemed to float in a detached sepia world that was all her own. A little china jar beside the picture contained some early daffodils.

The flowers had been placed there by Sarah Brown. It was she who had gently persuaded him to fetch the picture from the back of a cupboard beneath the winding staircase and set it up in its ebony frame here on the mantel. That had been in mid-March.

'It's time you let her come back, Saul,' she had said. It was hard to argue with her, but his eyes almost always avoided the photograph. He could never look at it without seeing a wall of raging flame, and hearing the wicked crackle of burning timbers. He could smell the spring perfume of the daffodils, but above them he was assailed by the phantom sickening stench of fire. That was why he had hidden the picture away in a cupboard all those years ago.

Charlotte Anne Jackson, aged twenty-nine.
Also Rebecca, daughter of the above, aged two years and three months.

Sarah stirred, like someone opening her eyes after prayer. Jackson hauled his watch out of its pocket in his waistcoat. He was proud of his grand array of gold watch chain with its pendulous medals. He flicked open the case and looked at the enamelled dial. Ten to eleven.

'It's time I was gone, Sarah,' he said. 'Dr Venner's having

himself driven over to the Volunteer, so I expect he's there now. I don't know when I'll be back, but if you want to get in touch with me they'll let you know my whereabouts in Barrack Street.'

It was only after he had set out along the lane in the direction of Thornton Heath and the Volunteer Inn that he asked himself why Sarah Brown should want to get in touch with him at all. It had been his suggestion, not hers. Her quiet smile had told him nothing. She had left the cottage by the orchard door, and when she had passed out of sight through the trees he suddenly realized that it was she who must have swept his dead hearth that morning, and kindled the welcoming fire.

The main thoroughfare of Ashgate St Lawrence sloped gently down from a bridge over the River Best, where it was known as Bridge Rise, to a wide and level road called, in the mysterious manner of such places, Sheep Pen Street.

At one o'clock in the afternoon of the day following Jacob Bagnall's discovery of the Dried-Up Man, the street was filled with the sudden noise and commotion occasioned by the arrival of the public coach at the Royal William Hotel. One or two regulars alighted, but there were some strangers too.

A strongly made man in a brown serge suit clambered down from the roof. He wore his coat open, revealing an ample waistcoat sporting a heavy watch chain hung with various seals and medals.

He was joined by a man who had travelled more comfortably inside the coach, a distinguished-looking man nearing sixty, clad in an immaculately cut black suit over which he wore a black frock coat. His silk hat reflected the weak sun of the hazy day.

A figure detached itself from a knot of onlookers and came towards the two passengers. Only his helmet and heavy serge uniform told them that this man was a policeman. He looked dusty and burnt out, and walked with a pronounced limp. He held his left arm close to his body as though it was paralysed.

'I expect you'll be Detective Inspector Jackson? I'm Joseph Bramble, sir.'

Bramble spoke with a sort of gasping wheeze, which caused Jackson's companion to look at him with keen interest.

'Sergeant Bramble, this gentleman is Dr Venner, the police surgeon. You did very well to telegraph me. You've no inspector here, I take it?'

'No, sir. Just me, and two constables. One of them's not much more than a lad, and we've never had detectives here, nor the need for them.'

Well beyond sixty, Jackson thought, looking at the weather-bronzed face with its old-fashioned fringe of white beard. Bramble, he suspected, was the old type of parish constable promoted to station-rank. He looked overdue for retirement.

'We'll just leave our things with the porter, Sergeant, and then we'd like to go straight away to the graveyard. I take it you've been able to leave the remains undisturbed?'

'That's right, sir. . . .'

Bramble's voice suddenly ground to a halt, and he was obliged to breathe deeply before he could continue.

'Pardon me, sir. The words don't always come easy. It's this chest. . . . Yes, sir, I've had the tomb guarded ever since the grave-diggers opened it. I've got a few trusted men there, and one of my two constables. Dr Phillips is there too.'

'Dr Phillips?'

'Yes, sir. He's chairman of the parish council.'

The old policeman's worn face suddenly creased into an attractively sardonic smile.

'You'll always find Dr Phillips hovering around when there's something important going on. Always very anxious to help, he is! So when you're ready, gentlemen, I'll take you down to the churchyard.'

A few minutes later the three men were walking up Sheep Pen Street, passing the thriving shops of the area. Jackson was acutely conscious of the curious eyes of passers-by fixed on them.

'This dried-up body – what makes you think it's murder? You didn't tell me much in your telegraph message, Sergeant Bramble.'

The limping policeman threw Jackson a guarded glance with a hint of amusement behind it. This sick man, Jackson thought, would very much improve on greater acquaintance.

'Old Thomas Eves – he's the grave-digger – let me take a proper look inside. Not that he had any choice in the matter, sir, but civility counts, I think. I saw something there that made me sure it was an old murder come to light.'

'What did you see?' asked the inspector patiently.

'Perhaps it'd be as well not to say, sir. I'll leave you to see it, and you can make up your own mind. Without prejudice, as they say.'

They climbed the gentle slope where the street changed its name and became Bridge Rise. There were a few fine eighteenth-century houses with red-brick fronts and white-sashed windows interspersed with small workshops.

At the top of Bridge Rise, they turned abruptly left into Ashgate Street and Sergeant Bramble passed through a gate into the garden of a tall, gaunt three-storeyed house. It was a curious place, Jackson thought. There were no painted signs to suggest that any business was carried out there, but there was an unmis-takable suggestion of trade. To the right of the double-fronted house all was genteel and opulently residential. But that part to the left of the front door – it had all the appearance of a work-place.

Jackson laid his hand on Bramble's arm.

'What is that place?' he asked.

'That's Dovercourt House, sir. Mr James Dovercourt lives there. They're a very old family, and that's a very old house by all accounts.'

'And we're going through this Mr Dovercourt's grounds?'

'Yes, sir. Mr Dovercourt very kindly lets folk cut through his gardens to get to the graveyard. It's a terrible long way round to the front if you keep going down Ashgate Street.'

'And Mr Dovercourt is in trade, isn't he?' asked Jackson shrewdly. Sergeant Bramble paused and looked up at the house before he replied. His whole manner seemed to be that of a man who had been personally affronted.

'Yes, Inspector,' he said gruffly. 'He's in trade. He's a merchant, and so was his father before him, and his grandfather before that. He carries on his business from the house, where he lives with his wife and son. And his daughter.'

In one of the little shops bordering Bridge Rise, a workman stood at a bench, carefully using a hand-punch and mallet to print lettering on to small crosses fashioned from tin. A cardboard box beside him held a large quantity of these little crosses, each with four arms of equal length.

So engrossed was the metalworker in his task that he was hardly conscious of the workshop door opening. It was the sudden onrush of weak sunlight across the shaded bench that caused him to pause in his task.

'Good day, Mrs Needham. What can I do for you?'

His voice was measured and quiet, holding great authority. He was a tall, well-knit man with dark bright eyes and curling black hair. It was generally agreed in Ashgate that he was not a man to be trifled with. He seemed to be one with his surroundings, with the cool whitewashed walls of the shop, with the scythes, plough-blades, lengths of railing and other signs of his craft, with the smell of metal filings and oil.

Mrs Needham was a young woman in her twenties, a gossipy contrast to the taciturn metalworker. He was conscious of her covertly appraising eyes, but had no time for such frivolities, however innocent. There was too much to be done.

Mrs Needham carried a basket full of provisions, which told him that she had made a detour from the main shopping area of

Sheep Pen Street to call on him. She put her basket down on a clear corner of the bench.

'How much are you asking for the ban-devils, Mr Littlechild?'

'Just a penny. They don't take much making.'

He drew an oil-smeared hand across his brow and stood back from the bench. He had to admit that Mrs Needham was a pretty young woman, even if she talked more than she should. Womenfolk, he thought, should guard their tongues.

'Did you see the policeman passing just before?' she asked.

'I did.'

'A detective, he is, from Warwick. He'll do his best, I expect, but he'll never know the truth of it, will he? Or about old Parson.'

Mr Littlechild did not make a direct reply, but his visitor heard him mutter to himself, 'Old Parson? Staunch and true, both him and me', and in the way of closed communities she knew what he meant.

Mrs Needham took a penny from her purse and laid it on the bench. She picked up a little tin cross from the box and looked at it. Stamped into the thin metal were the words:

CHRISTE VICTOR OPN

'Pretty little things, aren't they, Matthew? What do those words mean?'

'I don't know, Mrs Needham: I'm not skilled to read. But they've always been used at times like these. Get your man to nail it up on the lintel of your door.'

Mrs Needham put the cross carefully in her basket and covered it with a cloth. She lingered for a while near the door. Matthew was nice, but he never wanted to chat about things.

'It was young Jacob Bagnall who saw the rope around its neck. He told old Tom, and that's how the town heard about it.'

Matthew Littlechild gave a snort of disgust. He half turned back to his bench.

'Sometimes, Mrs Needham, the town can hear too much. But it's out in the open now, and the old sprites will be roused, which is why I started making the ban-devils straight away. It's not for the pennies, God knows. Well, I've work to do. There'll be more pennies than that one on the bench before the day's out.'

In the churchyard, canvas screens had been thrown up around Josiah Anderson's tomb. If it was to deter ghoulish onlookers, thought Jackson, it would be a forlorn attempt. Even as they crossed the dew-soaked grass he was conscious of staring faces among the trees.

When they reached the screened area, they were greeted by an earnest-looking man in a dark overcoat and bowler hat who came towards them with all the signs of eager impatience. Sergeant Bramble was able to introduce Jackson and Venner by name before the man in the overcoat burst into speech.

'Dr Ambrose Phillips, gentlemen, chairman of the parish council. That elderly man there is Thomas Eves, who is the senior grave-digger. The young man standing beside him is Jacob Bagnall. It was Bagnall who saw the . . . the body when he and Eves opened the tomb.'

Inspector Jackson nodded absently at the earnest doctor, but his eyes were occupied with other matters. He looked thoughtfully at the old grave-digger, and then back the way they had come towards the towering bulk of Dovercourt House, the glass of its rear windows a blaze of reflected sunlight. He turned and gazed up the very large sloping churchyard, letting his glance rest only briefly on the taller monuments until his eyes came to dwell on the enormous brown sandstone church with its pediment and columned front, and its pillared cupola. It rose proud and confident above the graves and above the houses on that side of the country town.

'What is that house, Doctor, just near to the church? It has a garden running down to the edge of the burial-ground.'

21

Dr Phillips seemed disconcerted. He had expected the detective and the police surgeon to take an immediate interest in the tomb and its grisly contents. Instead, the detective seemed to be captivated by the scenery, and the surgeon was content to stand patiently beside him. Dr Phillips was not used to police work.

'Well, that's St Lawrence's Rectory,' said Phillips. 'But aren't you going to examine the tomb?'

'Indeed we are, Dr Phillips,' Jackson replied. He was a genial man by nature, and he treated Phillips to a sudden, unexpected smile. 'I can understand you feeling impatient, sir, but we have our own peculiar ways of doing things. The police, I mean.'

He drew the elderly police sergeant aside and spoke to him privately for a minute or two. Sergeant Bramble saluted, and then limped off across the churchyard. Jackson's eyes followed him thoughtfully for a moment. Then he gave his attention once more to the eager Dr Ambrose Phillips.

'Doctor, I'd take it kindly if you'd stay with us while we conduct our investigation. Dr Venner, I think we're ready now.'

Dr Phillips looked pleased; Dr Venner smiled drily to himself. He and Jackson had worked on many cases together, and the surgeon was used to the inspector's ways. He turned to the little knot of men standing within the privacy of the canvas awnings.

'I will need two men who are not too squeamish to help remove this body from the monument. There will be nothing for you to fear. Who will help me?'

The young grave-digger, Jacob Bagnall, stepped forward, and another, older, man in a rusty black suit.

'You'd best let me help, sir,' he said. 'I'm the local undertaker. I've brought a coffin with me in the cart, and my premises in St Lawrence Square are at your disposal.'

'Excellent!' said Venner. 'Now, try to slide him out with as little disturbance as possible. You, young man – Jacob Bagnall, isn't it? – can you clamber inside? See if you can locate the shoulders, and then begin to slide the poor fellow out. Undertaker, you receive the body as Bagnall pushes it out.'

Dr Venner spoke in a virtual whisper, but his exact words had reached the watchers in the trees within a minute. They could see nothing but the occasional bobbing head above the canvas.

Everyone worked in tense silence except for little gasps of exertion and the scraping of boots on sandstone. Gradually the gruesome contents of the tomb-chest were slid out into the waiting arms of the undertaker.

Twisted and shrunk, like a gnarled tree blasted by lightning, the Dried-Up Man was brought into the light. It was not a skeleton, but a gaunt, mummified body, contorted and shrivelled, and clothed in a tattered suit of black. Jackson could see the mildew on the stained leather shoes.

The head and shoulders were almost covered by swathes of black cobweb.

The grave-diggers and their helpers stood in total silence for a moment, and then the undertaker pulled the cobwebs aside.

Cries of horror burst from the knot of helpers as the face and neck of the body were revealed. Venner looked up sharply, and the men tried to master what was evidently some kind of superstitious terror. It took only a minute for the watchers in the trees to hear that Jacob Bagnall's assertion was true: the body had a noose of rope around its neck.

Within seconds the watchers had dispersed. Matthew Littlechild was due for a not unexpected influx of customers.

Dr Venner had removed his hat and frock coat, and had knelt down beside the open coffin into which the undertaker and the grave-digger had placed the retrieved body. Venner grasped the edge of the coffin with his left hand and leaned so far into it that he was in some danger of joining its contents. He peered intently at the neck, and at the rope noose tied around it.

'Phillips,' he said, 'I take it that you're a doctor of medicine –

not one of these university people? Good. Take a look at the neck. What do you think?'

While Dr Phillips examined the neck, Dr Venner completed a preliminary examination of the rest of the body. He looked particularly at the hands. Then he straightened up and addressed the little group of helpers.

'I'd like to thank you men for all your help and your excellent work. I need now to confer with Inspector Jackson and Dr Phillips in private. Would you please withdraw out of earshot.'

There was a little move of disappointment from the observers, but nevertheless they did as Dr Venner asked. He sat down on an adjacent tomb and began to speak. From time to time he glanced at Dr Phillips for confirmation of what he was saying.

'The body now lying here dead, Jackson,' Venner began, 'is that of a man aged from thirty to thirty-five. The body, when placed in this monument, had not been embalmed, but the open aspect and the circulation of air has resulted in the body's being mummified.

'There is a noose of rope around the neck, tied loosely, and with what I believe is called a hangman's knot, but it is merely a ritual or cosmetic object. The cause of death was most certainly not hanging or any form of strangulation.' He glanced at Dr Phillips, who nodded a vigorous assent.

'A preliminary examination has not revealed the cause of death. I am not a detective' – Jackson smiled. How often he had heard Dr Venner preface his remarks with that phrase! – 'I am not a detective, but I would point out that the man might have died from natural causes and have been placed here secretly by relatives. On the other hand he might have been done to death by some means not immediately apparent. I will conduct a post-mortem, and I hope that you, Dr Phillips, will associate yourself with me in that enterprise?'

Jackson noted with wry amusement that Dr Phillips seemed overwhelmed by Venner's graciousness.

'You are too good, Dr Venner. I shall be honoured to assist you.

24

The undertaker – Mr Raymond, his name is – has placed his premises at our disposal. When you are ready, we'll call him back to close the coffin and convey the body to St Lawrence Square. That's just beyond the rectory up the hill over there.'

Inspector Jackson had remained silent until Venner had finished his verbal report. Now he asked him, 'How long has the body been in the tomb-chest?'

'Well, it's been hidden there for about four years. Three-and-a-half to four years. And of course, as you may have noticed, it is clad in the dress of a clergyman. I am not a detective, but I would point out that he might have been dressed as a clergyman in order to mislead.'

Venner saw the beginning of a familiar amused, pitying smile from Jackson, and hastily added, 'Of course, he may really have been a clergyman. Probably was. He was certainly a gentleman. The condition of his hands shows that.'

Jackson seemed to have lost interest in the proceedings. He stood motionless, staring upwards across the burial-ground at the distant rectory. Venner, who had resumed his frock coat and silk hat, moved out from behind the screens and sought out Mr Raymond, the undertaker. The time had come to close the coffin and convey the body to the funeral parlour.

Jackson recalled himself to the present.

'Dr Phillips,' he said, 'what was the name of that grave-digger? The older man, I mean. You did tell me, but it's slipped my memory.'

'Eves, Inspector. Thomas Eves.'

'Eves, yes. That was it. I'd take it kindly, Dr Phillips, if you'd go on ahead with the cortège. I want a brief word with Dr Venner. I shan't keep him long.'

Soon the sombre procession was making its way out of the churchyard and up the hill to the other side of the town. Jackson and Venner walked out of earshot into the tangled grass beyond Josiah Anderson's tomb.

'Well, now, Doctor, what do you think those cries of horror

25

meant? When they saw the noose around the neck? That's what Sergeant Bramble said he'd been shown. "An old murder come to light", as he put it.'

'I don't know what it meant, Jackson, but it was definitely seeing the noose that made them cry out, not just the sight of the body. There's something there that needs an explanation.'

'And here's another question, Dr Venner: why did you use the words "ritual object" to describe the rope?'

'Do you know, Jackson, I don't really know what made me say that. Wait a moment, though . . . yes! It reminded me of an archaeological dig I was invited to once in Wiltshire. There was a skeleton we found with some curious implements which they couldn't identify, so they said they were "ritual objects".'

Inspector Jackson frowned. The police surgeon allowed his longing glance to follow the grim procession toiling up towards the higher town. I know what he wants, Jackson thought. His fingers are itching to hold a scalpel!

'I don't much like this business, Dr Venner. There's something very sinister here. There are some very unpleasant questions that need to be asked, such as, how does one introduce the uncoffined body of a Church of England clergyman into a tomb in the middle of a vast town churchyard without somebody noticing? And if somebody did notice, why didn't they say anything? I'm going to stay here until some of my questions are answered.'

'Why did you ask Phillips for the name of the old grave-digger? Poor fellow, he has one of those port-wine-stain birth-marks. Nothing can be done about them, you know.'

A guarded look came into Jackson's habitually frank eyes.

'I fancy I met him once, years ago, Doctor. Thomas Eves. That was his name. It's nothing to do with this present business.'

Jackson saw Venner narrow his eyes against the sun and look back in the direction of the town. His next question showed that his thoughts had returned to police matters.

'Will you make use of this local man – Sergeant Bramble? Or

do you think he might be a jealous guardian of local secrets? You and I have encountered that kind of thing before.'

'He may well be, Doctor. For instance, he didn't like me suggesting that his Mr Dovercourt was "in trade". There's some kind of local loyalty there, I expect. In any case, I've had a brief word with Bramble, and he's more than content to leave this business to me. It's a detective matter. Sergeant Bottomley and I will manage very nicely in our own way.'

'Bottomley? That great shambling fellow? I didn't know he was here!'

'Oh, yes, Doctor, Sergeant Bottomley's here all right. I wouldn't be surprised if he hasn't been watching us all the time. Shambling or not, he has a knack of making himself practically invisible.'

Venner delicately flicked a speck of dust from his trouser leg.

'Sergeant Bramble's not in good health,' he said. 'In my opinion he shouldn't be working. That wheezing and gasping – it's emphysema. And I rather suspect he's had a slight stroke without realizing it. People do, you know.'

The surgeon glanced longingly in the direction taken by the macabre procession. It was time, thought Jackson, to let him get busy with his knives.

'What I intend to do now, Dr Venner, is call on the rector, on the off-chance that he's at home. Perhaps when you've finished with the Dried-Up Man, you'll call to see me at the rectory?'

Jackson watched the jaunty Venner as he hurried after the procession. The fact of death made little impression upon either of them. It was bound up with their daily work. But the means of death – that was a different matter. That twisted, stiff thing in tattered clerical dress could only have died in some vile fashion at the hands of someone who was mad or wicked. Or perhaps both. There was devilry in the air.

Had the sunlight reflected from the rear windows of Dovercourt House been weaker, Inspector Jackson might have glimpsed the slender form of Mr James Dovercourt's 17-year-old daughter, Deirdre, standing in the casement of one of the rooms, looking pensively out on to the churchyard.

2

'The Ungodly Bend
Their Bow'

'Extraordinary! I can't recall anything so peculiarly dreadful in twenty-five years of practice.'

Dr Venner made no reply until he and Dr Phillips had refastened their shirt cuffs and resumed their frock coats. It had been an interesting post-mortem, offering a few technical difficulties, but the results had been very satisfying.

'When you've been a police surgeon for as many years as I have, Phillips, you are not surprised at anything! But it *is* curious, I grant you.'

Venner, fastidious to the point of fussiness, peered into a mirror and adjusted the lie of a pearl-headed pin in his cravat. When it sat against the grey silk to his satisfaction, he packed away his instruments in his Gladstone bag. The two men left the room, and Venner locked the door behind him.

The undertaker was waiting expectantly in the front office of his funeral parlour.

'Thank you, Mr Raymond for the excellent arrangements. Let me leave this key with you. There's nothing else I can do here. I'd be better employed back at Warwick.'

'Are you able to draw any conclusions from your examination, Doctor?'

'Yes indeed, Mr Raymond.' Venner smiled at the man's attempt to fish for information. Only natural, in the circumstances. 'Unfortunately, Dr Phillips and I must keep the matter to ourselves until Inspector Jackson has been informed. Early tomorrow I'll send up a closed hearse from the Warwick police mortuary to collect the remains.'

The two doctors left the funeral parlour and crossed St Lawrence Square. A short flight of steps with a wrought-iron lamp above them led directly into the rectory garden. They passed over a rather ragged lawn bordered by tall beech trees and came out on to a terrace at the back of the rectory. The house, like the enormous church rising beside it, was an eighteenth-century building.

They crossed the terrace, but there were no signs of life at the back of the house.

'We'll go round to the front, Dr Venner,' said Phillips. 'Mr Goodheart is used to people cutting through his grounds to get into Old Town.'

'An apt name for a rector, I think,' said Venner, as they skirted the side of the house.

'Yes, indeed. The Reverend Harry Goodheart. Not *Henry*; he was christened Harry. I wonder what he'll make of your Inspector Jackson?'

Dr Venner smiled. 'For that matter, Doctor, I wonder what my Inspector Jackson will make of *him*? After all, this . . . this . . . abomination has been brought to light in your Mr Goodheart's churchyard.'

Inspector Jackson allowed the exuberant words of the Reverend Harry Goodheart to flow around him, giving occasional signs that some parts of the rector's description of life in his ancient parish had reached his ears. Mr Goodheart's study was a long room lit by three windows. Jackson stood at the right-hand window, sipping a cup of tea. He had half turned to face into the room, but his gaze was directed to the scene outside. The lingering light of the April afternoon flooded the extensive graveyard falling away from the front garden of the rectory. Across the expanse of tombs he could see Dovercourt House brooding on its crag-like eminence.

When Dr Venner had left him to hurry after the dismal procession to the undertaker's, he had lingered in the sunlit graveyard. It had been unusually quiet, as by some form of common consent the people of Ashgate St Lawrence had kept away from the place.

It had been different early that morning at Coldeaton. The swirling mist had not risen, and the short, sheep-nibbled grass had shone with beads of dew. Here at Ashgate, in this vast hollow cemetery, the grass was longer, and the sun glinted here and there on objects half hidden in the tangled growth.

He had stooped down and parted the grass at his feet to reveal a row of three small tin crosses arranged in a line and surrounded by an outline of straw plaited in the shape of a hollow fish. He had picked up one of the crosses and peered at the letters that had been stamped into it:

CHRISTE VICTOR OPN

A sudden chill of dread had clutched at him. It was as though a subtle voice emanating from those objects in the grass was speaking to him of some ancient knowledge known only to the folk of this town and shared with long-gone generations who had not known the rectory, or Dovercourt House, or indeed this old burial-place. Instead, they had visited a wide sunken valley with a rise to the east and another to the west. What was this place?

The mood had passed almost immediately, but a movement of something, or someone, on the periphery of his vision had caused him to glance up towards the right, where what was evidently St Lawrence Square lay high on its plateau above the town. A tall, athletic figure in black, a purposeful man with a wide-brimmed hat, appeared between the tall beech trees for a moment before disappearing from view. That man was talking to him now.

'Not that I'd call myself a scholar, Mr Jackson. If there's a gospel to preach, then preach it! If there's a life to live, then live it! So I get out a lot, and see a good many people. Try one of these. You're not eating, man!'

Jackson put down his cup and saucer on the wide window sill and bit into a buttered tea-cake that the rector had handed him on a small white china plate. He looked round the room, which was lined with shelves containing hundreds of books, arranged in the kind of untidy rows that spoke to Jackson of constant use. A man's view on his claim to scholarship, he mused, was a relative thing. Perhaps the rector preferred to see himself as an athlete. There were many photographs of rugby fifteens and cricket elevens adorning the walls. In all of them Goodheart's burly six-feet-four frame could be seen towering above other athletic men.

'No scholar, sir? That's a pity, because I was going to ask you to help me with a curious little mystery.'

Jackson smiled as his host readily rose to the bait.

'A mystery? Well now, Inspector, maybe I know a little bit about rather a lot of things, so what's your mystery? Have you drunk your tea? There's more there, in the big pot on the tray. Good, that's it. Now, what's your mystery?'

'Mr Goodheart, sir, as I walked through the churchyard to call here this afternoon on the off chance that you would be at home, I came across some little tin crosses half-hidden in the grass. They had some letters stamped on them, and were lying in a girdle of plaited straw shaped like a fish.'

The rector shifted uneasily in his chair and stared for a moment at the leaping flames in the grate. His fine honest eyes looked troubled. If I wait in patience, Jackson thought, he will want to share the burden of the mystery.

'The letters that you have seen on those little crosses, Jackson,' said Harry Goodheart at last, 'are *Christe Victor OPN*. Those are Latin words. The three single letters stand for *ora pro nobis*, and the whole thing translates: "O Christ, Victor, Pray For Us".'

'And why should these little talismans be so much in evidence in Ashgate St Lawrence, sir?'

For reply the rector strode to one of his bookshelves and returned with a massive tome bound in faded calf. Many dusty book marks protruded from the top edge. Harry Goodheart opened the book at one of the markers and began to read:

' "In some country districts tokens known as 'ban-devils' are still made and displayed whenever popular feeling senses a return of one of the pagan pantheon. They are buried near the walls of houses containing a fireplace, or are placed in grass or near running water. In Warwickshire and Oxfordshire they are nailed to the lintels of doors. Their use has persisted for centuries in areas where there were Hanging Groves of Odin in pre-Christian times. The specific charm here is the tin cross with its plea for protection to Christ as the victor over the pagan gods: *Christe Victor OPN*. Peasants often believe that these ancient deities, transformed to demons, are still worshipped by covens of devotees. Such superstitions deserve more than the condescending patronage of the enlightened, as they sometimes point to true abuses sanctioned under the varying names of antique magic".'

The rector closed the book.

'From Norton's *Superstitions of Old Britain*, written in 1774. There, Mr Jackson, is the explanation of your little tin crosses.'

Harry Goodheart rose from his chair and put the volume back on to the shelves. He crossed the room and stood gazing from the centre window at the vast churchyard below. He motioned silently to Jackson, who joined him.

'In ancient times, Mr Jackson, that graveyard was a Hanging Grove. In the caverns beneath the vaults of my church, I have seen evidence of ancient burials with ropes around the skeletal necks of the sacrifices. Do you know anything about the god Odin?'

'Nothing, sir.'

'He was the chief of the gods, the son of a frost giant called Bor.

33

His mother, Besstla, was a giantess. The river here, the Best, takes its name from her.'

Inspector Jackson withdrew his gaze from the scene lying before him in the quiet sunlight. He felt strangely disturbed.

'But surely, sir,' he asked, 'these things are not true?'

'True? Maybe not for us, Inspector. But perhaps they're true for others. Odin lived in a place called Asgard, and it is that place which gives the town of Ashgate its name. The whole area – the whole community of people – is imbued with the spirit of this ancient deity.'

'And do you think that this Odin still has secret followers?'

'I don't know. All that I've told you is from the old Icelandic chronicles. But I have seen those ancient victims of sacrifice. Maybe there are more recent ones. Odin demanded human sacrifice, which was achieved by hanging victims from trees in groves such as that one out there. I sometimes think—'

The rector stopped speaking as the sound of voices in the hall told him that further visitors had arrived. Jackson saw how the dark shadow disappeared from his host's face as the door opened. The rector sprang from his chair.

'Ah!' boomed Harry Goodheart. 'Dr Phillips, my able and devoted chairman of the parish council! And you, sir, will be Dr Venner. We've not met before. How are you? Tea's in, as you see. Please help yourself. Sit down somewhere. Mr Jackson, do you want me to go? I'll go if you like.'

'Why, no, Rector. Certainly not, sir! All this business has happened on your patch, as we say in the police, so you're to be in on it all! Now, Dr Venner, what have you and Dr Phillips got to tell us?'

Would Venner realize that Jackson needed this instantly like-able clergyman to be privy to their councils? Yes, his sharp glance showed that he understood. Jackson pulled an upright chair forward from the wall and sat near the window. Dr Venner began to speak in his measured, rather pedantic manner.

'Dr Phillips and I have examined the remains of the man found in the tomb. We confirm that his age was between thirty and thirty-five years, and that he has been dead for some four years. He was in general terms a healthy man, though he might have suffered with his teeth. At one time he must have sustained a fracture of the left wrist, but this had healed many years before his death.'

Venner glanced at his new disciple, Dr Phillips, who nodded his assent. The police surgeon continued, pleasurably assured of an entranced audience.

'He was wearing a black clerical suit, with white shirt and white tie in the older fashion for clergyman, black stockings, and black leather shoes. There was no sign of tearing or penetration of these outer garments.'

Dr Venner paused, and darted a dramatic glance at Jackson. For goodness sake, thought Jackson, why doesn't he just get on with it?

'On removing the outer garments, we found the body to be clothed in cotton combinations. This garment had been penetrated by an object, and on removing part of the garment with scissors, we were able to see the sawn-off shaft of an arrow sticking up from the lower part of the victim's back. We employed surgical techniques to remove this piece of arrow from the body, and can confirm that it was an ordinary arrow, such as is sold for use with the popular archery-sets that one may purchase for use in domestic gardens.

'The arrow must have been fired with great force,' he concluded. 'It had lodged itself between the third and fourth vertebrae.'

The four men sat in silence for a while, almost as though they were paying tribute to the dead man. The rector's clock ticked away merrily on the mantelpiece. The afternoon sun drifted lazily through the three windows.

The silence was broken by the strong but quiet voice of the Reverend Harry Goodheart.

' "For lo, the ungodly bend their bow, and make ready their arrows within the quiver, that they may privily shoot at them which are true of heart". Psalm eleven, verse two. I'm not given much to quoting verses, gentlemen, but that's what has happened here.'

The rector caught Jackson's keen glance and dropped his eyes. For a while he seemed to sink deep into his chair as though to hide from the banalities of evil.

'So it's murder, then,' said Jackson, 'murder most foul. And there was no damage to the outer clothing?'

'None,' said Venner. 'Which means, Jackson, that whatever clothes he was wearing were removed by his murderers, who then dressed him in fresh clothing. I think—' He stopped and frowned. The idea he wanted to express would not form itself properly in his mind. Inspector Jackson interposed.

'Let us suppose, Doctor, that the man was running – running away from something. He is pursued by someone who does not want others to hear the report of a firearm, or someone who picked up a bow and arrow that happened to be lying on the ground. Our man is running away . . . "The ungodly bend their bow" and fire. He falls. They wish to conceal their crime. They remove his outer clothing, and saw through the arrow-shaft. They dress him in a new suit of clothes. Where do they get it from? It must have happened in his own house, or in the house of a fellow-clergyman. Or— And why should they want to conceal their crime in that way when in the end they conceal it by hiding it in a tomb? What better way of disposing of a body than to entomb it in a churchyard?'

Inspector Jackson stood up, caught Venner's eye, and motioned almost imperceptibly towards the study door. Venner acted admirably on cue.

'Well, Jackson,' he said, 'I can do nothing more here. I've arranged for the remains to be conveyed to Warwick tomorrow. My man Gates has come over with the carriage, so that I can get home this evening. I'll call on you at Barrack Street with a full report when I'm ready. Come on, Phillips. I'm sure that Jackson here will want to chat with the rector about various matters. Rector, thank you for your hospitality. Perhaps we shall meet again on a less sombre occasion.'

In a few moments, Jackson heard the front door of the rectory closed after the departing doctors. He resumed his seat near the window. Harry Goodheart's honest face bore a strangely irresolute expression. This man, thought Jackson, is a stranger to deceit. He doesn't know how to dissimulate. He feels diminished by the burden of secret knowledge.

'Rector,' he said, 'when you quoted from the Psalms just now you mentioned "them that are true of heart". Do you know for certain that the dead man in the tomb was "true of heart"?'

He recalled the brief glimpse of this man returning to his house earlier that day. He had worn a distinctive wide-brimmed hat, which Jackson had seen thrown carelessly on the hall table when he had been admitted to the house earlier. By the time he had seen the rector returning, the body of the Dried-Up Man had been received into Mr Raymond's parlour. He must have persuaded the undertaker to show him the remains as soon as they had arrived.

When the rector did not reply, Jackson added gently, almost coaxingly, 'Do you, in fact, know who the dead man was?'

When the rector finally found his voice it seemed to be tinged with shame, as though he despised the knowledge that he had not as yet revealed. He looked at the fire as he spoke.

'*Everybody* knows who he is – except for Phillips, who only came to practise here two years ago. I had heard of your gruesome discovery before you came up here from Old Town, and I was in Mr Raymond's house when the cortège arrived. When the doctors retired to prepare themselves for the post-mortem, I asked Mr Raymond to let me see the body.'

Harry Goodheart seemed disinclined to say any more. He

37

clasped his hands together and sat gazing at the leaping flames, lost in recollection.

'And *did* you, sir? See the body, I mean.'

'Yes. The cruel hand of time had left its ravages, but I recognized him immediately. I met him more than once at meetings of the Evangelical Evidence Society in London before ever I came to this place.'

Jackson asked quietly, 'And who was he, sir?'

'He was the Reverend Samuel Wheeler, MA, former curate of this parish. He disappeared in very peculiar circumstances in 1888, and it was assumed by many that he had taken refuge in Florence.'

Jackson had produced a notebook in which he rapidly scribbled a few sentences with a lead pencil. He closed the book with a snap. He could feel the flush of anger reddening his cheeks. His voice betrayed the same sentiment.

'When you viewed the remains of the Reverend Samuel Wheeler, MA, did you notice, sir, that he appeared to have been hanged? Did you see the rope around his neck? And did that not suggest certain things to you?'

The rector went very pale. He nodded, but made no reply.

'Well, Mr Goodheart, you've told me everything and you've told me nothing, as we say in our part of the shire. I'm grateful for the facts, for the name and the identity. But you've not told me what I need to know. And I think I know why.'

'What do you mean, Inspector?'

'Well you see, sir, in our line of business – the police, I mean – we get to know things, and to store things, so that on future occasions we can make connections. So I can tell you about the Reverend Neil Green, missing from Birmingham since 1885, or Canon Sylvester of Lichfield, wanted for embezzlement since 1880. We remember these things. Any police officer here in the middle of England could reel off a whole list of missing clergymen in our patch. But I've never heard of the Reverend Samuel Wheeler, MA, aged 35, missing since 1888 and presumed to have gone to Florence. So I imagine I'm about to come up against one of those conspiracies of silence that clerical folk seem so very keen on.'

The Reverend Harry Goodheart turned his troubled face to Jackson. It showed no sign of anger, only a kind of anguished understanding. This man, thought Jackson, will never rise to high office in the church. He hasn't the craft.

'Mr Jackson, I stand rebuked by your candour. I will tell you at once all that I know about the Reverend Samuel Wheeler.'

The rector rose from his chair and stood in front of the fire. He squared his shoulders, and with his immense height and air of restless energy he seemed to dwarf everything in the room.

'Wheeler was a curate here at St Lawrence's for about a year before his sudden disappearance. It was before I came to this parish from my previous living in Northumberland. Samuel Wheeler was originally, I believe, from Exeter, but studied for the ministry at Oxford. He was, by all accounts, an interesting man with pronounced pastoral gifts, and an interest in the new theories of Darwin and people of that sort. He was, in fact, an amateur geologist of considerable repute.'

With a characteristic dart at the bookshelves Goodheart began rummaging through a motley collection of pamphlet boxes piled in a dark area of shelving near the floor.

'If you'll bear with me a moment, Inspector, I've got— Ah! Yes! Here we are. This was a sort of journal kept by the previous churchwarden, and there's a lot here about parish personalities in previous years.'

Mr Goodheart picked up some yellowing sheets from one of the boxes and resumed his seat. He put on a pair of gold-rimmed spectacles.

'Here we are. Wheeler came to St Lawrence's as a curate in January, 1887. It was his first appointment after his ordination to the diaconate. He never received priest's orders. He was well liked, and received many invitations to visit. It says here that he

39

was very popular with young ladies, whose spiritual characters he was always anxious to form.'

In spite of himself, Mr Goodheart smiled. Then his face grew grave once more, and he laid the papers aside. He made a great business of taking off his spectacles. Inspector Jackson waited patiently.

'In February 1888, a parishioner intimated privately that Mr Wheeler was too interested in his young daughter, aged thirteen. The father made no overt allegations, but stated firmly that the curate's attentions to the child were totally unacceptable. The father, it seems, had mentioned the matter to other gentlemen in the parish and in the wider district.

'Mr Wheeler solemnly denied any impropriety, but soon afterwards the child in question suffered an attack of brain fever. Her father had chastised her for some misdemeanour, and, though seemingly none the worse for that, on the following day, she fell into a feverish trance. Meanwhile Mr Wheeler had disappeared from the parish. It was from that time that word got round about his having left England to reside at Florence.'

Mr Goodheart stopped, and there was a heavy silence. Both men could hear the merry clock on the mantelpiece ticking away the minutes. Jackson had been writing rapidly in his notebook. Now he stopped, and addressed his host.

'He did not go to Florence, Rector. Instead, in some place unknown, he fled from a person wielding a bow and arrow who shot him in the back and killed him. A noose or halter was placed about his neck. He was murdered! I need hardly tell you that you must reveal the names of the father and daughter involved.'

'Yes, of course. All this happened before ever I set foot in the parish, so I am only telling you what I myself have been told. It will be for you, Inspector, to verify the value of this information. The man involved was Mr James Dovercourt, of Dovercourt House. The child was his daughter, Deirdre, who is now seventeen.'

*

The public bar of the Royal William, a sort of alcoholic fairyland of cut glass, silvered mirrors, clinking glasses and marble-topped tables, was fully furnished in the evenings with townsmen and women who desired to escape from the drab boredom of oil-lit cottages. All was gaslight and laughter, so all could be friends together, even big boozy Herbert, the red-faced man with the open purse who had come over on horseback early that morning. He told very funny jokes in a droll, quietly cheerful style that raised many people's spirits.

There was a burst of laughter at the end of one of his more risqué tales, and a man in the bar placed a pint tankard of ale on the table in front of him.

'Well, thank you very much, friend, I'll not say no. So what's all this about a stuffed man in the churchyard?'

His florid face was suffused with a combination of drink and curiosity.

'Not stuffed, Herbert,' said the man who had given him a pint, 'he were dried up, like a prune.'

'Dried up? Did you hear about the water-closet that dried up at the banquet? There were these three toffs—'

Five minutes later there was another gale of laughter and another complimentary pint of beer. The coarse-looking man smiled very boozily at one of the ladies present.

'And who was this dried-up prune? I bet he'd had a plum job when he was alive. Who was he?'

'One of old Parson Woodward's failures!' someone cried.

There was an uncertain laugh from the company, and the man behind the bar banged a tankard down sharply on the counter.

'I think that's enough about that, folks,' he said.

'I should think so!' said the beery voice of the stranger. 'It's a grave matter to talk about. Now here's something you may not know. There were three lighthouse-keepers one winter's night—'

41

By nine o'clock that night the air had thickened with tobacco smoke, and the general crescendo of conversation had put paid to any more stories from Herbert. Someone had commandeered a badly tuned piano, and was playing an endless mechanical composition evidently designed not to be listened to. No one noticed Inspector Jackson when he slipped into the bar and ordered a pint of mild. He carried it carefully through the throng and sat down beside the coarse-faced storyteller.

'Well, Sergeant Bottomley,' said Jackson, 'it's as I thought. It's like getting blood out of a stone. Everybody's very nice and helpful, but nothing's volunteered. How have you got on?'

Sergeant Bottomley stared fixedly at Jackson for a moment as though he could not recognize him. Then he shook himself rather like a terrier emerging from a pond.

'Hey? I've been in here, on and off, for most of the day. When I wasn't here, I was walking round the town, chatting to people. I've got the lie of the land, so to speak.'

Jackson sipped his beer thoughtfully, and then glanced with mock distaste at his sergeant.

'You'll get locked up one of these days. You're too fond of the bottle. Were you in the churchyard when we brought out the body?'

Herbert Bottomley grinned lopsidedly, and threw back the contents of a gin glass that had stood before him on the table.

'Yes, sir, I was there, but you didn't see me. Neither did anyone else, though I saw *them*. Dandy Jim was playing to the gallery for all he was worth.'

He suddenly assumed an incredibly educated tenor voice. ' "Dr Phillips, would you care to associate yourself with this here exhibition? Exhumation?" Yes, sir, I was there all right.'

Jackson laughed. 'You impudent man! What'll you have?' he asked.

'A measure of gin would be very welcome, sir. Thanks very much.'

'Now then,' said Jackson, when he returned from the bar, 'here's what I want you to do. There's high and there's low in this town. Find out what you can about the Reverend Samuel Wheeler, MA. He's the subject of this case.'

'The Dried-Up Man?'

'The Dried-Up Man. Find out about him. And anything else that a pint of bitter or a tot of rum can reveal.'

'Did Dandy Jim offer any suggestions?'

'He did. He suggested it might have been natural causes, and that the Dried-Up Man had been buried secretly by his relatives. "Dressed as a clergyman to deceive" was another of his notions. Mind you, he admitted that he wasn't a detective.'

A strange, strangled hoot of mirth came from somewhere inside the detective sergeant's deep chest. He threw back the measure of gin and put the glass steadily down on the table.

'Did Mrs Brown come in to see you off this morning, sir?' he asked.

'Mrs Brown? Yes, Sergeant, as a matter of fact she did. Why do you ask?'

'Don't you like her? She likes *you*, from what I hear. Esther – the wife, you know – met her the other day in Stratford Market. She was saying how clever you are. "Mr Jackson this, Mr Jackson that". I can't think why you don't like her.'

He looked at his superior officer with a kind of impish trucu-lence.

'What are you talking about, Sergeant? I *do* like her. Let's get back to the business in hand. I *do* like her.'

Sergeant Bottomley felt in his pocket and produced a battered cheroot, which he lit successfully at the second attempt. He puffed away almost absent-mindedly for a while, gazing glassily at his superior officer as though not entirely convinced that he was really there.

'Here's a name for you, sir. Parson Woodward.'

'Who's Parson Woodward?'

'I don't know, sir. But I tell a joke, see, and while they're laughing I ask a question. And that was the answer I got.'

Jackson finished his tankard of mild and wiped his mouth on a spotted handkerchief. Sergeant Bottomley looked critically at the butt of his cheroot, which had gone out. He dropped it into the dregs of Jackson's beer.

Inspector Jackson got up. His eyes gleamed with evident satisfaction.

'Parson Woodward, hey? Well done, Sergeant. I'll see you in the morning. I'm off on a little visit.'

'Where're you going, sir? It's gone ten o'clock.'

'I'm going to call on my favourite informant, and turn the screw a bit harder. There's something he hasn't told me yet, and it can't wait.'

'Mr Goodheart,' said Jackson, 'in all your account this afternoon of the Reverend Samuel Wheeler and his doings, you never once mentioned the name of his rector, who, I presume, was your predecessor. Would he, sir, have been known as Parson Woodward?'

Strange, thought Jackson, how a simple question could reveal another man's secret cross. He had walked up from the Royal William through dark lanes lit by a few winking lamps, back to the rectory, simply to ask that question.

The rector gave a long, weary sigh. It was as if, Jackson thought, he carried a burden not of his own making. And he noticed the terseness in Goodheart's normally cheerful voice when he replied.

'Yes, Mr Jackson. Parson Woodward. He was my predecessor here at St Lawrence's. He was an antiquarian of great note, and keenly interested in those things I told you about today.'

'And this Parson Woodward, can you tell me where he is now?'

'Upon my word, Mr Jackson, I've no idea where he is. We Anglican clergy, at any rate most of us, enjoy the freehold of our livings. We can move wherever the spirit urges us to go. So I don't

44

know where Woodward is now. After the disappearance of his curate he experienced certain diffculties, and decided to pursue his vocation elsewhere. The Archdeacon of Warwick will probably know where he went. Do you think it necessary to see him?'

'Well, Rector, you saw the late Mr Wheeler seemingly offered as a sacrifice to Odin. Wheeler was Mr Woodward's curate: I'd just like to make quite certain which god it was that Mr Woodward served.'

3

The Ghosts of Dovercourt

Inspector Jackson could hear the hectoring voice shouting at someone unseen. 'When I tell you to assemble an order, I expect you to do it properly. . . . Can't you read? Can't you check a simple list of items to make sure everything's there?'

Another voice, faintly suppliant, attempted a reply, evidently without success. A door banged shut, then another, nearer to where Jackson stood on the 'works' side of Dovercourt House.

He had been right about that. There was no trade sign outside the house, but in this bare-boarded passageway smelling of carbolic, Jackson recognized a place where business was carried on.

Another door banged and then from the end of the dim passage a tall man appeared, red-faced through recent anger. He sported a pugnacious black beard that spread over his chest and compensated for his sparse locks of black hair, arranged carefully across his balding pate. He favoured a black morning suit, so that the only relief from this impression of energetic gloom came from the glitter of the lenses in his gold-rimmed pince-nez.

'Mr Jackson? Dovercourt. James Dovercourt.'

The inspector winced as the big man shook hands.

'Come in here. I'm sorry that you had to wait in the works

passage. Why can't a simple process be carried out correctly? Where's the difficulty in putting fifteen bottles into a crate? Come into my office!'

James Dovercourt's office was a plain, neat room, filled with pale sunlight from a window high in the outer wall. The big man in black flung himself on to a chair behind a desk covered in ledgers and papers. There was a curious smell in the air, faintly acrid. Spices? No – chemicals.

Dovercourt frowned, and bit his lower lip, apparently in vexation. His voice was naturally loud and, when he spoke, Jackson wondered whether his words would carry to the other rooms of the house and their occupants.

'Is it true? About the man found in the churchyard? I knew you'd come here today. You've been closeted with Harry Goodheart, who probably prattled to you about things best forgotten. Dr Phillips was with you at the exhumation, or whatever you detectives call it, so I'm the only person of note in Ashgate left for you to see. So it's true, then?'

Jackson appreciated that this man could effortlessly intimidate others, but that he was making no attempt to do so at that moment. It was part of his nature to throw other people into the shade, but there was a certain sensitivity around the mouth, an almost hidden tremor of the lips, which suggested that Dovercourt was something more complex that a mere bully.

'It is true, sir. The body has been identified as that of the late Reverend Samuel Wheeler, aged thirty-five, at one time curate of this parish. I have proof positive that Mr Wheeler was murdered, and his body hidden secretly in the tomb-chest above Mr Josiah Anderson's vault.'

Dovercourt visibly paled. He held his hands together in a strange, supplicatory fashion, as though wishing to fend off the reality of the news.

'Let me say at once that I'm sorry to hear this, Inspector. Sorry and shocked.'

The merchant smoothed his thin black hair with the fingers of his left hand. He picked up a cardboard label and looked at it without seeing it. He glanced round the office at the glass carboys of acid in their straw coats, and at the few open crates standing amongst wood shavings.

'Yes. Sorry and shocked. They said he'd fled to Florence. I had reason to dislike Mr Wheeler. Very good reason. I expect you made Goodheart tell you the whole story, so you know what I'm talking about. But murder him? No. Not that.'

Dovercourt rose from his chair and crossed to the empty fire-place of the office. He ran his finger along the mantelpiece and gave a low growl of annoyance.

'Aniline,' he muttered. 'Why did the stupid clot bring that in here? I won't have it in the place. It turns everything blue.'

Jackson watched him. What was lurking in this powerful man's mind? He'd know soon enough. His lips were dry. When he'd moistened them, he'd speak.

'How . . . how did he die?'

'I'm afraid I'm not at liberty to say, sir. But there was a hangman's noose around his neck.'

'Ah! That!' Dovercourt sat down again at his desk. Jackson saw that the merchant's nervousness had been dissipated, to be replaced by a kind of impatient anger.

'A noose. So that fool Bagnall was right. A blabbing fool, feeding the fires of superstition. I suppose the rector added his measure of fatuities. Did he tell you all about Odin? And the groves? And the talismans? Well, did he?'

'Yes, sir.'

'Did he tell you about the sacrifices, and the charms, and all the other odious dunderheaded superstitions and retrograde grown-up fairy-tales?'

'Why, yes, Mr Dovercourt. I think the rector felt obliged to tell me all about those things. I don't suppose he believed them, though.'

'Oh, don't you? I tell you, Jackson, the folk in this town are pagans! The Christian religion passed them by in the olden times. Fortunately, there are just a few beacons of sanity scattered around the district. Ambrose Phillips is one of them. You've met him? Yes, of course you have. I'm another, and so is my son, Lionel. He's a graduate in chemistry from King's College, London. A scientist. It's the likes of him who'll drive away all this nonsense in the end.'

'So Mr Goodheart doesn't qualify as one of your beacons of sanity, sir?'

'What? No, I'm not saying that. You've seen what kind of a man he is yourself. It's just that he's one of the . . . one of the fraternity, if you like, open hearts and closed minds! Church and State. Well, Inspector, things can change. Knowledge is power! Why should position and privilege depend on rotten parchments, land deeds, and induction to benefices?'

The angry merchant seemed to recollect himself. He rose abruptly and opened the door, motioning to Jackson to follow him. They crossed the bare-boarded passage and went through an old warped door adorned with linen-fold panels.

The room they entered was panelled in drab fumed oak, and sparsely furnished in the style of the previous century. There was an old iron fireplace in which, so Jackson thought, no fire was ever lit. In the centre of the room was a small round table with a couple of straight-backed chairs beside it. Dovercourt sat down, and motioned Jackson to do likewise.

Facing him on the inner wall beside the fireplace, Jackson saw an oval portrait of a dark-haired, frowning man in a short wig. Dovercourt followed his glance and shifted uneasily in his chair.

'That, Jackson, is a portrait of one of my ancestors, Amos Dovercourt. This is the Haunted Room, the focus of all these gods, ghosts and bogies, and Amos there is the family ghost. I'll say no more about him, because I'm heartily sick of the subject.'

He was lost in thought for a moment. It was very quiet in the

Haunted Room, and Jackson could hear the distant ticking of a clock, and the occasional creak of old woodwork in dim corners. When he finally spoke, Dovercourt's voice was less strident and more confiding.

'Mr Jackson, I'm going to tell you the whole story of the Reverend Samuel Wheeler and my daughter. This unpleasant room is bound up with that story, which is why I've brought you here. It's a dark, dismal hole, and my wife and I are going to knock it through into the drawing-room.'

It was certainly a melancholy place, Jackson thought, a room that was walked through hurriedly and with aversion, unused, unloved. At that time of morning the sun was absent from the rear of the house, and the air in the room was dull. From the window you could see the grass and tombs of the burial-ground.

'Five years ago, Jackson, in January 1887, Samuel Wheeler came to this parish as curate. He had been in secular employment before his ordination. He was in deacon's orders. Had he lived, he would no doubt have gone on to the priesthood.'

Dovercourt paused and looked speculatively at Jackson. He removed his pince-nez and polished them vigorously with a yellow handkerchief.

'You policemen, I know, find out all kinds of things. Did you know that Wheeler was a friend of my son, Lionel?'

'I did not, sir.'

'Oh, yes. They shared similar interests, and even before his ordination Wheeler was no stranger to this house. I didn't know him well, but Lionel was very much taken with him. You've probably noticed that I'm a chemical merchant. I have a large warehouse away from here, and deal with many works and factories who need what I can supply. Lionel intends to expand our business into the provision of rare chemicals and reagents to universities and specialist laboratories. Lionel has a collection of many rare and curious substances, and a fine cabinet of geological specimens. He and Wheeler were both keen geologists.'

'And so, sir, five years ago . . . ?'

'Yes, Inspector. I'm digressing. Let me return to the point. Five years ago Wheeler came to this town, newly ordained as curate. He was a handsome man by any account, and a great favourite with the ladies. He was unmarried.'

Dovercourt, who had resumed his pince-nez, now began to fiddle with the fringe of the cloth draped over the little table near which he sat. He looked both angry and embarrassed.

'Mr Wheeler, as I say, was very interested in geology, and he would often bring specimens of minerals and rocks for Lionel to see. He – Wheeler, that is – had collected many of them on walking tours in Wales and Cornwall. He and Lionel made such a tour together in – when was it? – May or June, 1885.

'Wheeler had become very friendly with my daughter, Deirdre, who was then only thirteen – a little girl, you understand. Deirdre is an unworldly child, who is not, I fear, mentally robust. I don't mean that she's lacking, just that she's given to fancies. There are times when she can't distinguish fantasy from reality.'

Suddenly the merchant's face flushed red with a deeply remembered anger. He writhed his fingers together until the knuckles showed white. They were strong fingers, Jackson noted, their power somehow accentuated by the heavy gold signet ring that he wore.

'Such children, Jackson, are readily – how can I put it? – readily imposed upon.

'One day in February 1888, Wheeler came across here with a mineral specimen to show Lionel. He had also brought with him a particularly fine opal to give to Deirdre. We were all next door in the drawing-room. It was a bright afternoon. Wheeler suggested that Deirdre and he should come in here to look at the opal, as the sun was shining here. There's no window on this side in the drawing-room.

'So they came in here. After a while, I remembered something that I wanted to ask Wheeler – some parish matter. I opened the door. Wheeler was clasping Deirdre to his bosom. It was not just an affectionate hug, Jackson: there was movement, struggle . . . her back was towards me.

' "Deirdre!" I cried. Immediately she screamed and fainted. Wheeler just stood transfixed, letting the child sink to the floor. "You villain!" I shouted, "what were you doing to that child?" Wheeler was as white as a ghost. "It is not as you think, Dovercourt", he said. "What must I think, then?" I asked him. He made no reply. I lifted my daughter in my arms and carried her through to the drawing-room. I told Wheeler to leave my house and never to return.'

There was a profound silence in the Haunted Room when Dovercourt had finished his story. He seemed to have purged himself of the spasm of physical anger that had shaken him, and he sat calmly, his great black beard bristling, his strong white hands unclasped.

'Was Miss Deirdre excited when she saw that she was to have a present?'

'What? Yes, she was excited. It was a fine opal on a gold chain.'

Dovercourt looked surprised. It was not a question that he had expected.

'You have told me, sir, that your daughter is easily swayed. Has this made you particularly protective towards her?'

'Protective? Yes, I suppose it has. I'm not a sentimental man, Jackson: life's too stern a business for that. But I love my girl very much. I have been a strict father, but a just one. Neither of my children will tell you differently.'

'Will you let me speak to Miss Deirdre when the occasion offers? I won't do so if you don't wish it.'

'Very considerate of you, Jackson, but if you feel you must question her, then I won't say no. You might care to talk to Lionel when he returns to Ashgate. He's staying with a friend at the moment. My wife expects you to talk to her this morning. She's through that far door, which opens into the drawing-room.'

Another silence descended on this most silent of rooms. Here, thought Jackson, is a man sensitive as to his origins, with a scarcely concealed bias against landed and clerical privilege. A member of that ruling caste attempts to violate his young daughter. What does he do? He is a strong, powerful man, a man capable of allowing his outrage to fester into vengeful hatred.

Here is a man surrounded by lethal poisons. What exactly were those 'rare and curious substances' assembled by Dovercourt's son Lionel? The rear garden of this man's house led into what could be seen as a private cemetery. Had Venner, Jackson wondered, tested the remains of the Dried-Up Man for poison? But surely Wheeler had been killed by an arrow? Or was that some kind of deliberate pointer away from the truth?

James Dovercourt still sat motionless at the table. The light had grown stronger, and the lenses of his pince-nez were like two mirrors. Jackson fancied that he could see playing about the corners of the merchant's mouth the beginnings of a decidedly unpleasant smile.

Inspector Jackson stood near the blazing fire and surveyed the cheerful drawing-room of Dovercourt House. Modern floral wallpaper, gilt mirrors, a cluster of photographs on the piano. A pleasant room, he thought, all shadows banished by the fire-light. His hostess had risen to greet him, and then sat down in a chintz-covered armchair.

'I'm a practical woman, Mr Jackson,' said Mrs Dovercourt, 'and I find myself extremely vexed by all this superstition. I married into a family burdened with an ancestral ghost, and have to endure this nonsense of the Haunted Room. It was useful when the children were little, of course, to frighten them into behaving themselves. Now it's outgrown its usefulness. But since you want to hear the tale, I'll tell it to you.

'My husband had an ancestor called Amos Dovercourt, who was born in this house in 1742. He was a desperately wicked man, given to drinking, dicing, and . . . and other things. On the morning of the twentieth of December, 1784, he gambled away all he possessed to one of his drunken titled cronies.'

Despite her declared distaste of the subject she told the tale with a certain relish. Jackson watched her as she spoke. A striking woman, he thought, with fair hair pulled back into a bun. Her features were fine and regular, her face virtually unlined. How did one define her kind of elegance? It spoke to him of a slight inequality of background in the marriage of Mr and Mrs Dovercourt. His was an old and respected mercantile family, but she, he suspected, was a daughter of the Landed Interest. He would make it his business to find out.

'That very evening, Mr Jackson, at a quarter past eight, Amos Dovercourt shot himself in what has ever since been called the Haunted Room. Before he died, he whispered some words to his attendants, and they were these: "You may carry me where you will, but I will dwell here forever". And ever since that day, he has been glimpsed in the house. So there it is, Mr Jackson. The ghost of Amos Dovercourt. But I expect my husband has told you of other lurking superstitions stifling the air here in Ashgate?'

'He has, ma'am. So has Mr Goodheart. The business of Odin and the Hanging Groves.'

Mrs Dovercourt shuddered, more in disgust than fear, it seemed to Jackson.

'The business of Odin, as you call it, is a far graver nuisance than poor Amos. Learned and wise men lend their weight to it by writing serious volumes and conducting excavations and all the rest of it. So naturally the lesser sort of people believe it to be true. That can be a dangerous thing.'

Mrs Dovercourt stopped speaking and looked at Jackson expectantly. The preliminaries, he realized, were over. She wanted to hear about Samuel Wheeler.

'I'm inclined to agree with you, ma'am. These old fancies can indeed be dangerous. But let me get to the point of my visit. As you will have heard, the body of the Reverend Mr Wheeler has been discovered, and I have reason to believe that he was murdered. For professional reasons I cannot reveal the cause of death, but I can tell you that there was a noose around the neck. The rector told me that the ancient folk used to hang people as sacrifices to Odin, and there is a possibility that some such abomination was behind this murder.'

Rather to Jackson's surprise Mrs Dovercourt took a handkerchief from her sleeve and dabbed her eyes. She seemed truly upset, not over the details of the noose, but, he felt sure, by the fact of murder itself.

'Murder? Oh dear, Mr Jackson, I am truly sorry for that poor man. We all thought he had gone to Florence, and all the time he was stuffed into that monument without Christian burial. Now you say it may have been a pagan sacrifice! What have you done with his body?'

'He has been taken to Warwick, ma'am. There need be no haste in burying him, because he has been preserved by the elements, and it should be possible to trace his family without difficulty.'

'Family? How very odd! Do you know, he never mentioned any family, though of course he must have had relatives somewhere. I only ever thought of him as someone Lionel was friendly with. He was a bachelor, of course. Poor man!'

Mrs Dovercourt wiped her eyes again and looked at the leaping flames of the fire.

'Poor man!' she repeated softly.

'If I may say so, ma'am, you show great forbearance towards the late Mr Wheeler. It does you credit, if I may say so. Your husband has told me the sad story of his imprudent affection for your daughter, Miss Deirdre, and its consequences.'

'Forbearance? Yes, I suppose that's true. His was a venial slip, for which he has paid dearly. Find out who did it, Mr Jackson, and bring them to judgement! He had much promise, and would eventually have made some woman a good husband. He was already an engaging preacher, though he did not live to take priest's orders.'

She added rather cryptically, 'Men like to make a fuss about trifles. Women see things differently. I sometimes wonder whether men can see anything very clearly.'

Jackson had expected to find a vengeful and outraged mother. Mrs Dovercourt's views were startlingly at odds with what he had imagined. It was time to change the subject.

'Mrs Dovercourt,' he ventured, 'this is an old crime, going back four years. One person essential to my investigation is no longer in this town, someone whom it is vital that I should see and talk to—'

Mrs Dovercourt anticipated Jackson's words before he could form them.

'Have you noticed how no one mentions him? The Reverend Hezekiah Woodward – Parson Woodward, as he was called. A strange, crack-brained man – saving his cloth – who preached cautious despair and neglected his flock. Many a night you'd look from our rear windows and see the candles lit in that great barn of a church, and you knew he was there, struggling against demons of his own creation.'

'He would hold services in the night?'

'Oh, yes. And more than that. Down in the bowels of the earth he'd delve, and when he'd done that he'd consult the old musty books in his study, books he'd ordered from London.

'Parson Woodward had a maggot in his brain about Odin. Disgusting. He'd preach about him from the pulpit, warning the folk to flee from him! People who'd never heard of Odin started to be curious about him, and so there were more people added to the flock of Satan. Now to my way of thinking, Parson Woodward was a worse man than Samuel Wheeler. Why did his curates leave? Or *did* they leave? Are there others lying hidden in that churchyard?'

Mrs Dovercourt suddenly recollected herself, and looked up at

Jackson with some embarrassment. She attempted a cheerful smile.

'Thank you, ma'am, for speaking so frankly to me. I hope at some time to have a talk with your daughter, Deirdre, and also with Mr Lionel Dovercourt when he returns. I hope you'll have no objection to that?'

'None at all. Lionel is staying at the moment with a friend. Perhaps you would like his address?'

'If you please, ma'am.' Jackson took a notebook and pencil from his pocket.

'Lionel may be found care of Mr Rollo Bateman, at Park House, Old Penfold, Warwickshire.'

Mrs Dovercourt waited until Jackson had written the details down, and then pointed to a chair near the fire. She seemed to have made some kind of private resolution.

'Sit down there, Mr Jackson. That's right. My husband has no doubt told you that Deirdre is not entirely – well, not mentally robust. Girls, Mr Jackson, require a certain kind of understanding which men like James can't always give. Lionel thrives in this house, because he shares his father's energy and – explosiveness, if there's such a word. Deirdre wilts under it, and withdraws into a world of her own. She is a romantic child, who has always been captivated by the family ghost. Lionel laughs at her for being superstitious, but that's not really fair. She is timid and shy. After all, she's only just seventeen.'

'Be assured, ma'am, that I will be very careful when I talk to Miss Deirdre. Young ladies of her age need special consideration when it comes to asking questions.'

Mrs Dovercourt looked at Jackson with a suddenly kindled new interest.

'Are you, perhaps, the father of daughters yourself, Mr Jackson?'

He could see the flames again. . . . He heard Mrs Dovercourt's sharp intake of breath: his panic and agony must have shown fleetingly. He was quite unable to reply for nearly a minute.

'I am a widower, Mrs Dovercourt,' he said at last. 'My wife perished in a fire when she was only twenty-nine, and my little girl died with her. But I understand what you've told me about Miss Deirdre, and when I speak to her I'll do so, as I said, with special care.'

It was a relief to get out of Dovercourt House and breathe the fresh April air. Jackson's steps took him along the shale path of the long narrow garden at the rear of the house. He pushed open the creaking gate in the railings and stepped into the churchyard.

Bottomley was about, somewhere. They needed to confer. The time had come for positive action away from Ashgate St Lawrence. The mystery of Parson Woodward had to be brought out from its dark vaults of suspicion into the light of day.

Jackson had penetrated deep into the ancient burial-ground before he heard the sound of someone singing tunelessly to himself. He turned a corner between two gaunt tombs and saw the figure of the old grave-digger breaking fresh ground with a mattock. He straightened up, stopped singing, and touched his forelock to the inspector. Jackson raised his hat in acknowledgement.

'Good day, master,' said old Thomas Eves. His gnarled hand hovered for a moment over his disfiguring birthmark.

Jackson seemed not to hear. He looked hard at the aged, weatherbeaten face, and saw that the old man had recognized him. The grey eyes regarded him with a kind of resignation, an acceptance of the vilenesses that came to human life. The flames, a wall of fire, the screams, screams. . . .

In his mind's eye, Jackson saw the faded photograph in the back office of the police station in Barrack Street, a photograph that he had wrapped in cloth and tied with tape, and kept at the back of a drawer. The blackened ribs of a crucked cottage burned out, like the skeleton of a calcined beast, or a ravaged whale cast up on a beach. Six stern men standing grim-faced before the ruin, the old photography of those days giving them a blackened, almost demonic look. One of the men carried a dark birthmark across cheek and forehead.

'Mr Jackson, isn't it, master? I remember you well, sir, though it's long years ago. And you'll remember me, as like as not, because of the birthmark I carry. I lived on your side of the county in them days, sir, and I dug graves for the old church at Coldeaton.'

Thomas Eves sat down on the end of a tomb and filled a short clay pipe. Jackson watched him. He had recognized him immediately, despite the passage of years. Somehow it seemed right to talk to him.

'Yes, master, I remember the fire at Paul's Copse. You were just a constable then, and in uniform. 'T was I that dug the grave for your poor lady. Years ago, now. Did you ever wed again, master, asking your pardon?'

'No, Mr Eves, I never did. I don't suppose I ever will, now.'

Thomas Eves said nothing, but puffed away thoughtfully at his pipe. There was an unspoken bond between the two men, no longer just detective and grave-digger, but participants in a hideous tragedy. Eves had searched the ruined croft, and had helped to extinguish the flames.

'Years ago it was, master. It says in the Good Book that them as is in Heaven neither marry nor are given in marriage. But it don't say nothing like that about the folk still here on earth. Quite the contrary, as I've always understood.'

Old Thomas Eves glanced briefly at Jackson, knocked out his pipe and picked up the mattock. It was time to get back to work.

Deirdre Dovercourt stood solemnly in front of her full-length mirror and contemplated her green sprig-muslin dress. It had been a mistake to ask Mama for that yellow linen thing: with her blonde tresses it made her look like a corn dolly. This green was better.

'Should I wear a sash with this, Annie?' she asked.

Annie, her 14-year-old maid, was as dark as she was fair, with black ringlets peeping from below her little lace cap. She stopped her task of arranging some flowers in a vase and cast her brown eyes appraisingly over her young mistress.

'No, Miss Deirdre. It's well taken in at the waist, and brings out the line of your figure. You don't need a sash.' She turned again to her flower-arranging. Deirdre picked up a book and spread herself gracefully on the upholstered window-seat of her small sitting-room on the third floor front of Dovercourt House. It was a dreamy, insubstantial place, light and airy, with a lot of pale fabrics and bamboo furniture.

'Miss?' asked Annie at length.

'What?' Deirdre did not look up from her soft-leather edition of Keats.

'What are you reading?'

'It's a poem by John Keats. It's called *La Belle Dame Sans Merci*, and it's about a knight who falls under the spell of a ghostly lady. She takes him to her magic grotto, and pretends to have fallen in love with him.'

Deirdre sighed, and turned the page.

'What does it say next?'

'He went to sleep, and all the ghosts of her dead victims warned him to fly for his life. Listen:

> *"I saw their starved lips in the gloam*
> *With horrid warning gaped wide,*
> *And I awoke and found me here*
> *On the cold hill's side." '*

Annie glanced at her mistress with a look that was as old as the hills. It held amusement, affection, and a sort of good-humoured contempt.

'Ghosts! Tell me about the ghost you saw when you were thirteen. Were you frightened? Did you make an awful fuss?'

Deirdre threw her book down in vexation, and sat up straight on the window-seat.

'You impertinent minx! Don't you ever mention that horrid business again. Yes, I *was* frightened. You would have been, too. You'd have screamed and screamed if you'd seen old Amos climbing back in his tomb in the ghostly light he shed. Now go about your business.'

Deirdre picked up her book, but Annie's question, and the pictures conjured up by the poem, had rekindled frightening images that were best buried and forgotten. . . .

One night, four long years ago, when she was a little girl of thirteen, she had looked out of the window of the Haunted Room into the churchyard below. She had always made up pictures in her mind of old Amos Dovercourt walking among the tombs, and that night she had seen him.

He had been half in and half out of a tomb, and there had been a light like that of a lantern, which seemed brighter than the candle she had held. He had been getting out to go a-haunting, or he had just returned. She could still remember it, and how frightened she had been.

Frightened? It had been worse than that, and she had stayed in thrall to the room for an hour. She could no longer distinguish the pieces of the tableau in the graveyard, and had no wish to do so.

No one ever stayed long in the Haunted Room, and the curtains were never drawn at night. That was why she had been able to see Amos Dovercourt's ghost.

She had told Papa. He had become very angry. He had shouted, held her at arm's length by the wrist and smacked her legs. How she had cried! He had gone to Mama in the sitting-room, and she had heard him saying, 'You must stop making the child mad with that talk of ghosts, Grace. She is already frantic as a result of what Wheeler did to her. I fear that her mind is not very strong, and now she is seeing things.'

61

Next day he had come and found her and hugged her, and given her a box of sugar plums. The same evening, something had burst through the barred gates of her memory and driven her into a feverish trance, from which she had recovered some three weeks afterwards.

There had been other ugly visions in subsequent years, all best driven down and forgotten. She had heard from Annie about the grisly find in Josiah Anderson's tomb, but had no desire to get involved. Let them do as they liked in the churchyard. She would take no notice. . . .

Annie had shown no inclination to 'go about her business'. For the last minute or two she had been idly pulling petals off some of the flowers.

'Miss?'

'What?'

'It's not poems you should be interested in. Or ghosts.'

'Well, what *should* I be interested in?'

'Lads.'

Annie treated Deirdre to another of her dark-eyed glances that spoke more eloquently than all her mistress's volumes of poetry.

Deirdre blushed. She let her long hair fall over her face while she sat quite still, clutching her book so tightly that her knuckles turned white. She watched Annie through her hair, and saw her look with avid curiosity at the dressing-table. Had she been rooting in there? Had she seen. . . ?

Annie gave a cruel little smile.

'Maybe you can deceive your papa and mama, but you can't deceive me. I know all about you, miss, and I'll make you share your secrets with me. I won't tell anyone. Tell me about Mr Wheeler. What—'

Annie never finished her sentence because the other girl, with a scream of rage, had flung herself like a fury from the window-seat and hurled her to the floor. She knelt over the terrified little maid, supporting herself on the floor with one hand while the nails of the other hovered over Annie's white face.

Deirdre was panting with anger, and her blue eyes blazed with fury. Annie had never seen her like that before. She lay quite still, feeling sick and frightened. She tried to speak, but no words came.

'You little cat! You jade! I'll kill you. Nobody will miss you. Don't you ever mention that man again, do you hear? If you do, I'll kill you. I'll slit your throat while you're asleep. Or I'll smother you.'

Annie suddenly began to cry. Immediately, Deirdre sat up, hauled the younger girl off the floor, and cradled her in her arms. She pressed her cheek against the black ringlets. Annie clutched at her and sobbed.

'Oh, there, you stupid girl,' said Deirdre. 'I'll not hurt you. I don't know what I'd do without you. But don't pry too much, or you'll get hurt. Come on, hold your face up so I can kiss you. Then straighten yourself in the mirror.'

She kissed Annie's cheek, and the younger girl, with the resilience of her years, soon managed a smile. She adjusted her cap and smoothed down her black dress and white pinafore. Then she dropped Deirdre a little curtsy.

'Sorry, miss.'

'Oh, go *on*, Annie! Go and do some sewing.'

The little maid left the room, quietly closing the door behind her. Deirdre sighed. It was not the first time she and her maid had fought. Despite the difference in age and station they were very close. But she must not pry. If she played with fire then her fingers would get burnt. . . .

Deirdre opened a drawer in her dressing-table, and from under a pile of clothing she extracted something wrapped in tissue paper. Carefully removing the paper, she revealed a tinted photo-graph in an ebony frame. It was the image of a young clergyman, posing solemnly in front of what appeared to be the entrance to the Crystal Palace. The stiffness of the pose could not disguise the handsome features and the general air of attraction attaching to the man.

Deirdre gave the photograph the undivided attention that she had recently given to Keats's pallid knight. She sighed again.

'The Dried-Up Man,' she whispered, and returned the photograph to its hiding-place in the drawer.

Sergeant Bottomley's reputation as a cheerful, homely man had spread through the town, and he had begun to receive friendly nods and smiles as he went about his business. He was also regarded with some puzzlement, as he never seemed to ask any direct questions about the Dried-Up Man. He just chatted.

Adjoining the 'works' side of Dovercourt House there was a small garden enclosed by railings. It was only a few square yards in area, enough to contain a plot of grass and a bright flowerbed. Sergeant Bottomley stopped in the road and looked through the railings, where a young dark-haired girl in the uniform of a maid sat on a kitchen chair in the sun, munching an apple. She gave him an old-fashioned glance, but said nothing.

Bottomley cleared his throat noisily.

'Good morning, miss,' he said, sweeping off his hat and bowing low. 'You must be Miss Deirdre Dovercourt. Honoured and pleased to meet you, miss.'

Annie laughed, and bit into her apple.

'Go on, mister! You know I'm not Miss Deirdre. I'm her maid, Annie. She and me have just had words, so she's upstairs reading her book until we both recover.'

A look of profound disappointment crossed Sergeant Bottomley's face. He shook his head and turned away.

'Miss Deirdre's maid? Oh, well, *you're* no use! You won't know anything about the family and its doings.'

Annie sprang up off her chair and came close to the railings. She put her apple in the pocket of her pinafore and grasped the bars.

'That's where you're wrong, mister! I know all about the family. Especially Miss Deirdre. She's kind and beautiful and has lovely clothes. Some of her things come from London.'

Sergeant Bottomley scratched his head. What a big soft thing he looked!

'Kind and beautiful? I thought you'd just had words with her?'

'So I have, but that doesn't make her any less beautiful, does it? It's my fault for not knowing my place and speaking out of turn.'

Annie retrieved her apple and bit into it noisily. Bottomley winced and shied away as though in alarm.

'So you're her personal maid, are you? I expect she takes you with her when she goes visiting to all her rich relatives?'

The brown eyes regarded him over the apple.

'You being so pretty, like, and knowing all about her,' Bottomley added.

'Visiting? She doesn't do much of that. And they're not rich. They may be grand folk, but there's no money there, if you ask me.' She laughed. 'Their butler had a brown suit instead of black, and you could see it'd been a cast-off of his master's. And their velvet curtains are full of moth-holes!'

Sergeant Bottomley looked anxiously along the road.

'I feel uneasy speaking to you like this through the railings, Annie, in case your young man comes by. I don't want any trouble.'

'There'll be no young man come by. What a thing to say! Missus would never allow it.'

'Strict, is she? I don't blame her, not with you in the house. No wonder she keeps you behind railings, Annie. She's lucky that your Miss Deirdre doesn't bother with young men, she being a bit simple, so I've been told.'

Annie loosed her hold on the railings and stepped back on the grass plot. She looked angry, and her interested gaze changed to a glare of defiance.

'Miss Deirdre's not as daft as she makes out. And she lets her eye rove when she's so inclined. You wouldn't understand. Miss Deirdre's a lady, you see.'

Annie retreated to the chair and gave all her attention to her apple. She bit it savagely, and stared at her pinafore. Sergeant Bottomley looked helpless.

'There's a funeral tomorrow,' he ventured. 'Someone's being buried in the grave where they found the Dried-Up Man.'

'I know that,' said Annie. She had been amused by Bottomley's behaving like a big soft lad instead of bullying and hectoring, and decided to resume the conversation.

'Somebody called Perkins, I understand,' said Bottomley.

'Well you're wrong there, because it's Mr Loxley Anderson's cousin, and his name's Gregg. They call him a cousin, but he was really Mr Loxley Anderson's wife's nephew. They're the folk Miss Deirdre and me stayed with that time. Over at King's Leyland.'

Bottomley made a valiant effort to keep all these facts in mind. If he put a foot wrong the little maid would clam up. He took off his hat and scratched his head in mock perplexity.

'You and Miss Deirdre went to stay with this Mr Perkins?'

'No! With Mr and Mrs Loxley Anderson at King's Leyland. It was lovely there, and young Mr Elmore came. Miss Deirdre was very taken with him. So was I, for that matter.'

'I expect Mrs Dovercourt went with you both, didn't she? To keep an eye on Miss Deirdre, like.'

'Why should she? She'd enough to do here. That was the whole idea of Miss Deirdre and me going on our own. Mr Loxley Anderson is Mrs Dovercourt's brother.'

Sergeant Bottomley sighed contentedly. He gave Annie a kindly, avuncular smile.

'Well, I'll say good day, Annie. Thanks for the conversation. I'd give you a kiss, but these railings make it very difficult!'

Annie laughed. 'Oh, go on, mister! I know who you are, you know. You're the detective man who tells rude stories in the William. My dad told me.'

'Me? Rude stories? Your dad's got the wrong man. I'd never do a thing like that! Goodbye, little chick.'

Bottomley raised his hat with mock solemnity, and walked gravely away. Annie followed him with her dark eyes. A little smile hovered about her lips.

'No,' she said softly, 'Miss Deirdre's not as daft as she makes out.'

4

Death by Drowning

Parson Woodward knelt down on the stony shingle of Polwarthan Cove and looked at the drowned man. The sea had not yielded up its dead, for the man's legs and body pointed towards the village. Only his head and shoulders lay beneath the choppy water worrying the margin of the Cornish shore.

It's as though he'd run towards the sea to escape, mused Parson Woodward. He turned for a moment to look up inland at the straggle of grey slate roofs bordering the workings of the lead mine. Little wonder if he had fled from that ungodly place! Polwarthan, unlovely, unvisited by trippers, nursed its brood of evil, and imposed its murderous silence even on him. There were times when he could no longer remember things that he had done, or things that others had done. And now a man lay dead. . . .

It was neither easy nor pleasant to grasp the drowned man by the ankles and pull him by main force further up the shingle. The jacket of the man's serge suit was weighed down by something heavy in the pockets . . . stones! Large, ugly, irregularly shaped stones of unusual heaviness, sufficient to anchor the corpse to the beach. Had it been the man's intention to commit suicide, burdening himself with rocks and then running into the sea?

For a while his powers of sight and hearing seemed to desert him, and there was a hollow calm. Then the world rushed back as suddenly as it had left him, and he heard the sullen slapping of the darting eddies of grey water among the rocks.

Suicide, then? No. One further glance revealed the halter round the neck. For every victory there was a defeat. His life was to be spent and burnt out in this crusade, where the sounds of the blows were silent, and the clash of arms unheard. Carefully he removed the halter, and concealed it in his pocket. That was part of his psychic battle, nothing to do with the law.

The parson rose to his feet, and pocketed one of the stones that he had been holding. Other, sharper minds must be summoned to unravel this mystery. He had merely come out for his usual lonely evening walk and had stumbled on this tragic burden clinging on to the sea-girt margin of his wild parish. Parson Woodward began the steep ascent from the beach that would lead him to Polwarthan.

Constable Polk, morose and surly by nature, was taciturn by conviction. He lived on the edge of the slate-grey village in a two-roomed cottage standing in an overgrown vegetable patch.

Parson Woodward had stumbled on the body shortly before half past eight in the evening. He reached Polk's house at twenty-five to nine. In answer to his knock, the door was opened by a dark-haired, surly woman in a flannel gown, who looked at him with very little favour.

'Yes, Parson, what is it? Polk's out at the moment. I don't know where he is.'

Woodward stood patiently in the muddy patch before the door, composing his reply. He was never invited into the houses of these people: isolation and suspicion seemed to be their way of life. The parson was there for funerals, and the few weddings that took place. No one brought a child for baptism.

'Good evening, Mrs Polk. Please tell the constable when he returns that there is a body washed up on the shingle near to the ruined boat-house. He will want to look at it and make arrangements.'

'I'll see to it, Parson,' said Mrs Polk, and closed the door. She had shown neither surprise nor interest.

Each in his own little world, thought Parson Woodward. Even Constable Polk was treated as a pariah, so it seemed. Was he local, or not? It made no difference. He had committed the crime of belonging to a body of folk who existed outside the confines of this cursed hell-hole, this place of ancient slaughter in its valley between two hills. . . .

Polwarthan Parsonage was a substantial stone building a few hundred yards from the village. It seemed to be choking in a grove of gnarled oak trees that had grown too near the house. The ground was mossy and dank, and the walls of the parsonage seemed forever damp and green. The door, like all the external woodwork, was unpainted and cracking.

Woodward pushed open the door and entered the chilly passage of his dwelling. He fumbled in the gloom for a while, striking a tinder-box until he had a flame for the candle. With that to light his way, he went into his sitting-room, and prepared to light a fire. He had no domestic servants, because no one in the village would work in that capacity, and no one from Truro, the nearest town, would have dreamed of working in such a benighted spot.

By nine o'clock, the light from the fire and several candles had banished some of the perpetual gloom of the place. Half dozing, he recalled the image of the drowned man, heavy and wet, struck down, so it seemed, fleeing towards the sea, and round the neck a halter. . . .

He saw hands slipping the rope over the soaking head – or that rope was a sign, a token of sacrifice, not the cause of death itself. But what hands had placed the noose around the dead man's neck? Why did his memory lapse, so that at times he remembered nothing, and would surge back, shocked, to the present? What hands?

70

A hammering on the door jerked him back to wakefulness. It was Constable Polk. Woodward glanced at the clock and saw that it was five past nine. He pulled on his heavy serge cloak and opened the door. He knew that there was no point in asking Polk to enter the house. Instead, he greeted the man, who stood immobile and unresponsive in his damp blue uniform and helmet, then accompanied him along the track leading from the parsonage to the shore.

When they came in sight of the body sprawled where Woodward had left it, Constable Polk laid his hand on the parson's sleeve.

'That's far enough, thank you, Parson.' His voice conveyed remorseless indifference to life or death. It might have been a sack of coal washed up from a wreck for all the emotion he showed.

'I'll see to this alone, as is right and proper. Good night, sir.'

Hezekiah Woodward made no reply, but merely turned away and retraced his steps. He heard few words from that man, but those he did hear always stirred some unpleasant memory. Just for a fleeting moment he wondered how long he could endure this alien existence. Then even that thought was lost in a host of speculations, an escape into the brilliantly lighted chambers of the imagination.

As he approached the parsonage, heavy, chilling spring rain began to fall and form pools among the stones and scree.

'Polwarthan? I don't know the place, Mr Jackson, but the name stirs a faint memory. So *that's* where Woodward ended up! Cornwall. A wild, remote corner of Britain, Inspector. I went there once, years ago, to a place called St Ives. But I've read about Polwarthan somewhere recently, or someone has mentioned it to me. . . .'

Harry Goodheart sat lost in thought for a while.

This rectory, thought Jackson, is a kind of sanctuary. Or rather its occupant, the unfailingly generous Harry Goodheart, makes it

71

so. The merry clock still ticked away. The untidy rows of books had not been straightened. More than that, they looked as though they had been mercilessly consulted very recently.

The rector stirred and looked at the tea trolley, which was groaning under its weight of sustaining fare.

'I can see no valid theological reason, Inspector, why two men should starve themselves at tea-time just because they wish to speak on serious matters. That seed cake is very good, if you'd care to try some.'

'Thank you, sir. I'll have some presently.'

'So you're going to Cornwall? What will you do? Will you arrest Woodward?'

Jackson contrived to look horrified.

'Arrest him? Good heavens, sir, what for? I've no evidence that he was in any way concerned with Mr Wheeler's murder. No concrete evidence, that is. But it'll be obvious to you, sir, that I must have a talk with Mr Woodward. He was Mr Wheeler's rector, and I think it very likely that he was still rector here when Mr Wheeler's body was hidden in that monument. Yes, he and I must talk together.'

Harry Goodheart thoughtfully spread some raspberry jam on a scone, and added a blob of cream.

'It will be a long, tedious journey to Cornwall, Mr Jackson. Gloucester, Bristol, Exeter, and from there to Saltash. It's near on two hundred miles.'

'Yes, sir, it's a long haul, but I think it will be worth the trouble. When I spoke to the Archdeacon of Warwick he suggested that I should call on Mr Woodward's bishop in Cornwall. He's already written to him, and given me a letter of introduction in case the post miscarries. The Bishop of Pentreathan, he's called. He'll be able to tell me a good deal about Mr Woodward's past career. At least, that's what the archdeacon hinted.'

Jackson permitted himself a half smile. He had taken other measures with different authorities, measures that would ensure a very eager co-operation from the Cornish bishop. It would do the good rector no harm to think that he was relying totally on the church's compliance.

'The Bishop of Pentreathan,' said Harry Goodheart. 'Hope Sutherland, his name is. Quite a decent sort of man, by all accounts. He has friends in high places—'

He broke off, and looked speculatively first at the serried ranks of volumes on his bookshelves and then at Jackson.

'You know, Inspector, I can't think why the name Polwarthan should be so familiar. Perhaps I knew someone who came from there, or who'd been there. . . .'

Jackson helped himself to a slice of seed cake. It was an idle exercise not to join in the rector's generous tea-times.

'I came here today, sir, in the hope that you'd be able to answer a question that's been puzzling me ever since the archdeacon told me where Mr Woodward had gone. Why Cornwall? Is it because it's well out of the public eye?'

The rector frowned and shifted in his chair. He threw Jackson a shrewd glance.

'You mean is it another clerical conspiracy? Well, perhaps it is. I don't know. Maybe the Bishop of Pentreathan will enlighten you. As for Polwarthan . . . oh! I remember now! I knew I'd read about Polwarthan somewhere!'

The rector unfolded his six feet four frame and crossed to one of his bookshelves. He brought down a large volume, which Jackson recognized.

'Yes, Inspector. it's Norton's *Superstitions of Old Britain.*'

He rapidly turned over a number of pages and then gave a little sigh of satisfaction.

'Here we are. Just listen to this extract:

"Those enthusiasts for the cult of Odin were wont to gather many years since at a place in Cornwall called Pole Werthan, which the antique sages boasted as the chief shrine or altar of the pagan

73

deity. Antiquities of great interest were shown there at one time, but now dispersed or buried. There is a well there, and a chamber, and all lies in a vale between hills, but the mining of lead and the mechanical engines have combined with the bans of the church and its ministers to drive these old forms from the remembrance of many".'

Harry Goodheart closed the heavy volume and sat quietly for a few moments. He looked grave and troubled. The gentle afternoon sun filtered lazily into the room.

'I don't much like the sound of this, Jackson,' he said at last. 'I'm fairly certain that someone's offered Woodward a quiet backwater to escape from what I suppose could be called his notoriety. Maybe Bishop Hope Sutherland knows about that. But no one seems to have realized that they were plunging poor Woodward deeper into his world of demonic fantasy.'

'You mean—'

'I mean that he knew from his years of study that Polwarthan was once the chief centre of Odin worship. That, Inspector, was why he accepted the living of Polwarthan. He was haunted enough here, poor man. There, I fear, he will have found fresh spectres ready to greet him.'

Sullenly, as though unwillingly, the train from Exeter bringing Inspector Jackson and Sergeant Bottomley into Cornwall clanked and clattered at a snail's pace over the Royal Albert Bridge. Jackson huddled in a corner of the carriage, savouring the damp smell of horsehair and stale smoke.

He hauled his watch from his waistcoat pocket and flicked open the cover.

'We'll be in Saltash in a few minutes, Sergeant,' he observed. 'We've been an hour and six minutes.' Bottomley, slumped in the opposite corner, looked glassily at Jackson, but made no reply.

The carriage windows were buttoned with large raindrops,

blown uneasily into filmy tracks by the wind. From a black and green lowering sky, heavy rain came flying down like fury. Cornwall was greeting the visitors with its traditional festal array.

The train groaned to a thankful halt at Saltash Station just beyond the bridge, where the shining hoods and saturated horses of a few cabs were huddled together. A huge pall of steam hung over the grimy engine and its string of carriages, adding greatly to the pervading gloom.

'This Bishop Hope Sutherland,' said Jackson, standing up, 'lives at Pentreathan Palace, which I'm told is only a few miles from Saltash. There's a livery stables here. We'll be able to hire a conveyance of some sort to take us out there.'

Sergeant Bottomley hauled himself up from his seat. He rubbed the misted window of the compartment and peered out at the gaunt ironwork of the bridge as it seemed to glide past the lumbering train.

'I don't much like the look of this place, sir,' he said. 'The sooner we're back in that snug little boarding-house in Exeter the better. Somehow I don't think that Cornwall and me are going to agree together.'

Bishop Hope Sutherland opened his copy of *The Cornish Weekly Gazette* and smoothed the pages flat on the green morocco leather top of his desk. The unthinkable had happened. Hezekiah Woodward, for the third time in his lugubrious career, had contrived to be in the neighbourhood of a suspicious death. That, he supposed, was the most charitable interpretation. But he wondered privately whether the Reverend Hezekiah Woodward was going off his head.

He would have to reread what the *Gazette* had reported about the matter. In less than half an hour these detectives from Warwickshire would be calling, and he would need to be armed with some convincing answers. He turned his attention to what the *Gazette* had called the 'Mysterious Drowning at Polwarthan'.

Wednesday 6 April – Today the body of a man was found drowned upon the margin of the sea at Polwarthan. The melancholy discovery was made by the Reverend Mr Woodward, vicar, at about the half-hour after eight o'clock in the evening. Constable D. Polk was summoned, and the vicar confirmed that the man had been lying with his head and shoulders in the sea. It appeared that he had been fleeing from someone in pursuit, but Constable Polk ascertained that the body had in fact been dragged face downward to the water. The toe-caps of the man's boots had left grooves across the shingle.

Bishop Hope Sutherland stirred restlessly. Why did these barbaric things have to happen? He looked round the long, low study of his mock-Gothic eighteenth-century palace, with its tall, pinnacled and fretted bookcases filled with old calf-bound volumes. This fanciful palace was a tenuous sanctuary from the savageries lurking beyond its gates.

A thin, mean rain had begun to spatter against the diamond panes of the poppy-headed casements. He rose from his desk, crossed to the hearth and placed another log on the fire. It was always cold in April in Cornwall. He watched the sparks fly upward, tried to recall a text about it, and failed. He resumed his seat at the desk and continued to read.

Later. – The body was conveyed to Truro, where Dr H.J. Lewis, Surgeon to the Board of Guardians, confirmed that the cause of death was drowning. Dr Lewis also stated that the man had drowned in fresh water, not in the sea, as had at first seemed apparent.

Drowned, but not in the sea. A mysterious affair – and a very inconvenient one. Old Woodward had vegetated quite happily for the past few years at Polwarthan. Surely this drowned young man was not another obscene sacrifice? At any rate, he was not in Holy Orders.

What else had the *Gazette* had to say?

Later. – Mr Reuben Calderdale, general manager of the mine, was summoned by Constable Polk, and confirmed his suspicion that the unfortunate deceased was Mr Robert Elmore, aged 25, surveyor and agent for Redcott, Caradyne & Co. Major Giles Redcott of St Jude's, a partner in the firm of Redcott, Caradyne & Co., owners of the Polwarthan Lead Mine, has been informed of the unhappy circumstance. The investigation is now being conducted by Inspector Tregennis of Truro. We hope that the active exertions of Constable Polk will be seen by him as deserving of commendation.

The door of the study opened to admit a young and deferential chaplain. He carried a cardboard folder tied with purple ribbon.

'My Lord,' he said in a low voice, 'the detectives are here. Detective Inspector Jackson, and Detective Sergeant Bottomley.'

'Excellent! Show them in, Lander. I am not to be disturbed for any reason while they are with me. What . . . what kind of people are they?'

'Well, My Lord, they seem decent men of rural background. The inspector reminds me of a country solicitor I once knew in Mevagissey. He was quite genial and confiding. He and his sergeant, he told me, are lodging in Exeter. They've come across here today by railway. The sergeant's quiet enough, but rather a rough-looking man, I'm afraid.'

'Well, we must take the rough with the smooth. Bring them in. Dean Fellowes will be here in about an hour to discuss the repairs to the aisle of the south choir. I should be finished with these policemen by then.'

The chaplain handed Bishop Hope Sutherland the cardboard folder.

'All the relevant letters about Mr Woodward are there, My Lord.'

When the chaplain had left the room, the bishop settled himself further back in his chair. He had a smooth, pink face, of which he was proud, and his blue eyes twinkled like beads on a child's necklace. Bishop Hope Sutherland looked like a bishop, or rather looked as he thought a bishop should look.

He glanced cursorily at the collection of letters – an old one from the Archbishop of Canterbury, a later commendation from the Bishop of Oxford, the recent cautious request from the Archdeacon of Warwick, a private note from the Archbishop of York ... and yesterday's almost peremptory letter from the Lord Lieutenant of Cornwall, asking him earnestly to tell these detectives all that he knew about Hezekiah Woodward. ... Very awkward, to say the least.

'And that, My Lord,' said Inspector Jackson, 'is what brings me down here to this secluded part of Cornwall. A young clergyman done to death in a manner which I'm not at liberty to reveal, and his body concealed in a tomb-chest. A young man who was curate in the parish of which Mr Woodward was then vicar. I am inviting you, My Lord, to tell me what you know about the Vicar of Polwarthan, the Reverend Hezekiah Woodward.'

This bishop has a bright eye and a good presence, Jackson thought. But there's a weakness about the jaw that no amount of thoughtful stroking with his beringed hand can disguise.

'Upon my word, Inspector,' said Bishop Hope Sutherland, 'it's a difficult invitation to accept! What am I to say? Maybe Warwickshire is an open book, with a straight choice of saints and sinners. You'll find it very different here in the see of Pentreathan. It's a diocese of men who shun the fierce light of day, a strange Celtic sort of place, where perhaps the dividing lines between virtue and vice have become blurred. There's not much fraternizing among the parsons. They're all very fierce defenders of their freeholds in Cornwall.'

Yes, Jackson thought. And there's not much missionary activity, by the look of things. It's not only the clergy who have turned inward upon themselves. Their bishop seems to have given them a lead.

'Indeed,' Hope Sutherland continued, 'you'll find it a far cry from Warwick. This palace of mine, Jackson, clings on to civilization like a limpet to a ship's hull! Out there' – he waved his hand vaguely towards the diamond-paned windows – 'out there lies a harsh and savage world of mines, unyielding earth, and poverty. Truro, now – our neighbouring diocese – is a paradise compared with Pentreathan!'

Jackson waited patiently for the bishop to come to the point.

The bishop closed the file of letters on his desk, and sat up in his chair. He seemed to have come to a definite decision.

'Mr Jackson – and you, Mr Bottomley – I have decided to tell you all I know about Hezekiah Woodward. My duty is to protect and shepherd my clergy, but you have mentioned the word "murder". In that context, I think, the secrets of all hearts must be revealed. I don't much care for the idea of Woodward being mixed up with dead bodies of young men.'

'No, My Lord. So let us hope that what you are going to tell me will help to show that the Reverend Hezekiah Woodward is innocent of any crime.'

'Hezekiah Woodward,' the bishop began, 'was one of a hopeful crop of scholars from Sidney Sussex College in Cambridge who graduated in 1849: "the Parnassian Band", they were called at the time, all with brilliant Firsts in the Classical Tripos. You've heard of them, perhaps?'

'No, My Lord.'

'Well, they really were a rather special group of men. Some are retired, others are dead. People like Dr Jouste, Professor E.A. Paterson, Charles Miller. I can't remember them all. Well,

79

Woodward was one of that number. He read for Orders, and was ordained deacon and priest by the then Bishop of Ely.'

'So he was what I would call a learned man, My Lord? Somehow, I'd imagined that he was sunk in superstition and idle tales.'

'To some extent, Inspector, you were right. But the "idle tales", as you call them, had their foundation in some sound scholarship on Woodward's part. He'd become very interested in the study of Norse mythology, and published a number of learned papers on the subject in various journals.'

'Could he not have become a fellow – is that the right word? A tutor at Cambridge or Oxford?'

'He could have done that, Mr Jackson, but I suppose he felt the call to parish work. He held a number of small livings in quick succession. He was only a mediocre parish priest. Most of his preferments came through the influence of patrons.'

Inspector Jackson smiled. The bishop, he noticed, frowned slightly before continuing. He had evidently understood the smile, and had not liked it.

'Then, in 1876, Woodward was appointed vicar of St Edward the Confessor, Thirlwood Parva, a fairly prosperous parish near Harrogate, in Yorkshire. He had a curate there, a young man called Percy Field. Hezekiah Woodward had discovered that Thirlwood Parva had in ancient times been a place of worship dedicated to Odin, and that sacrifices had taken place there.'

Inspector Jackson leaned forward in his chair. So there was, after all, a pattern. Woodward was to be found where there were sanctuaries of Odin. It would be interesting to hear why the bishop had mentioned a young curate at Harrogate by name. What, he wondered, had happened to Percy Field?

The bishop stopped speaking and began to polish his glasses. He glanced across at the inspector, who sat apparently in rapt attention. He put his glasses on again and leaned forward confidentially in his chair.

'Now I'm not saying, Jackson, that Woodward was in any way directly responsible for what happened. Not at all. But he had taken to thinking that the ancient gods whom he studied still lived, and that they were engaged in a battle for mastery with the church. It was the beginning of a dangerous eccentricity that was to lead him down troubled paths.'

'I've heard something about those "troubled paths" at Ashgate St Lawrence, My Lord. Some familiar bells are beginning to ring, if I may put it like that.'

'No doubt, no doubt. He began to preach about these gods and their struggle for domination. He mingled Holy Writ with pagan legend, and told his flock of the ritual hangings offered to Odin by his worshippers. The Archbishop of York was alerted by a member of his congregation, and Woodward was threatened with inhibition. Less educated people at St Edward's became frightened.'

'I'm not surprised,' observed Jackson drily. 'What *does* surprise me is how long this kind of thing was allowed to go on.'

'Well, Jackson, things came to a very dramatic head in this case. The young curate, Percy Field, was found hanging in the grove of birch trees sheltering the apse of the old church. Someone had placed a silver token and a "fish" fashioned from straw at his feet.'

Sergeant Bottomley uttered a strangled oath. Inspector Jackson's eyes flashed with sudden anger. He was beginning to be repelled by what his reason told him was manic nonsense, while something deeper than reason whispered an undefined fear. The bishop noted these responses without comment.

'There was widespread hysteria in the district, even though it was proved beyond reasonable doubt that Percy Field had taken his own life for personal reasons connected with an emotional failure. At the end of that year, Hezekiah Woodward was persuaded to resign the living and seek a parish elsewhere.'

Jackson and Bottomley exchanged glances. The bishop shifted uneasily in his chair. He knows I'm reading his unspoken thoughts, Jackson said to himself. And I'm perfectly aware that he's reading mine.

The bishop winced visibly when Jackson asked bluntly, 'Who persuaded him to resign? And, more to the point, who encouraged him to seek a parish elsewhere?'

The bishop glanced desperately at the ornate gilt clock on the mantelpiece.

'Eh? I'll answer that question presently, Inspector. Just let me finish what I have to say about Woodward. He moved from Yorkshire to Warwickshire, to St Lawrence's, Ashgate, a fine church, as I think you know, with a good tradition. Again, he was very fortunate to be appointed rector of such a living. The same pattern of obsession and parochial neglect emerged. Complaints were received, and his bishop hit upon a possible way out of trouble.'

'And what was that, My Lord?'

'His bishop considered it would be a shrewd move to bolster his ministry by sending a very popular young man as curate there, the Reverend Samuel Wheeler. That was in 1887. Wheeler was an immediate success, but then the church was threatened with a hideous scandal over his relationship with a girl of school age. I expect you know all about that?'

'I do, My Lord. And up to a point I know what happened after that. Mr Wheeler, so it was supposed, fled to Florence. Mr Woodward continued for a while in his own eccentric ways. I'm told that he began to hold services behind locked doors, playing the organ himself, and chanting what sounded apparently like Roman Catholic prayers. . . .'

'Exactly. And the outcome of it was that a petition for his removal was lodged by prominent parishioners, and so . . . well, he came here, to fill the advowson of Polwarthan.'

The bishop glanced keenly at Jackson.

'You're reading my mind, aren't you, Inspector? Yes, Woodward didn't just come here by chance. The Archbishop of

Canterbury wrote to me, asking for my help. That's another story, which I'm *not* going to tell you!'

Sergeant Bottomley had been sitting slumped on an upright chair near the door while Jackson and Hope Sutherland were speaking. The bishop secretly wondered whether the amiably smiling man was not slightly intoxicated. It came as something of a shock when the shambling figure suddenly sprang to life.

'Very interesting, My Lord Bishop,' said Bottomley, 'everything that you've told us about Mr Woodward. We're very discreet, my guv'nor and me, sir, and that's why you can tell us any secret that you want. We're also Crown Officers of the Law. So perhaps you'll change your mind just for once and tell us?'

'Tell you what, Sergeant?' the bishop stammered, in reply to what he felt was a menacing cheeriness.

'Why Mr Woodward came down here especially. To Polwarthan, I mean.'

'Very well, Sergeant. I don't usually breach confidences in this way, but since you have asked me especially, I shall tell you. Mr Woodward had to leave Ashgate St Lawrence without being dismissed. To have dismissed him would have created a fine old row. So Dr Benson, the Archbishop of Canterbury, contacted me. I always try to help in these cases, especially as this little diocese has a lot of trouble in attracting clergy. Accordingly, I offered Woodward the living of St Petroc's, Polwarthan.'

The archbishop, he reflected, had asked him to give Woodward a parish as a personal favour to him, and he had complied. Benson's requests were never without an ultimate, unspoken, purpose. Bishop Hope Sutherland was just beginning to suspect what that purpose was.

'Why did the archbishop contact you in particular, My Lord?' asked Jackson.

'Why? Because Dr Benson, Inspector, was the first Bishop of Truro. He was appointed to that new see in – when was it? – 1877. He was Chancellor of Lincoln before that. So he knows Cornwall,

83

which is a remote corner of Britain, better able to contain scandal than places like Ashgate. And, of course, he knows *me*. I was able to offer Woodward a choice of three parishes, and he immediately accepted Polwarthan.'

Of course he did, thought Jackson, and you never even thought to wonder *why*.

Bishop Hope Sutherland sighed. Suddenly, Jackson thought, he looked older than his years. The colour, he noted, had drained from his face.

'Then, as I read in the papers, the mummified body of Samuel Wheeler was found at Ashgate, hidden in a tomb-chest. No details have been released to the news prints, but you tell me that it was murder?'

'Yes, My Lord. Murder most foul. And so, I think, you'll understand the drift of things. First this Percy Field who you've told me about, then Samuel Wheeler. Both young men, both in Woodward's parishes, which were both shrines of this pagan abomination.'

The bishop hesitated, and then said in a low voice, 'Polwarthan, too, Inspector, was such a shrine.'

'It was, My Lord, as the rector of Ashgate explained to me, and I find it difficult to believe that anyone would have let Mr Woodward go to such a place again. Fortunately for all of us, no mysterious death has taken place there during Mr Woodward's incumbency.'

The bishop looked both abashed and puzzled. He picked up the copy of *The Cornish Weekly Gazette* from his desk and handed it to Jackson.

'Surely, Inspector,' he said, 'you would count this unfortunate business of Robert Elmore as a mysterious death? We've evidently been talking at cross-purposes. I assumed that it was this bizarre drowning that had brought you here to Cornwall.'

'Robert Elmore. I wonder, sir, if that could be the Mr Elmore that little Annie told me about? When she and Miss Deirdre stayed with the Loxley Andersons a young man called Elmore came to visit.'

Jackson registered what his sergeant said, but made no reply. Another Odinic shrine. Another young man dead. Wherever this half-crazed parson went, a young man died.

'We must act now, Sergeant,' he declared, 'before more lives are lost. This article in the bishop's newspaper will serve as a useful blueprint. There are three things we need to do. First, we must make ourselves known to the constabulary here. The time for discretion has gone. What was the inspector called? Tregennis. We'll need to let him know we're on his patch. Secondly, we need to see this mine owner, Major Redcott. There's bound to be someone here at the palace who knows where he lives. He'll be able to tell us something about Polwarthan, and what goes on there.'

'And thirdly, sir?'

'Thirdly, Sergeant, we must interview the Reverend Hezekiah Woodward. That is becoming more and more imperative by the minute.'

The Bishop of Pentreathan had left the two detectives alone to read the account of the finding of Robert Elmore's body. In doing so he had, Jackson thought, revealed a kindly understanding of their bewilderment, and their need to confer in private.

Presently both men heard the crunch of carriage wheels in the drive. At the same time the bishop returned. He glanced towards the rain-spattered window looking out on to the palace carriage-drive.

'That is Dean Fellowes arriving, Mr Jackson. He's due here on a matter of business concerning the cathedral fabric. Have you resolved what you will do? My chaplain, Mr Lander, is a local man, and he'll be happy to help you in any way he can. I've told him to place himself at your disposal.'

'That's very kind, My Lord, and sincerely appreciated. Yes, I can see my way forward now, though I don't like what I've heard, and I very much fear that the church's anxiety to avoid scandal may have led it into even graver trouble. I am myself a member of the Church of England. So is my sergeant there. But that will not prevent either of us delving for the truth when murder is the subject.'

'You are right, of course, Mr Jackson, but I beg that you won't think too badly of the church. Dr Benson's actions, and those of his agents, have been a sincere attempt to ensure that Hezekiah Woodward has never to endure the catastrophe of being unfrocked.'

'A worthy purpose, My Lord,' said Jackson drily, 'and one that I can understand. But let me remind you of the Dried-Up Man - the Reverend Samuel Wheeler. He, too, was a clergyman, but no sanctuary was found for him in his time of trouble. Yet the Reverend Hezekiah Woodward has been hidden from sight here in a remote part of Cornwall, where he is apparently at liberty to do whatever he pleases.'

With his hand on the latch of the study door, Jackson turned to Hope Sutherland and added, 'I sincerely hope, My Lord, that the Reverend Hezekiah Woodward may never have to endure the catastrophe of being hanged.'

When Jackson and Bottomley left the bishop's study they found that their pony and trap had been brought round beneath the *porte-cochère* of the bishop's palace, and after they had climbed into it the young chaplain, Mr Lander, gave them clear and concise directions.

'Major Giles Redcott, Inspector, lives in a big granite-fronted house on the main street of St Jude's. That's a little working town about ten winding miles from here. There's nothing much at St Jude's, you'll find, apart from a small iron foundry and a carpet mill. There's a livestock market, a dissenting chapel, and a couple of fine terraces of housing put up a hundred years ago.'

'You're very kind, Mr Lander,' Jackson said. He was attracted to the dark-haired, fair-skinned young man in the black frock coat. There was something honest and open about him that sent the inspector's thoughts flying back to the rectory at Ashgate St Lawrence.

'This Major Redcott – have you heard of him?'

'Indeed yes, Inspector. Major Redcott is very well known and esteemed in this part of the world, but you may find him a little . . . well, difficult.'

'I'll bear that in mind. And have you heard of Inspector Tregennis?'

'I have, sir. You'll find him at Truro. Major Redcott and Mr Tregennis are both true Cornishmen, and so am I, which is why I know them both. The bishop, of course, is a foreigner!'

Lander treated them to a friendly smile and released the pony's bridle.

5

The Mines of Odin

The skies had been threatening rain all morning, and well before they reached St Jude's the heavens opened. Merciless oblique curtains of rain descended on the two men as they urged the open trap along the stony tracks. By the time the wet slate roofs of the glum little town had come into sight they were soaked through to the skin.

They quickly located Major Redcott's house and, as they alighted from the trap, a man with a split sack over his head ran out from an alley to lead horse and vehicle to the rear of the terrace. In response to their ring on the bell, the door was opened almost immediately, and they all but fell into a tiled hallway.

A huge slab of a man in butler's attire watched without emotion as a widening pool of water fell from them, and spread into a sort of pond on the tiles. He relieved them of their soaking coats, and asked them their business. Jackson produced his warrant card. Slab's eyebrows rose a little, but he said nothing until he had crossed the hallway and opened a door on the right. Standing back in a kind of dramatic pose, he announced in a loud voice, 'Detective Inspector Jackson, Warwickshire Constabulary', and motioned them to enter.

The room was heavily furnished, but surprisingly cheerful. The stone floor was covered with a sumptuous Indian carpet, and there were quantities of shining Benares brassware displayed on shelves and in cabinets. There was a bright fire burning in the grate, above which lowered a rather alarming African tribal mask.

In a high winged armchair on the left of the fireplace sat a woman in her sixties, busily knitting. She gave them an appraising glance and a welcoming smile, then returned to her clicking needles.

Opposite to her sat a big elderly man with a yellow face and snow-white hair. A copy of *The Times* lay across his knees, and it was evident from his slightly bemused manner that he had just woken from a doze. An elaborately carved walking stick lay near his left hand on the floor. He let his eyes focus for a while on the visiting-card that Jackson handed him.

'Well, Inspector, you may as well sit down somewhere. And your friend – oh, Sergeant, hey? Well, him too. Bring a chair over here so I can hear you properly. I'm a bit deaf, you know, and my legs have gone.'

The old major's voice was lively enough, thought Jackson, but it seemed to come from somewhere far away. Perhaps Major Redcott couldn't always hear his own voice very clearly.

'When I say my legs have gone, of course I don't mean they've gone literally. I mean I can't use them properly any more. They're still there – well, you can see they are – but they don't always do what I want them to.'

Inspector Jackson brought a chair and sat down.

'You are Major Giles Redcott?' he ventured.

'I don't deny it,' replied the other. 'Now, then, Inspector, what can I do for you? I must confess, this is an unexpected visit.'

'Major Redcott,' said Jackson, 'I am a police offlcer, concerned with the investigation of a crime that took place in Warwickshire. I came to Cornwall to make certain enquiries. I have just left the Bishop of Pentreathan's palace, where I heard about the death of the unfortunate Mr Robert Elmore at Polwarthan. As my own investigation must take me there, I thought you might be able and willing to tell me something about the place.'

The major's faded eyes leapt briefly into life. He seemed enormously relieved. He'd forgotten something that he should have remembered, and in some way I've jogged his memory, thought Jackson. Was it age, or something else, that had started to close a few of the gateways of the major's mind?

'Elmore? Yes, dreadful! Somebody came and told me about it. Such a nice young man. He came here to see me, of course. It's a courtesy that they show me. For old times' sake, I suppose.'

'For old times' sake, sir?'

'Yes. You see, Inspector, I don't have much to do with the business. My father was an oil merchant – wasn't he, Maude? Very wealthy, he was. It was my father who put up the money for the mining company originally. Redcott, Caradyne and Company. That's . . . that's what it's called – isn't it, Maude?'

The major's eyelids drooped, and his head fell on to his chest. His wife put down her knitting.

'What my husband is telling you is all true, Mr Jackson,' she said. 'His father put a great deal of money into the mining venture, which was started by old Mr Caradyne, who was an engineer. He's been dead these many years. My husband retained his financial interests in the company, but embarked on a military career. We spent many years in India, and then in The Gambia.'

Mrs Redcott glanced briefly at her dozing husband. Jackson waited. She was, he realized, forming a resolution to tell him something.

'Mr Jackson, while we were in The Gambia my husband contracted what is called sleeping sickness, or Gambia fever. It wasn't so bad while we lived in Georgetown and then Serukunda, but later we had to move up-river among the Serahuli people. That's where Giles caught the fever.'

'And so he resigned from the army, ma'am?'

'Yes, he did. And we came here to St Jude's. I've told you all that because my husband looks and behaves much older than he is. I thought you should know.'

Jackson looked with interest at the major. A sleeping partner? The words perhaps had greater significance in his case.

'Thank you, ma'am, for telling me that. You mentioned the name Caradyne. Are there still any Caradynes in the business?'

'Caradynes? Indeed yes, Mr Jackson. Old Mr Caradyne's son, Mr Martin Caradyne, is most actively involved in the venture. He trained as a lawyer. They say he's very clever.'

Major Redcott suddenly woke up with a start.

'What? Did someone mention Caradyne? He comes here once a year in person, to show me the books. He explains it all to me. I don't see too well, so it's a mercy just to sit here and listen to him. There always seems to be some money for us! Not that we're really dependent on the mine. I've money of my own – haven't I, Maude?'

Mrs Redcott blushed very becomingly and sat up in her chair.

'My husband has always had a good income, Inspector, because his father was very wealthy. You may as well know, too, that I brought a large parcel of Great Western Railway stock into the marriage. My father was a trusted business associate of Mr Brunel, who established the railway.'

Major Redcott had been eyeing Jackson critically for the last minute. He looked mildly puzzled.

'You're a police inspector, aren't you? What is it? Some black-guardry, I expect. You hear of these Thugs—'

'Don't be silly, dear, that's India.'

'All the same, Maude, you never know. So what did you want to ask me?'

'About Robert Elmore—'

It was only a name, but not a common one. Sergeant Bottomley remembered little Annie, the maid, saying that a Mr

91

Elmore had visited the Loxley Andersons. It was a point well worth pursuing.

'Elmore? Dreadful! I remember now. Somebody wrote to me. Was it you? They found him drowned on the seashore. Poor lad. Now why should a young fellow of that age commit suicide? The mine manager – that man with the beard – he thought it was suicide. I wrote— Maude? What was that letter I wrote?'

Mrs Redcott's face suddenly looked strained. She's worrying about her husband, Jackson thought. We're tiring him.

Mrs Redcott rose from her chair and rang a brass handbell. The door opened immediately to admit Slab. He evidently knew the reason for the summons. Without waiting for orders he crossed the room and gently helped the major to his feet.

'Indeed yes, sir, indeed yes,' he said, 'a little nap would do you good. It's all this rain that's tiring you. Indeed yes, sir, indeed yes.'

The door closed silently behind them. Mrs Redcott resumed her seat. Somehow, with her husband out of the room, she was able to reveal a stronger, more determined, personality.

'O'Hare is very good with my husband,' she said. 'He was his batman out in Africa. He's very protective of poor Giles.'

She sat up in her chair. Time, thought Jackson, to change the subject.

'Now, Mr Jackson, you are evidently here on confidential business, so I won't ask any questions that you won't answer. But do you intend to stay in Polwarthan? If so, I can be of immediate help.'

'Indeed yes, ma'am. I'd originally intended to make just a brief visit, but I think a longer stay is indicated. My sergeant and I are lodging in Exeter at the moment.'

'Can you return to Cornwall tomorrow? I will have our groom ride over on horseback to Polwarthan today and prepare the mine manager, Mr Reuben Calderdale, to receive you both. There's no problem about accommodation at the company's premises, and my husband would want you to stay there until your investigation is finished. Meanwhile, when you arrive at Saltash tomorrow morning, you'll find one of our company's vehicles awaiting you.'

When Jackson and Bottomley arrived next morning at the station beyond the bridge they both saw a heavy closed van bearing the name Redcott, Caradyne & Co. standing in the station yard. A big cart-horse waited patiently between the shafts. A stolid police constable in uniform emerged from the rain, saluted the inspector, and introduced himself as Constable D. Polk. He motioned towards the van.

'This will get us fairly dry to Polwarthan, sir. It's a cruel drag from here, so let's be thankful for the shelter. Mr Calderdale, the manager of the mine, will be there when we arrive. I'm the constable at Polwarthan, sir. It seemed only right and proper that I should come to fetch you.'

It seemed to Jackson that this man Polk was wilting under the burden of holding office. He had a firm, heavy face, essentially expressionless, and with eyes that seemed too uninterested to lift themselves much from staring at the ground. He pushed his words out grimly, as though not much used to talking to anyone.

Polk climbed into the van, and when the two visitors had hauled themselves up, he let down the canvas flaps and tied their strings.

In this conveyance, driven by a saturated man in oilskins, the three policemen were taken on a seemingly interminable journey up sharply inclined lanes and across stony wastes, through stunted and dripping copses and along coarsely metalled roads until they descended into the village of Polwarthan.

There was nothing picturesque in the scene that confronted them when they had scrambled down from the van. The village seemed to rest on a raft of broken stones and scree, from which rose a single row of slate-roofed cottages. There was a beetle-browed alehouse with a faded sign and moss-covered roof, and an old stone church in a ragged churchyard with tombstones like broken teeth. Above all these buildings lowered the mine workings, and the vast engine shed.

Bleakness. . . . There's something alien and daunting about this rain-soaked place, thought Jackson. It's not just the rain: there's something forbidding in the very atmosphere. He glanced at Bottomley, and guessed that his sergeant was having similar thoughts.

Standing outside the alehouse was a giant of a man clad in an ankle-length gabardine secured at the waist by a wide leather belt. Beneath the brim of a high-crowned hat, two fierce grey eyes blazed at them. The rest of the man's features were obscured by a wide black beard. The gigantic man strode towards them. For the first time since he had greeted the two officers at Saltash, Constable D. Polk found his voice.

'This is Mr Reuben Calderdale, the general manager of the mine. Mr Calderdale, this is Detective Inspector Jackson.'

Polk turned an impassive face in Bottomley's direction. It was the nearest he came to asking the sergeant his name. Bottomley treated Polk to a dangerously tolerant smile.

'You'd better tell Mr Calderdale that I'm Detective Sergeant Bottomley, Constable. Then he won't forget, will he? And neither will you.'

'Well, well,' said Reuben Calderdale testily, 'never mind the formalities. I expect you'll be talking to Constable Polk later. In the meantime, come up to the mine-house, and I'll show you your quarters.'

Jackson was surprised at Calderdale's mild, educated tones. From his appearance he had expected someone far more gruff and intimidating. He was also disturbed by Bottomley's sudden truculence towards Polk. What, he wondered, did *that* portend?

As they walked up the stony path towards the mine-house they were joined and then escorted by two lines of silent, surly men who had appeared on the edges of the street. They stared sullenly and unblinkingly at the new arrivals, paying no attention to the rain tormenting their eyes.

Jackson felt an unaccustomed alarm. There was something terrifying in the vicious blankness of their hostile stares. This, surely, was not an aimless act?

Calderdale himself began to notice the unwanted escort, and made an impatient attempt to wave the men away. They took no notice. Jackson heard the giant manager mutter something to Polk, who stopped in his tracks and turned his impassive face in the men's direction.

However taciturn, Polk seemed to have no difficulty about exerting his authority. The threatening escort melted away as though by magic, and the moment of rising panic subsided.

The mine-house proved to be a morose, grey stone building of three storeys, with an array of grimy square windows and a heavy coffered front door. The rusting ends of iron tie-bars showed here and there through the façade, which was stained from roof to ground with runnels of brown rust.

The day-long rain had contrived to depress the thick smoke belching from the chimney of the neighbouring engine-house, so that the whole area of the mine and its buildings seemed enveloped in wet fog. There was a taste of soot in the air they breathed.

Constable Polk saluted, and left them at the door. Calderdale motioned to them to enter.

Inside, the general impression was of gloomy neglect. A dim, brown-panelled entrance hall contained a gaunt staircase. There were dark passages, uncarpeted, and with patches of bare plaster above the wainscot. There were brackets for oil lamps, and a few tin candle-sconces nailed here and there.

'This way, if you please,' said Calderdale, his boots echoing on the bare boards.

He led them to the rear of the house, where he had a dark business-room. Its sole window looked out on to the blank wall of a shed. There was a desk and a few chairs, a number of books connected with mining arranged neatly enough on a shelf, and a padlocked cupboard. A clock fixed to the wall had stopped at twenty past seven on some dreary morning or evening in the past, and had never been rewound.

'Sit down for a while, Mr Jackson, and you, Mr Bottomley. This is my office when I'm away from the mine-workings. Put your bags on the floor over there. In a minute I'll show you to your quarters, but for the moment I'd better tell you a few things about Redcott, Caradyne and Company. I gather that you've seen old Major Redcott? His groom rode over here yesterday afternoon.'

'Yes, Mr Calderdale. I've seen Major Redcott. He was not, I think, in the best of health.'

'You are right, Inspector. Major Redcott is frail through Africa fever, though he's sharper than many would think. His partner, Mr Martin Caradyne, is more active in the business.'

'I was hoping to meet Mr Martin Caradyne,' said Jackson.

'Indeed? He's away at Derby at the moment. He travels to various places around the country for most of the year. Mr Caradyne's a lawyer by training. He has a lot to do with land deeds and other things that often impinge upon our business.'

'And what exactly is the nature of that business, Mr Calderdale?'

Reuben Calderdale picked up a paper-knife carved from a piece of slate, looked closely at it without seeing it, and put it down again. He stroked his great black beard nervously with his right hand. The fingers, Jackson noticed, were slender, but the nails bitten and broken.

'Essentially, Mr Jackson, we're merchants. The principals of the firm are not trained mining engineers, which is why we employ specialist engineers and mineralogists on contract. We trade in lead, some tin, and in various types of shale for use in road-building. We've thought of trying to break into coal, but it's really too much of a risk.'

'And the mine here at Polwarthan is a lead mine?'

Calderdale threw Jackson an appraising glance. For a brief moment Jackson imagined that the bright eyes of the giant manager betrayed an inner alarm. Nevertheless, he answered readily enough.

'You'll understand, Mr Jackson, that there are various different kinds of activity that can all be lumped together and called "lead mining". What we're mining here is a stuff called galena – sulphide of lead, it is – and the yield of lead from that is only sixpence an ounce. It's a poor return for the company, and a thankless task for me. But come, I'll show you to your quarters.'

Reuben Calderdale led the way back along the drab passage towards the front of the mine-house, where they began to climb the steep staircase. The landings were tall, unfurnished and forbidding, with festoons of cobwebs hanging from the ceilings. There was a strong smell of mildew.

When they reached the third storey, Calderdale stopped and threw open the door of a long room containing three truckle beds, two of which had been made up with straw pallets and blankets.

'This is where you'll stay,' he said. 'I expect you've had little to eat today. There'll be a meal ready in the mess downstairs in half-an-hour's time.'

Calderdale stood with his hand on the door, watching the two men as they began to unpack their valises. Jackson paused in his task and looked at the great bearded man towering in the doorway. For some reason he's afraid of us, he thought, and yet at the same time he's fascinated by us. Later, maybe, he'll ask us what we're really doing here. . . .

'Yes, Mr Jackson, it's a thankless task. The men are a hangdog lot, sullen, and dangerous when they're drunk. They know there's not much lead left in the seams here, and that in a year or two's time the mine'll be closed down. There's no profit here worth talking of.'

'It seems a benighted kind of spot, Mr Calderdale,' said Jackson.

'It's a sorry place altogether, Inspector. Mr Martin Caradyne wants the company to withdraw from the enterprise. Maybe it will.'

Calderdale lingered gloomily at the door of the barely furnished room.

'Some folk say that the place is cursed – Polwarthan, I mean. They say that the mines were once sacred to Odin, and that a miasma of evil pervades those ancient galleries.'

Calderdale did not miss the knowing look that passed between the inspector and his sergeant. He gave a rather shamefaced laugh.

'Idle tales, Mr Jackson, as you obviously appreciate. And yet bad things have happened here. We'll talk of these things later, I expect.'

Calderdale left them abruptly, and they both heard him clattering off down the stairs.

'So, Sergeant Bottomley,' said Jackson, 'what do you think of Polwarthan?'

The sergeant had been looking out of the single grimy window, where he could see the squat brick chimney of the engine-house and its pall of black smoke. The leaves of the trees beyond the works were black and singed.

'I think it's a trifle damp, sir. Nowhere's got the right to be as damp as this in April. I wish we were back home and dry in Warwickshire! And I think—'

Bottomley stopped in mid-sentence. Far below, he could see the stolid, caped figure of Constable Polk intent on some bleak errand. Two men, bent double in the rain, were pushing a wooden wagon laden with stone along a tramway.

'And I think, sir,' he concluded, turning away from the window, 'that some of the damp has got into people's heads in Polwarthan. There are folk walking round here, sir, with rotting minds.'

The mess, as Calderdale had called it, was a kind of dining-room and kitchen combined. Here a sullen maid-servant served the men a meal of beef stew and dumplings, and a large jug of beer. There was a coal fire in the wide stone grate, which lent some cheer to the place.

Calderdale had eaten in silence for the most part. He mopped up his plate with a slice of coarse rye bread and drew on his tankard, wiping his lips delicately with a handkerchief. His measured, educated voice sat ill in the rough surroundings of the mess.

'You'll want to be knowing about poor Robert Elmore. To my way of thinking, his death was a private matter – suicide, in fact. He came down here to check the books and to see that all was fair and square. He was an interesting man. He knew something about minerals, whereas the other two were just book-keepers.'

'The other two?' Jackson interrupted. 'Who do you mean by that, sir?'

'What? Oh, there were two other agents, Mr Jackson, who came down here and fell foul of lurking ruffians. One was very badly beaten, and left the company soon afterwards. The other was pelted with stones whenever he ventured into the mine-workings. Mr Martin Caradyne instigated a vigorous enquiry on that last occasion, but we never found out who was responsible.'

Calderdale moistened his lips. He stared ahead of him as though reliving some unpleasant experience. His hands, Jackson noticed, were clasped steadily on the table, but there was a vein throbbing in his temple. His nervous agitation was almost contagious.

'And then came this business of poor Elmore. He's a great loss. There was something personal churning around in his mind that made him rush into the sea and drown himself. As Shakespeare said, "What private griefs they had alas! I know not that made them do it". You'll find the answer to this mystery in Redruth or Exeter, not here.'

Inspector Jackson smiled a little wearily, but said nothing. Sergeant Bottomley, who had poured some of the contents of his hip flask into his drink, addressed the manager in a loud, beery and friendly voice. The manager jumped in alarm.

'Very choice and poetical, what you've just said, Mr Calderdale. Mr Elmore drowned in the sea! Why do you say that when we all know it's not true? Mr Elmore was drowned in fresh water, and carried to the sea afterwards. That's a fact, established by the medical evidence. So why keep saying he drowned in the sea?'

He fixed the manager with a disconcertingly glazed smile. Calderdale was clearly nonplussed by Bottòmley's thick, loud voice, with its finely controlled edge of impudence.

'It may have seemed perfectly obvious to you, Sergeant, that this was murder,' Calderdale replied haughtily, 'but to the inexperienced – those of us who are not examining murders daily – it certainly looked like suicide when poor Elmore was found on the very margin of the sea, and weighed down like that.'

'What my sergeant says is true, Mr Calderdale,' said Jackson quickly. 'When the autopsy was done at Truro the surgeon found water in the lungs, as you'd expect. But it wasn't sea-water, sir. It was fresh. Robert Elmore had drowned, but not in the sea.'

'How do you know all this, Inspector Jackson? You've only recently come down here from Warwickshire, so I gather.'

Jackson smiled. He knew that Calderdale's question was more an expression of pique than a genuine request for information.

'I know all this, Mr Calderdale, because there's an excellent police station at Exeter, and they were happy to tell me everything I wanted to know. They also allowed me to use the electric telephone, and I spoke at great length to Inspector Tregennis at Truro. I don't normally use those telephones – I prefer the telegraph – but it was very useful on this occasion. Very useful indeed.'

'I see. And what else did your colleagues tell you about Elmore? Or mustn't I ask?'

'They told me, sir, that Mr Elmore was found with only his head and shoulders in the water. Now, when people want to make away with themselves on beaches they don't usually lie gingerly down on the edge of the sea and dip their head in the water. That in itself was sufficient to show that this death was not suicide.'

'But—'

'And there's something else, sir, if you'll let me finish. When Constable Polk finally arrived on the scene – and he took his time about it! – he had the wit to see that poor Mr Elmore had been dragged to the sea's edge from somewhere else. Dragged there by his murderer, aided perhaps by accomplices.'

Calderdale's eyes glimmered with what Jackson felt was an inner desperation. The more they talked about Elmore's death, Jackson saw, the more agitated this man became.

'I must agree with you perforce, Mr Jackson. Poor Elmore was murdered! But by whom? And to what purpose? It's a mysterious business altogether.'

When the thick and friendly voice of Sergeant Bottomley suddenly filled the quiet room again, Jackson saw Calderdale flinch almost in fear. It was clear that he was unable to cope with this seemingly befuddled man whose mind was as sharp as a pin.

Bottomley's red, flushed face was turned to the mine manager with a rather terrifying expression of affability.

'A mysterious business altogether, as you so rightly say, Mr Calderdale. And to my way of thinking, the biggest mystery of all is Robert Elmore himself. As far as I can make out, sir, he appears to have come into this world without kith or kin. He seems to have an identity down here in Cornwall, and he's floated briefly into our notice up in Warwickshire. But who is he? What is he? Or rather, what *was* he?'

101

Calderdale refilled his tankard. He seemed suddenly relieved and more relaxed. That, thought Jackson, is because Bottomley's drawing the conversation away from the fact of murder. . . .

'Well, Sergeant Bottomley, as to that, I think I can provide you with some answers. Elmore was certainly a skilled geologist, and a fully trained professional mining surveyor. He had all the necessary qualifications from the School of Mines at Redruth. He had worked for the company for over two years.'

Bottomley gazed fixedly at Calderdale without speaking. It was rather disconcerting, and Calderdale's discomfiture returned. It was not lessened by Jackson, who in turn had fixed his eyes expectantly on Bottomley. Bottomley noisily cleared his throat.

'Did this Mr Elmore have a brother? And – wait a minute! – was he a half-brother?'

'Why, yes, I believe that's so. How on earth could you have known that? There *was* a half-brother, a much older man by all accounts, who had also studied at the School of Mines. Poor Elmore was never willing to speak about family matters, but I gather that this elder brother had been involved in some scandal. I can say no more, because of course I don't know any more. I'm not an inquisitive man by nature.'

The bearded mine manager rose abruptly from his chair and stood by the fireplace. His face had regained its usual passivity. Producing a short clay pipe from his pocket he lit it with a spill of paper and inhaled thoughtfully for a while.

'In five minutes' time, Mr Jackson,' he said, 'I must get back to my work in the mine. But something struck me very forcibly just now. We've talked at great length about poor Elmore. *Why*? This case has been investigated by Constable Polk, and by Inspector Tregennis from Truro. I'm beginning to wonder what *your* connection is with the affair. I believe the police have their own etiquette about who should solve cases. Didn't this Inspector Tregennis at Truro object to your involvement?'

Inspector Jackson smiled, and Sergeant Bottomley made a

strangled noise that may have been a suppressed laugh.

'Very shrewd of you, Mr Calderdale, very perceptive. It's rather more than etiquette, sir, it's a matter of legal requirement and the independence of constabularies. But, you see, I've not come down all this way to the West Country just to get under Mr Tregennis's feet. I'm here on quite a different errand, which just may or may not involve the late unfortunate Robert Elmore.'

'Will you tell me what that errand is?'

'No, sir. I'm afraid that wouldn't be possible. But then, as you told me before, you're not an inquisitive man!'

There was no malice in Jackson's retort, and Calderdale smiled. It was the first time they had seen him do so. He turned to the door.

'I must return to the mine, Inspector. What do you intend to do now?'

'Well, sir, Sergeant Bottomley here will go now to talk with our colleague Constable Polk. What I'd like to do is see over the mine-workings, if that's in order.'

Calderdale's grey eyes widened in surprise.

'You want to go into the mine? By all means, Mr Jackson. I'll send a man across for you in about a quarter of an hour. But you must take care on the ladders. Mines are dangerous places.'

'That was very perceptive of you, Sergeant. About Robert Elmore and his half-brother. Remarkable, the way you suddenly see these connections.'

The two detectives had remained in the mess after Calderdale had left the house. They had both seen him striding across the stony waste in the grey drizzle. For a moment the mine-house seemed to be deserted.

'I've got a good memory, sir, and I never forget anything I'm told. I'm not as stupid as I look.'

'No,' said Inspector Jackson.

'Miss Deirdre Dovercourt's little maid, Annie, told me that she and Miss Deirdre had stayed together at King's Leyland with the

Loxley Andersons. I don't know when or why they went there, but it couldn't have been just after the earlier business with Mr Wheeler, because Annie would have been too young to be in service. But whenever it was, sir, Annie told me that "young Mr Elmore" came. The way she phrased that – "young Mr Elmore" – suggests that they'd met him before.'

'If that's true, Sergeant, then it was probably at Dovercourt House. They all seem to have been geologists. This Mr Elmore was probably yet another friend of Mr Lionel Dovercourt. An unfortunate young man, Sergeant: his friends seem to get themselves murdered. I wonder why Elmore called on the Loxley Andersons?'

'As you said, sir, they were all geologists. That's how I made the connection. Mr Elmore was a geologist; Mr Wheeler was a geologist. They were both murdered. Could they be related in some way? The different surnames would mean they were stepbrothers. It looks as though I was right.'

Jackson nodded absently. He was thinking of something else.

'What did you think of our mine manager?'

'Mr Reuben Calderdale? He's the ruins of a nice man, sir. He can't abide any mention of murder. He wants to pretend that Elmore's death was suicide. He's hiding something.'

'He certainly is, Sergeant! Did you hear him betray himself?'

'I did, sir. And very nicely you hurried him on after he did it! I'll make it my business to find out what he meant by those words.'

'Do, Sergeant. "Weighed down like that" – those were the words he used. Find out what they mean.'

Throbbing and threshing, the gleaming rods of the engine plunged and reared, plunged and reared, with an almost mesmeric and manic passion. The place seemed pervaded by the greasy smell of train-oil, and beneath that an earthy, lung-chilling dampness.

Inspector Jackson stood looking down into the pit below. He was standing perilously near to a void, falling away before him from the wet and greasy platform where he stood, clutching the flimsy handrail. The noise from the great steam-engine was deafening, and everything seemed to be shuddering in fear of its mighty force.

The pit, or shaft, held black, steaming water. Jackson could see a film of oil moving and shifting uneasily on its surface. He clung more tightly to the handrail. That water below him had accumulated from the condenser of the great engine: it was fresh water, and Robert Elmore had drowned in fresh water. . . .

Inspector Jackson was not an unduly imaginative man, but he could not fail to sense the menace in the air. There was something, a sort of electric tension, which began to clothe the blackness of the mine with a mantle of fear. Iron ladders led up from the platform, and the shadowy figures of silent miners seemed to have positioned themselves on rungs above him, where they stood motionless, looking down at him where he stood near the peril of water.

The educated tones of the gigantic Calderdale floated down to him above the crashing of the engine. The man's voice, adjusted to rise above the din, sounded like the thin bleat of a goat.

'Mines are dangerous places, Mr Jackson. One false step, one careless slip, and you're dead, or maimed. Be careful how you go. Poor Robert Elmore stood where you are now the other day, and nearly went over into the pit. Luckily I was right beside him.'

Jackson made no attempt to reply. He tightened his grip on the handrail, and peered into the impenetrable gloom of the galleries. A grotesque thought came to him unbidden. Had the miners dug too deep, and opened up the altar of Odin?

The goat's voice floated down again.

'It doesn't do to meddle, Mr Jackson. Some things are best left alone. Mines are funny places. A man can be lost in a tunnel, or a turning, and nothing heard or seen of him again.'

Jackson was now more attuned to the manic threshing of the great pumping engine, and at the same time his eyes could more effectively penetrate the gloom. He saw with a sense of shock that other dark shapes had appeared on the ladders and perilous platforms below him, having insinuated themselves into the scene from hidden galleries.

They said nothing, but from the way they stood it was clear that the conversation was of great interest to them. The inspector suddenly knew that it would be fruitless to investigate any further in the mine. All that needed to be seen would be hidden away through the skills of these mute watchers. The time had come to get out into the air, and consult with Sergeant Bottomley.

Sergeant Bottomley put his arm around the stooping shoulders of Constable Polk and gently propelled him through the ale-house door on to the village street. He had been in the dim bar long enough to see that the majesty of the law was kept well at arm's length in a dark nook near the door, where he had sat, staring glumly into his glass of ale. The few other grim and dusty men in the beery hovel appeared to regard Constable Polk as some sort of implacable foe.

'Well, now, Polk, my friend and comrade, let you and me go for a stroll down to the beach. I can see that you tend to be on the periphery of things in this rural spot. But now's the time, Constable Polk, to serve the Queen with all your might and main.'

Chatting in his usual agreeable fashion, the sergeant piloted his morose colleague down across the stunted grass to the edge of the stony beach. They sat down on a rocky outcrop, and Bottomley produced a minute notebook from the pocket of his coat. He moistened the thumb and index finger of his right hand and noisily turned over several pages.

'Here we are, then. Wednesday, April 6th, 1892. Body found on beach at Polwarthan by the Reverend Hezekiah Woodward, vicar, at about thirty minutes past eight in the evening. Constable Polk summoned to scene. Arrived at ten past nine. Noted that body had been dragged down to the edge of the sea?' It was a statement, but voiced as a question.

'Yes, Sergeant. This poor Mr Elmore had been surveying the works for two days, and showed no signs of going away. Very interested in everything, he was. Well, somebody done for him, and then tried to make out that it was *felo de se*. Devilry, that's what it was.'

'And what did you find in his pockets?'

Constable Polk seemed startled by the question.

'His pockets? There was nothing in his pockets. Jacket, trousers – nothing.'

Sergeant Bottomley produced his hip flask and treated himself to a nip of brandy. He seemed disinclined to offer his comrade any refreshment, despite Polk's earnest glances in his direction. Bottomley treated him to a beatific smile.

'Why did it take you forty minutes to get here that night?'

Polk moved restlessly on the rock and looked sulkily out to sea.

'Parson couldn't find me at first,' he muttered.

'Why not? Weren't you at home? Where were you that the parson couldn't find you?'

Polk made no reply, but his hands began to tremble slightly. Sergeant Bottomley looked at him with shrewd calculation.

'You'd been waiting for him, hadn't you? For Robert Elmore, I mean. Up in the woods, or somewhere like that. He'd been to see you, hadn't he, earlier that day? Said he'd want to talk to you seriously that evening, and so you went out to the woods, or wherever it was, and waited for him. But he never turned up, because he was dead. I'm right, aren't I?'

'Yes, you are, Sergeant, though how you knew that, God knows. He came about twelve o'clock to my house that day, and said he'd want to speak to me at about eight-thirty in the evening.

We arranged to meet in the skirts of the wood above the church-yard. But he never came.'

Perhaps it was the chilly atmosphere that made Constable Polk tremble. Or perhaps he too was afraid of the dire spell of Polwarthan. Bottomley's tone became more confiding.

'I suppose you've no idea who did the deed? Just private, between you and me.'

Constable Polk looked keenly at the sergeant before glancing away at the sea.

'I'll not make any accusations, Sergeant, not without proof. All I'll say is, it hadn't got to be someone here on the spot. Someone could have crossed into Cornwall by train from Exeter, murdered Mr Elmore, then got a train back. We're off the beaten track here, but we're not as isolated as all that.'

'Very interesting, my good Polk: food for thought, as they say. Anything else?'

'No, Sergeant. Mr Tregennis, the inspector over at Truro, paid us a visit, and conducted a very sound investigation. He conveyed Mr Elmore's body away.'

Sergeant Bottomley looked positively cheerful. He treated the constable to a gleaming display of teeth and a friendly nod.

'You don't like answering questions properly, do you? You're too coy, Constable, too much of a shrinking violet. But I'll give you another chance. The question I asked you was, "Anything else?" '

Polk scowled murderously at the darkening horizon.

'Only this, Sergeant Bottomley, since you insist. Keep an eye on our parson. He's cracked. He spends too much time in that church of his, muttering prayers or charms or whatever it is he does. He wanders about at night. In the churchyard, or up in the woods. Mr Calderdale wants it to be suicide, but we know better. It was murder. The answer may lie somewhere in Exeter, but don't forget our cracked parson. Parson Woodward. A man's cloth shouldn't save him when it's murder.'

Sergeant Bottomley seemed struck by this remark.

'You know, Constable Polk, that's very true. No matter how mightily a man may dress, if it's murder he's done, then he'll come to the gallows.'

6
Dark Days in Holy Week

The next day dawned dull and misty, with uneasy cloud scudding across the sky. It was Maundy Thursday. Inspector Jackson had already decided to see the vicar on that day, before the succeeding Good Friday took him inexorably into the Easter season, the busiest time of a clergyman's year. The forlorn clinking of a bell came to Jackson's ears as he and Bottomley emerged from the gloomy mine-house after breakfast.

Reuben Calderdale, who had left with them, plunged into the opening of a grim, brick-lined pit where an iron stair led to the nether regions. He had glanced at the two men before beginning his descent, but it had been impossible to judge what he was feeling. His great bearded face and staring eyes told them nothing.

'Our parson evidently maintains the full services here, Sergeant,' said Jackson, listening to the bell's faint invitation. 'It might be as well if we were to attend the service. Perhaps then Mr Woodward will emerge as something more than just a name and a set of rumours.'

The church of St Petroc looked as though it had long ago tried to burrow itself into the rising hill behind the village, and partly succeeded. It would have been difficult to date the ancient building, but those interested in such things would have seen fragments of Roman work reused in the thick Saxon masonry. The

110

nave was pierced with a number of narrow windows, and there were traces of others bricked up in earlier centuries. There was no tower, but a small bell-turret, heavily weathered, clung to the roof at the west end of the building.

The two detectives groped their way down half a dozen uneven and dank steps until they stood on the hard brick floor of the nave. The church was crowded with ancient box pews, some still with doors, others gaping doorless into the aisles. There was a smell of damp and disuse, and only a little dim light slid furtively in from the narrow windows.

Parson Woodward sat in his stall behind an old carved and pinnacled screen, the lower panels of which were adorned with dim medieval paintings of saints. The Prayer Book lay open on his desk as he waited in silence to begin the service.

It was ten o'clock. No one had joined him in the church: no wife from the cottages, no servant from the mine-house. No one ever comes, Jackson thought. Maybe that bell had been rung as a personal summons to *us*? He glanced at Bottomley, and sensed that the same thought had crossed his sergeant's mind.

Gaunt and stooping, with silvery hair and an intellectual brow, the Reverend Hezekiah Woodward looked reassuringly normal. He wore a spotless surplice over his cassock, with the black scarf of an Anglican clergyman placed carefully round his neck. Whatever his eccentricities, in the matter of clerical dress he was strictly orthodox.

They sat down in the front pew, and placed their hats carefully on the ledge before them. Presently the parson sighed, and fixed them with a troubled gaze. It was then that they glimpsed something of his inner torment, the unending burden of his crusade against the ancient demons of the north.

'I know who you are, gentlemen,' said Parson Woodward, 'and when the service is over I expect that you will want to speak with me. For the moment. though, I will say the office of Morning Prayer.'

His voice was well modulated, but there was a hint of hysteria in some of the cadences. It was a voice with the potential for rising in fear, panic or anger. He turned over a number of pages, and began the office. It was clear that he knew most of the text by heart, as his earnest gaze rested on Jackson rather than the book before him.

In due course the Gospel was read from a great lectern Bible. Once again, the priest's gaze never left Inspector Jackson's face. His voice gained in power, and seemed to echo from the dark spaces above the open rafters of the church.

'Here beginneth the thirty-third verse of the twenty-first chapter of the Gospel according to St Matthew.

' "There was a certain householder, which planted a vineyard, and hedged it round about, and digged a winepress in it, and built a tower, and let it out to husbandmen, and went into a far country. And when the time of the fruit drew near, he sent his servants to the husbandmen, that they might receive the fruits of it. And the husbandmen took his servants, and beat one, and killed another, and stoned another. Again, he sent other servants more than the first: and they did unto them likewise".'

The parable continued: the sending of the son, and his murder in order to steal the inheritance, and the ultimate wrath of the owner.

' "He will miserably destroy those wicked men, and will let out his vineyard unto other husbandmen, which shall render him the fruits in their seasons".'

When he had finished reading, he closed the Bible, but instead of returning to his desk he walked slowly up the nave, followed by his congregation of two puzzled men. Why had he not finished the set form of Morning Prayer? Why had he stopped so abruptly at the end of the Gospel? And, thought Jackson, why *that* Gospel?

Jackson's eyes had become accustomed to the gloom, and he could see now that the walls of the church were covered with a pattern of fantastic memorial tablets from past centuries, curling stone shields, lozenges of incised slate, stained marble plaques with the remains of gilded heraldry and sombre carved skulls. Among a welter of proud Latin he glimpsed some Cornish names – Trevannion, Wolcot, Polwhele – and for a moment imagined an earlier Polwarthan where families of substance had been proud to live.

Parson Woodward had paused for a while at the dark west end of the church. Jackson saw that he was looking down at a deep rectangular tank set in the old pavement. It was full of clear water, and he could see a constant shivering of its surface, as though something in its depths were agitating the water. Another Bible image came to Jackson's mind, though he could not place it: an angel who came down to stir the surface of the waters at a healing pool.

Parson Woodward spoke, half to himself.

'This tank is an ancient font for total immersion at baptism. Its construction is lost in the darkness of the old Celtic church, when the priests knew that the power of Odin still stalked the land. They who are submerged in this tank are buried with Christ, and then rise with Him. Oh, that I could immerse the whole of this wicked generation of vipers in this cleansing pool! It is ever fresh, as a spring runs through it, bringing the cleansing power of baptism to the sinner.'

The old clergyman's eyes shone with a partly rekindled zeal which lasted but a moment. Then his shoulders stooped and he sighed, mounted the six steps and emerged into the overgrown churchyard.

The morning light surrounded them at once, driving away some of the choking claustrophobia that had pervaded the church. Jackson heard Bottomley give an audible sigh of relief. He turned his attention to Woodward.

'Sir,' said Inspector Jackson, 'today is Maundy Thursday, but I noticed that you did not read the Gospel set for this day. Perhaps

I'd be right in saying that you'd chosen that particular story especially?'

It was as much a statement as a question, but it required some
acknowledgement.

'Those that have ears to hear, let them hear,' said Woodward. A
spectre of a smile hovered around his mouth. 'I see that you are a
man of discernment, Inspector.'

Inspector Jackson inclined his head. He had been reared in a
strict Church family, and had grown to manhood with the
cadences of the Book of Common Prayer ringing in his ears. He
glanced briefly at Sergeant Bottomley, who now addressed the old
clergyman.

'Reverend sir,' he said, 'I've been asking various questions of
various people with respect to the death of Mr Robert Elmore. I've
gathered that you were the person who found his body, and there's
one question I'd like to ask you: what did you find in his pockets?'

As always, there was an edge of truculence to his voice that was
belied by his genial smile. The parson seemed in no way surprised
by the question.

'Stones, Sergeant,' he said. 'Great heavy stones in his pockets,
weighing him down. I was reminded of the offender against children: better that a millstone were hung about his neck, and that he
were cast into the midst of the sea. I wondered then if the man had
planned his own death. But you will know as I do the wickedness
of men. This is a desolate, abandoned spot, where the Devil can
flourish. "A fruitful land maketh he barren: for the wickedness of
them that dwell therein".'

'These stones, sir,' said Jackson, 'can you describe them more
particularly?'

Parson Woodward stood in thought for a moment, and Jackson
wondered if he had heard his question. The clergyman fumbled in
the pocket of his cassock and took out a large rusty key.

'Come with me, Inspector, and I will show you one of those
stones.'

At the east end of the church, almost buried in gorse and bramble, was the external curve of the ancient apse. At the base of its centre wall, and thus immediately behind the altar, a dark damp stair led downward into some unknown crypt. Jackson remembered how, on the previous day, he had descended into the mine pit with Calderdale. Now it was the parson's turn to take him below the earth.

The stairs were very steep and wet, and they descended in total blackness. They could hear a murmuring, like the sound of voices engaged in a quiet but serious altercation. There was a smell of mould.

Woodward had evidently prepared himself for this visit, as he brought out of his pocket a box of matches. He struck a match and lit several candles arranged on an iron stand. As the yellow light spread out, the policemen saw that they were in a large stone chamber. Moisture dripped from the roof.

'What is that murmuring sound?' Jackson found that he was whispering.

'It is the murmur of the stream that feeds the baptismal font above. It has the power to cleanse, and to wash away sins in the waters of baptism. Whenever I hear that sound of the rill, I am reminded of the words of the beautiful hymn for children:

There is a fountain filled with blood,
Drawn from Emmanuel's veins.'

'Very beautiful, sir,' said Bottomley, 'very cheering, I've no doubt, especially for infants.'

The parson's steps echoed on what proved to be a paved floor. Jackson saw that parts of the pavement were tessellated, while other sections were made of compacted brick. Here and there fragments of marble shone dimly.

Woodward reached the centre of the chamber, where a raised brick altar stood. It looked like a place of sacrifice, its shape being subtly different from that of a Christian altar. Carved into its surface was the figure of a one-eyed being, arms spread out, and hands clutching spears. Various Prayer Books and stumps of candles were scattered over the surface of the brick table, which was coated thickly in candle-grease.

Parson Woodward felt among the Prayer Books and picked up a large stone, which he gave to Jackson.

'There you are, Inspector. I found that I had absent-mindedly put that stone into my own pocket when I stumbled upon the unfortunate gentleman. I placed it here in this devil's sanctuary to keep it safe from light fingers. No one but I dare venture into this pagan chamber.'

'A Hanging Grove of Odin,' said Jackson softly, and heard the old clergyman draw in his breath sharply.

'You know about such things? You are even wiser than I thought, Mr Jackson.'

'One day soon, sir, I hope to talk to you about these matters, but not just yet. I must concentrate all my faculties on investigating the death of Mr Robert Elmore.'

Parson Woodward sighed. His refined features suddenly held an infinity of sadness.

'I was more sorry than I can say, you know. He was a respectful, quiet-spoken man of good education. I have sometimes thought that he and I had met somewhere before, though he never showed any recognition of me. Whatever his origin, I suspect that he was a gentleman.'

'You spoke with him, then?'

'Certainly. As a matter of fact it was on the morning of his death, and he was holding such a stone as that in his hand. I was much preoccupied by troubles of my own, and did not pay much attention to what he said. I think that someone had startled him in some way, as he said something about a "glance", and that "proof of deceit would soon be forthcoming".'

The parson made a conscious effort to think more coherently.

'He used the expression "a silver glance" – rather fanciful, I thought – and said that he would make the mine yield up its evidence that very evening. He seemed rather pleased with himself, as I recall. I hope that these recollections will be of some value to you?'

'Yes, indeed, sir, very valuable and interesting. We will speak further on matters that will be of considerable interest to you at a later time. For the moment, though, I expect you will soon be immersed in the duties of the Easter season.'

Woodward treated Jackson to a wry smile. He began to extinguish the candles.

'All will be done as the church enjoins, Inspector, but it will, I'm sure, be done to an empty church. Empty, that is, but for me and the Holy Spirit.'

Jackson looked at Bottomley, who almost imperceptibly nodded in agreement with his unspoken question. He turned to Woodward.

'My sergeant and I will certainly join you for the Good Friday service, Mr Woodward, whatever our duties may dictate. And who knows? Others may be tempted to follow our example.'

Woodward smiled, but shook his head. He knew the Polwarthan folk too well to expect even small miracles where they were concerned.

They began their ascent of the steep stair, Woodward holding aloft one of the candles which he had taken from the stand. Jackson noticed a band of marble let into the wall as part of some ancient repair. It had engraved on it a clear script older than Gothic, and carved, perhaps, when Charlemagne had ruled as Holy Roman Emperor. Inured as he was by then to the affairs of Odin, it came as something of a shock to discern the surviving letters as they passed up the stairs:

. . .TE VICTOR ORA PRO N. . . .

Inspector Jackson and Sergeant Bottomley made their way to the lonely beach where the body of Robert Elmore had been found. They stood on a rocky outcrop rising from the stunted grass near the edge of the water.

'So what it amounts to is this,' said Bottomley. 'This agent Robert Elmore found out something here, and got himself murdered for his trouble. He told the parson he'd seen a "glance", maybe a look between Calderdale and some other person unknown – which betrayed a guilty secret.'

'What would that have been, Sergeant?' asked Jackson.

Bottomley made no reply for a moment. He was looking out towards the sea. Jackson listened to the water fretting the edge of the shore.

'Sir, this is a benighted place, that could turn men's minds. Reuben Calderdale lives in fear of something, and I wonder whether it isn't connected with this business of human sacrifice.'

'What do you mean?'

'I'm thinking of the Drowned Man and the Dried-Up Man. They were stepbrothers, and so in touch with each other. They both came to an ancient sanctuary of Odin, they both became acquainted with Parson Woodward, and they were both killed. Maybe Calderdale knows something, and is afraid to speak.'

'Maybe Calderdale himself offered the sacrifices. Have you thought of that, Sergeant?'

'Yes. sir.'

Inspector Jackson produced a briar pipe from his pocket, filled it from a pouch and lit it. He smoked silently for a while, looking out to sea. His eyes came back to the shingle.

'It's an odd way to murder a man, Sergeant, to fill his pockets with stones, and then lower him into fresh water.'

Sergeant Bottomley paused with his silver flask halfway to his lips. His eyes narrowed, and he put the flask down untasted.

'Why did you say that, sir? Why did you say "lower" him into fresh water? Why not "throw"?'

'Well done, Sergeant! Yes; it's because I'm thinking of that convenient tank at the church, a tankful of fresh water . . . I've an image in my mind of *someone* – or *some two* – lowering the unconscious Elmore into that tank. Or maybe – I wonder. . . .'

The inspector gazed out to sea again.

'I know what you're thinking,' said Bottomley. 'You're thinking of our reverend friend, the parson, who may be off his head, baptizing folk against their will, and doing it a bit too thoroughly. When they come floating up to the top, he puts stones in their pockets to make sure they stay safely down until he decides it's time for them to rise with Christ. Then he drags them down to the edge of the sea. . . . What was it he said? Something like "I'd like to baptize all these vipers if I could". Constable Polk reckons he's cracked. Maybe he's right.'

'Maybe he is. But I'd be very chary, if I were you, Sergeant, about believing everything that Constable Polk says.'

Jackson sighed. The air of gloom about Polwarthan he found acutely depressing. He looked around him at the rocks and trees and the waste of stones. What a benighted place! A picture came unbidden to his mind: a comfortable, book-lined room, a blazing fire, toast on a china plate – the lively voice of Harry Goodheart. Was there really such a world? He brought himself back to the bleak present.

'Do you remember that brick altar that Parson Woodward showed us? He'd put the stone from Elmore's pocket there. Did you see what else was lying among the candle-ends and prayer-books?'

Bottomley took a sip from his flask and wiped his mouth with his sleeve. So the guv'nor had understood his hint about Woodward after all. He shot Jackson a shrewd glance.

'Yes, sir, I did. It was a noose – a hangman's noose, very like the one someone had tied round the neck of Robert Elmore's half-brother, the Reverend Samuel Wheeler, MA, aged thirty-five.'

*

Constable Polk was deep in conversation with Reuben Calderdale when the two detectives reached the straggling village street. The mine manager towered over the constable, but there was about him the same stooping, defeated quality that they had seen in Parson Woodward. Maybe it was the air of the place, thought Jackson, that so rotted away a man's character.

It wouldn't be long now. Soon he and Bottomley would be out of this vile, threatening place and back in the warm familiarity of Warwickshire. For a moment he reminded himself of the fruitful orchard behind his cottage, and the figure of Sarah Brown crossing the grass. . . .

Jackson had seen and suspected enough. It was time to put a plan into action. 'Constable Polk,' said Jackson, 'I want you to come with me to the mine-house. I've official business to talk with you.'

Polk seemed relieved that Sergeant Bottomley no longer wanted to ask him questions. He felt on surer ground with the more affable inspector. Together they walked purposefully towards the gaunt dwelling beside the engine-house. Bottomley ambled off on business of his own.

'I want you to go into Truro, Constable Polk,' said Jackson, when they reached Calderdale's gloomy office, 'and deliver this letter to Inspector Tregennis. It sets out clearly what I have discovered so far, and makes some requests for assistance.'

He passed a sealed letter to the constable, who stowed it carefully away in a breast pocket of his uniform jacket. Jackson pointed to two small sealed boxes on a table. One was tied with string, and the other sealed with wax.

'Do you remember telling Sergeant Bottomley that there was nothing in Robert Elmore's pockets when you found him?'

'Yes, sir.'

'Well, when I questioned Mr Woodward, the vicar, he told me

120

that he had found a large stone in Mr Elmore's pocket. He kept that stone, and gave it to me. It's a very curious stone, Constable, to my way of thinking, and it needs to be looked at by a specialist. So when you've seen Inspector Tregennis I want you to make your way to Redruth with that little box – the one with the sealing-wax – and deliver it to the chief assayer at the School of Mines. It contains the curious stone. There's a letter inside the parcel, asking the Chief Assayer to identify what kind of stone it is. I want you to impress on him the urgency of the matter. You are to wait for a reply.'

Constable Polk was silent for a moment: he was working something out.

'Sir, tomorrow is Good Friday; the School of Mines will be closed.'

'That had occurred to me, Constable. But you could get to Truro today, and deliver that letter to Inspector Tregennis. We'll give tomorrow a miss, and you can set out for Redruth early Saturday morning.'

Constable Polk seemed very much relieved to hear Jackson's arrangements. Something approaching a smile hovered around the constable's lips.

'Shall I take the parcel now, sir?'

'No. You can call for it early on Saturday. I'm up very early, so you can come for it at any time.'

Constable Polk's eyes were fixed on the second parcel, which Jackson had not even mentioned. He was clearly curious to know what it contained. Well, there could be no harm in asking.

'And the second parcel, sir – do you want me to deliver that?'

'Hey? Well, Constable, that little parcel is destined for quite a different quarter. But if you would be so good as to post it for me at Truro this afternoon, I'd be much obliged. Just in the ordinary letter-post: it's nothing very special.'

Polk stood up and took the parcel from the table.

'Very well, sir. I'll be getting off now for Truro. I should be back before dark.'

Polk saluted the inspector, and left the room. He seemed cheered and encouraged by the conversation, and pleased with the errands upon which he was to be engaged. He glanced at the name and address written on the parcel that he had offered to deliver, but it meant nothing to him. As the inspector had said, it was destined for quite a different quarter: someone called Mr Rollo Bateman, of Park House, Old Penfold, Warwickshire. Some rich gentleman, no doubt, with a fancy name and house to match. None of his business.

Sergeant Bottomley watched Parson Woodward emerge from his house among the gnarled trees and make his way along the track to St Petroc's Church. When he came to the edge of the burial-ground he caught sight of the sergeant and stopped abruptly. He was a little afraid of Sergeant Bottomley. He looked like a profane, debauched fellow, and yet he wasn't. His rather glazed eyes would suddenly turn shrewd, and you saw that he was looking through your defences to your inmost heart. . . .

Sergeant Bottomley removed his hat and bowed. Parson Woodward acknowledged the bow with a brief inclination of his head.

'I've been looking for you, Parson! I expect you're very busy today. Easter-time's always a rush for the clergy. Perhaps we could go inside the church for a little while?'

'That, in fact, is where I was bound, Mr Bottomley. I am about to strip the Holy Table of its cloths in preparation for tomorrow. It's Good Friday, as you know.'

'Yes, sir.'

Woodward preceded Bottomley into the church, descending the steps into the gloom. The very faint murmur of the stream running through the baptismal tank could be heard, together with a creaking and settling of timbers.

The parson entered the dim little sanctuary of the church, and began to remove the altar coverings. A cloud of dust rose into the air.

'Good Friday, Mr Bottomley, is also called Black Friday by some. The ancient Anglo-Saxons used the term *Langfridai* – Long Friday, which I imagine had something to do with the solstice and the lengthening days. You should read Bishop Catania's paper on *The Names of Easter* in the Journal of the Pontifical Academy of Reims. Or there's something quite useful on the subject in Migne's *Patrologia Latina.*'

Woodward had folded the dusty cloth and laid it on a stone sill to the right of the sanctuary. Now he removed what was called the 'fair linen cloth', folded it, and added it to its fellow. He stood back and surveyed the old Jacobean altar table.

'Good of its type, Mr Bottomley, though you'll have seen better work. It came from the chapel of Polthean House, so I'm told. The old stone altar from pre-Reformation times is buried around here somewhere.'

'Sir,' said Bottomley in a loud, clear voice, 'did you place a hangman's noose around Robert Elmore's neck? Or did you find such a noose, and remove it?'

Parson Woodward stood quite still before the stripped table. His voice came faint and tremulous, and he remained with his back to the sergeant as he spoke.

'There are times when I forget that I have done things, and then find them done. I live only partly in this world, you see. I have enemies unseen by all but me; shadows of the old gods who wish to ensnare me. They cannot, of course, do so. But their assault is continuous and relentless.'

He came down from the sanctuary and stood at the lectern, where he began to place the markers in the great Bible for the readings of the following day.

'Here, Mr Bottomley, is all that I can say with certainty. There was indeed a noose around Mr Elmore's neck. Whose hands placed it there? Mine? I cannot say. There are ancient rituals that

123

remove the curse of this pagan sacrifice, and in order to render them effective, the token of the sacrifice must be present. I carry such a noose at all times in my pocket. I have found the noose already around the necks of victims. Others may have placed them there, or even I myself in some kind of divinely sanctioned trance.

'Whatever the truth of the matter, the rope was around Mr Elmore's neck, and that told me that he had been a sacrifice to Odin. I have seen that sign before. I considered it a personal thing, part of my crusade against the demons that have come into this world. And so I removed it. It is on the brick altar below the chancel, the chamber in which I struggle against those ancient powers.'

Sergeant Bottomley sighed. He bade the parson farewell, and walked slowly back through the nave.

'That settles it, I think,' he said half to himself. 'There's nothing much left now that we need to know.'

He walked thoughtfully back towards the mine-house. They had seen all they needed to see in Polwarthan. Soon they'd be back in Warwickshire, where the burgeoning spring was stirring the fields and woods. He would be comfortable again with Esther and the girls in his rambling home on the heath, with the mud and slurry, the pigs and hens, the dogs and the kittens. . . .

He saw Constable Polk emerge from the mine-house, clutching a parcel, his heavy boots churning the mud of the village track. The glance that the constable gave him held all the expressionless indifference of a reptile.

When Jackson and Bottomley entered St Petroc's Church at ten o'clock on Good Friday morning they found to their surprise that they were not alone. Despite Parson Woodward's prediction to the contrary, a congregation of sorts had assembled.

In the front pew, almost hidden by the pulpit, Reuben Calderdale sat, his eyes staring into the gloom of the sanctuary as though he saw something there concealed from the others. Across the aisle from him, Constable Polk sat upright and stern in his rain-dampened blue serge.

The two detectives slid quietly into a pew halfway up the nave.

The presence of this congregation, small though it was, seemed to bring out Woodward's latent powers. His voice gained in firmness and conviction as he read the Good Friday service. He asked them to pray that all heretics would be saved among the remnant of the true Israelites. He told them how it was not possible for the blood of bulls and goats to take away sins.

Jackson saw Reuben Calderdale shift nervously in his pew. It was as though the gigantic man was trying to shrink into his greatcoat in order to shut his ears to the mysterious utterances of the priest.

Polk has noticed, too, thought Jackson. He had turned and looked sharply across the aisle at the uneasy manager. Calderdale appeared to be trembling.

Had Parson Woodward, too, sensed that Calderdale was ill at ease? It seemed so: he was looking fixedly at him as he intoned the words of the day's Epistle:

' "Let us draw near with a true heart ... having our hearts sprinkled from an evil conscience, and our bodies washed with pure water. . . ." '

Before Woodward could finish the reading, a hoarse scream from Reuben Calderdale shattered the solemnity of the service, bringing it to a dramatic end.

'It was fresh water!' he shrieked. 'He was drowned, but not in the sea!'

The tall, powerful figure rose to its feet, stared at the parson with wide-eyed terror, then pitched forward in a dead faint.

Constable Polk walked through the chill, dank churchyard with Parson Woodward. Neither man seemed to notice the fine, cold rain. Polk had moved swiftly to shepherd the old clergyman out of the church while Jackson and Bottomley tended the unconscious mine manager.

'Leave him be, Parson,' Polk had said, 'leave him to the law. There's something weighing heavy on his conscience, by the look of things.'

'You mean—?'

'Mr Elmore's death, I shouldn't wonder. He was drowned, you know, but not in the sea. That's a mystery, to my way of thinking.'

This was the longest speech Polk had ever made to Parson Woodward. The old clergyman had a distinct feeling that he was, at last, being treated as an equal member of the community. It loosened his tongue.

'There was a noose about Robert Elmore's neck. It's always a sign, Polk, a sign that sacrifice had been made to the Abomination. Who could have done such a thing?'

'Who indeed, sir? We must wait and see what Mr Calderdale says and does when he comes round from his faint. It may mean nothing. Or it may mean everything.'

'He was always a still, sufficient man, "walking as the Gentiles walk, in the vanity of their mind, having the understanding darkened". I will do as you say, Polk, and leave him to the law. We shall see, in the fullness of time, if Reuben Calderdale has been the secret priest of Odin in this cursed sanctuary.'

The two men walked in silence towards the vicarage. There was no sign of Calderdale or of the two detectives. When they reached the vicarage gate, Polk saluted Woodward and went on his way. He wondered what the parson had meant about Odin. Someone in the history books, he seemed to remember. Best not to ask. It would only be another of the parson's cracked fancies.

Hezekiah Woodward stood lost in thought at his gate, oblivious to the rain. He thought of the tantalizing quality of Polk's voice now that he was hearing more of it. What memory was it stirring? His mind was still darkened by many shadows, but somewhere in its deeper recesses there was developing a glimmer of new light.

7

The Devil's Brew Boils Over

At seven o'clock the next morning, Constable Polk, looking very official in his many-buttoned uniform greatcoat, called at the mine-house to collect Inspector Jackson's parcel which he was to take to the School of Mines at Redruth. The inspector was eating a solitary breakfast of bread and dripping in the mess-room, and the parcel was waiting for Polk on the table. Jackson pointed to a bench.

'Sit down there, Constable Polk, while I remind you what I want you to do. Deliver this parcel to the chief assayer in person, and see that you place it yourself into his hands. I'm taking no chances with it.'

'That other packet, sir. I posted it on Thursday at the post office in Truro. I think the gentleman it was addressed to should get it today.'

Polk was fishing for information when he said this, and was slightly surprised when he found he had made a catch.

'Yes indeed, Polk. It's nothing directly to do with this business of Robert Elmore. The gentleman I sent it to, Mr Rollo Bateman, is very interested in specimens of moss and lichen, so I sent him some in that little box. As a matter of fact, I owe him a favour! But the important business is this parcel that you are to take to Redruth. I firmly believe that the solution to the murder of Robert Elmore lies in this parcel.'

'The stone that Parson Woodward found in poor Mr Elmore's pocket, sir?'

'Yes. I can't tell you more than that here, Constable Polk, because I believe that walls have ears. Once you've delivered the parcel you can come back here, and watch a little surprise that Inspector Tregennis and I have concocted for the particular villains of this piece.'

Polk got to his feet and took the parcel off the table. He stood rather uncertainly near the door, which he had opened. He ventured a few words.

'What happened to Mr Calderdale yesterday, sir? After he fainted in the church? There was neither sight nor sound of him for the rest of the day.'

'Sergeant Bottomley and I got him out into the air, and he recovered straight away. It was very dramatic in the church, as you know, but it was only a faint. We accompanied him back here, and he retired to his office. He spent most of the day there, reading account books and writing notes. He appeared for meals, but didn't say very much. He was embarrassed, as you'll appreciate. He went to bed early. As far as I know he's still there. In bed, I mean.'

'Thank you, sir. I wondered, when he shouted out like that, whether he knew something about Mr Elmore's death. I told Parson Woodward that Mr Calderdale was worried in his mind. I'd keep a close eye on Mr Calderdale if I were you, sir. He looked that desperate yesterday that I wondered if he'd try to do himself a mischief. Well, I'll be on my way, sir.'

'Now that Polk's gone on his travels, Sergeant, there's nothing much left for us to do here. We'll spend one more night in this place – we'll have to do that – and then tomorrow, Sunday or not, we'll get out of it to Truro.'

Sergeant Bottomley cast a critical glance around the room that

129

Calderdale always called the mess. It was comfortable enough in a faded sort of way, he thought, but a lick of paint wouldn't do it any harm. Or much good either, come to that.

Bottomley got up from the table and straightened a picture that was hanging askew on the wall. It was an engraved black-and-white view of a stretch of countryside mounted behind cracked and flyblown glass. It looked like the ghost of scenery.

'You don't like this house, do you, sir? You've been on edge ever since we came here.'

'I *don't* like it, Sergeant, you're quite right about that. There's something – I feel as though there's a great weight suspended above me, waiting to crash down. I feel as though I'll choke if I have to stay here much longer.'

Towards mid-morning the two men left the mine-house and walked through the village. They could hear the drumming of the steam-engine in the vast shed as they passed through the low-lying pall of dense black smoke from the chimney-stack. The area around the mine-workings seemed alive with miners, their clothes blackened with soot and soaked with rain.

'A regular hive of activity, sir,' Bottomley observed, 'considering that the mine's supposed to be played out. Very keen on mentioning the fact, is our Mr Reuben Calderdale.'

Jackson caught Bottomley's shrewd glance, and smiled.

'The point had not escaped me, Sergeant. Businessmen don't usually advertise to all and sundry that they're not doing well. And if they do, no-one ever believes them.'

They walked up the main street of Polwarthan. Every door was closed, including that of the alehouse, and there were no signs of life. No smoke rose from the cottage chimneys. Somewhere they could hear the plaintive whining of a dog.

In a few minutes' time they reached the mouth of the road that had brought them into Polwarthan. It was, they knew, the only way into and out of the village, which was surrounded by tangled woodland on three sides, the fourth side being the margin of the sea. They heard the murmur of men's voices, and walked through the trees to investigate.

Fifty yards along the track, a group of men were standing around an overturned iron-tyred lorry that had shed its load of stone, blocking the way out from Polwarthan. One man held a trembling horse by the bridle, and Jackson saw that the traces had been cut to free the animal. Other men held wide, shallow spades.

When the men saw the two detectives they stopped and turned their grimy faces towards them. No one spoke, or offered any words of explanation. Jackson and Bottomley walked back to the village street, and from there to the gloomy confines of the mine-house.

Jackson hauled his watch from its pocket in his waistcoat and flicked open the cover.

'Nearly eleven o'clock,' he said. 'Polk should be in Truro by now.'

They had found the mess empty, and there seemed to be no one else about. Bottomley had thrown some coal on the fire, and had found where the barrel of beer was kept in a small scullery. The two men sat uneasily with their tankards of rather flat beer at the table, where the remains of their hurried breakfasts still lay.

'That accident on the road,' said Jackson, 'what did you make of that?'

Bottomley drained his tankard and set it down on the table.

'There was a frightened horse at the scene, sir, which suggests that it was a genuine mishap. I remember how steep the road was when we came down it into Polwarthan the other day. On the other hand—'

Jackson finished the sentence for him.

'On the other hand, Sergeant, the best way of faking a convincing accident is to do the job properly, which in this case would mean hàving a horse at the scene.'

'And if they've deliberately blocked the road, sir, then it may be to prevent someone from coming in. Like this Mr Tregennis from Truro. But it's more likely intended to prevent someone getting out. Us, for instance.'

Jackson felt the strange sensation of the whole weight of the mine-house resting tenuously on his shoulders. Three storeys, rising above him, resting, waiting to move.

'When I was fifteen or so, Sergeant, I was taken to Birmingham to hear Mr Charles Dickens read from some of his books. There was one about an old, rotten house that suddenly collapsed while a man was looking at it. I can't remember what it was called. That's what this place feels like.'

He looked absently at the table, and something began to stir in his mind.

'Sergeant, it looks as though Calderdale hasn't come down yet. There's no sign of him having breakfasted. I wonder. . . .'

'It's after eleven, sir. He must have left the house earlier. He probably gets something to eat and drink in the mine-workings.'

'All the same, Sergeant, I'd like to make sure. There's something unsettling me about this place. Where are the servants? There's no one here, yet the fire was made up. It's like a house of the dead. I think it's important to find Calderdale. To . . . to *place* him, if you get my meaning.'

They looked first in Calderdale's dark office, and then in the other rooms on the ground floor. Moving into the hall, they mounted the stairs to the next storey.

One room on the first floor proved to be Calderdale's bedroom. It contained a brass bedstead, a clothes cupboard, and a rough dressing-table on which stood a shaving mirror, a Bible, and a copy of the complete works of Shakespeare. The bed had clearly not been slept in.

'Look, sir,' said Bottomley softly, nodding towards a picture above the bed.

It was a large engraving of a human eye, open and staring,

above which were some characters in a script neither man recognised. Beneath the eye, in English, were the words:

THOU, O GOD, SEEST ME!

They searched the warren of bare chambers on the other floors without success. It was virtually certain that Reuben Calderdale was nowhere in the house.

Calderdale was not at the mine. A surly overseer had answered Jackson's enquiry with a palpable unwillingness that could not conceal his own personal anxiety. He was obviously speaking the truth, and was himself uneasy at Calderdale's non-appearance.

'If he didn't sleep in his bed last night, Sergeant, then he may have been holed-up somewhere in the village. Why? Maybe he was planning the little accident we saw on the road earlier on.'

The alehouse was open when they arrived at it, and a slatternly woman in a canvas apron was busy in the dim tap-room washing ale-pots in a wooden tub. She turned a surly face in their direction.

'What be you wantin'? My man's not here.'

'I'm looking for Mr Calderdale,' said Jackson.

'He's not here. There's been neither sight nor sound of him this morning. Bad luck to him! There's men waiting to work the seams that can't do it without his say-so.'

Jackson and Bottomley left the alehouse and hurried through the fine rain. They struck out across the stone and scree of the village street and through the soaked grass that skirted the churchyard.

Was Polk right? Calderdale could have murdered Robert Elmore, perhaps for some reason completely unconnected with the mine. Was his own carefully crafted case too clever by half? Jackson felt the unease rising from somewhere near the pit of his stomach. He was not quite sure why they were going to the

133

demon-haunted church. It seemed the inevitable place to search. Perhaps Calderdale had been drawn back to the place, a sanctuary for a man whose mind was disturbed by the terror of guilt.

Jackson pushed open the heavy door of St Petroc's. It was as gloomy as ever inside the old church, and it took the two men some time for their eyes to grow accustomed to the dim light.

'He's not here, sir,' said Bottomley. 'Maybe he's slipped away through the woods.'

'I wonder? It doesn't make sense, Sergeant. There's something yet that I haven't understood.'

Jackson stood halfway along the nave and listened. He could hear the gentle murmuring of the stream running through the ancient baptismal tank. Bottomley, he remembered, had suggested that the font had been used for unholy purposes. He had seen Parson Woodward as the crazed performer of lethal baptisms.

The inspector walked slowly down to the west end of the church and stopped near the ancient baptismal tank.

Had Calderdale, then, been the perpetrator? Had Robert Elmore been drowned in this deep font, his lungs filling with the fresh water meant for baptism? Had Calderdale fled that very morning from the scene of his crime?

In his mind's eye, Jackson saw a human form rising slowly up through the dark, fresh water, vague at first, and then focused, a large, dead, bearded face with open staring eyes, the clear water giving them a silvery look – a silver glance. . . .

Bearded? Jackson jerked to attention, and peered into the depths of the tank. Looking earnestly back at him with unseeing eyes was the dead and drowned face of Reuben Calderdale

'So this is the end of it: a life for a life. Well, perhaps it is for the best. This is the fruit of remorse. I knew that this would happen. I knew, you see, that he had murdered Mr Robert Elmore.'

Parson Woodward had come into the church to say the morning service, and had silently approached Jackson and Bottomley, who were standing in stunned immobility near the baptismal tank. Woodward showed no sign of surprise at what was floating in the tank. Jackson saw him glance briefly at the body and then turn away. He spoke as much to himself as to his companions.

'I fear that Calderdale was the servant of Dark Powers, and that he had offered Mr Elmore as a sacrifice. Constable Polk suggested as much. That is why I am not surprised that the wretched Calderdale's desire to make reparation has brought him, too, here to death by water.'

Inspector Jackson took the parson's arm and steered him away from the font and its awful contents. His voice was quiet but firm.

'How did you know, sir, that Reuben Calderdale had murdered Mr Robert Elmore?'

'I knew, Inspector, because I heard him confess! It was here, standing by this now desecrated font, that he gave himself up to Constable Polk. It was about three o'clock in the morning, a time when few in Polwarthan are stirring. They did not know that I was in the church: I am often here, praying in dark corners.

'When I heard Calderdale begin his confession I moved out through a private door. Although confession is one of the concerns of a priest, in this case it was not mine to hear. It was a confession of guilt in the face of the law to an officer of the law. In any case, it offended me to be an eavesdropper at such a moment. I slipped away through the graves and so back to my parsonage.'

'And can you, sir, remember any part of Mr Reuben Calderdale's confession? What had he begun to say to Constable Polk before you moved away? You see, sir, it's important that I establish the facts.'

'I remember quite clearly what he said. "I've asked you to come here, Polk", he said, "because we are not likely to be

135

disturbed. I tell you again I cannot go on. I cannot lie any more. You have seen how my soul was tormented at the Good Friday service. The truth of Robert Elmore's death is crying out to be known. Better that I was dead than to carry the burden of this secret".

'What awesome words those were! I crept away. What Calderdale had to say was for Polk's ears alone. I gather that you have sent him away today on police business. When he returns from that errand, ask him, and he will tell you all.'

Parson Woodward found himself faced with tasks far more tangible and immediate than his accustomed struggles with demons. He had watched while Jackson and Bottomley had attempted to lift the heavy body of Reuben Calderdale from the font, and had seen how the task would be impossible without help. When the half-soaked inspector turned to him with an unspoken request written in his face, he was ready to make a reply.

'If you will wait for five minutes, Mr Jackson, I will fetch a man whom we can trust, and he will help you. I, alas! am too frail to give you any physical assistance.'

'Who is this man?'

'His name is Nicholas Stadie. His right leg was crushed in an accident, and he's employed as a surface-worker. He's a man who at least manages to mutter a greeting whenever he crosses my path. He'll even meet my glance when I look at him. He will help you.'

Without waiting for a reply, Parson Woodward hurried from the church. A few minutes later he returned, followed by a thin, balding man who walked stiffly and with a swinging limp. He was, nevertheless, strong and wiry and, with his help, the lifeless body of the manager was removed from the baptismal tank.

Stadie had alerted some other men, and a hand-cart was manoeuvred along the narrow church path. The two detectives and Stadie placed the body on an unscrewed door that was brought down into the church, covered it with an altar-cloth, and carried it out to the cart.

The churchyard was crowded with sullen, unshaven men. There was the reek of drink in the air. No one uttered a single word. Four men came forward and received the body, placed it in the cart, and began to drag it away to Calderdale's house. Above the rumbling of the iron tyres it was now possible to hear vicious mutterings and oaths, accompanied by threatening glances at Nicholas Stadie.

Jackson motioned to the crippled miner to return with him and Bottomley to the church. As Stadie turned from the path a stone came hurtling across the churchyard to strike him in the small of the back. He gasped, but did not even turn round. It had been a signal to him that he was now seen as a deserter, a collaborator with those outside their closed circle.

There's danger here, thought Jackson, danger for us all. Some devil's brew is coming to the boil. Being in Polwarthan is like being in a cell. The door is being slammed shut and the locks turned. . . .

Inspector Jackson looked long and hard at the thin, nervous man in the threadbare clothes splashed with water. Unshaven and bleary-eyed like the others, he nevertheless lacked the air of desperate hardness that characterized most of the men in Polwarthan. Jackson addressed the man without any preamble.

'Nicholas Stadie, I know what has been going on here. *Know*, you understand, not guess. Will you confirm that I am right by telling me yourself?'

'I will not, mister. I'll tell you nothing. I have a wife, and a daughter of eight years.'

'Will you go on foot with a letter to a place in Saltash for me?'

'I will. But you must pay me. I am poor, and now Mr Calderdale's dead I'll lose my place. It'll be the workhouse or the prison for me.'

'Here is half-a-crown,' said Jackson. He took a sealed envelope from his pocket and gave it to the man. 'Take that to the tele-graph office at Saltash, and tell the operator to send the message enclosed in this envelope immediately. Can you read?'

'No, master.'

'Well, that writing on the outside is my name, Detective Inspector Jackson. Tell the operator. If you do this successfully, I will see what can be done for you and your family. I know what's going on here, Stadie, and I believe you to be innocent.'

The miner looked Jackson straight in the eye for the first time.

'Thank you, master. I'll not let you down.'

Stadie knew all the tracks and hidden ways out of the village, and he was able to gain the Saltash road without being seen. Although he limped, he was a strong man, and the journey would pose no problem. The resentment of the stone flung at his back still rankled. He would help this man in spite of them. Perhaps there was a different kind of world waiting somewhere beyond the confines of Polwarthan.

The body of Reuben Calderdale lay on a long table in a bare room at the front of the mine-house. Jackson folded down the sheet from the bearded face and turned to Bottomley, who stood beside him on the bare boards of the usually empty room.

'Stones, Sergeant – he made the mistake of letting us know that Robert Elmore's pockets had been full of stones, and that put us on the track.'

' "Weighed down like that" – they were the actual words he used, sir. When Parson Woodward found Robert Elmore's body the pockets were stuffed with stones. But when Constable Polk arrived at the beach all the pockets were empty. At least, that's what he said.'

'Yes, that's what he said. So Calderdale had seen Elmore's body after the vicar had stumbled upon it, and before Polk arrived on the scene. Elmore was drowned in the baptismal tank

138

and then dragged down to the beach. They were going to throw him into the sea so that it looked like suicide. But – well, Sergeant?'

'They were interrupted, sir, by Parson Woodward, out for an evening stroll. They had to beat a hasty retreat, leaving the stones in Elmore's pockets. Parson Woodward knew that Elmore had been murdered. He's no fool, even if he does like speaking in riddles.'

Jackson sighed. He looked at the still face, dignified in repose, no longer tortured by conscience and remorse.

'Look at him, Sergeant Bottomley. Think what people are going to say about him! How he had murdered Robert Elmore, and how the Reverend Hezekiah Woodward had heard him confess the murder to Constable Polk.'

Bottomley smiled slightly, and shook his head.

'People say all sorts of things, sir, because people can suffer from misconceptions, such as the idea that Mr Calderdale murdered Robert Elmore. Mr Calderdale murdered no one, sir.'

'Precisely, Sergeant. Which brings us to the other misconception, the one about Parson Woodward hearing Mr Calderdale confess to Polk. Parson Woodward heard no such thing.'

It was towards one o'clock that Inspector Jackson realized how he and Bottomley had become isolated in the mine-house. The sullen maid, and another woman who had worked in the house, had brought them some salt beef and beer, and then disappeared. Presumably, thought Jackson, they felt no obligation to remain in the house now that their master was dead.

'Sergeant Bottomley,' said Jackson, 'our aim now must be to get out of this place before something happens. I don't like the feel of things, and I don't just mean the feel of this tottering, top-heavy house. Let's search through Calderdale's things. After that, we'll either lie low until Stadie returns, or make a break for it.'

In Calderdale's dark business-room at the back of the house, Sergeant Bottomley deftly unscrewed the hasp and staple from the padlocked cupboard and looked inside. The cupboard contained an array of tools and drills, all carefully oiled, and a number of instruments and gauges fashioned in brass.

'Nothing sinister there, sir,' he said, and closed the cupboard door. He joined the inspector at Reuben Calderdale's desk.

Jackson had taken a mass of papers from the desk, and was quickly and rather nervously turning them over. Most of the documents seemed to be straightforward paperwork connected with the running of the mine. There were receipted bills, invoices, estimates for building work and a number of ledgers.

'Hello, Sergeant, what have we here?'

He had rummaged around at the back of the desk and had found a tin box containing a number of letters and scraps of paper. He arranged them on top of the desk.

'These seem to be private letters, Sergeant. Here's one dated 1878 and signed "Paulina". It's to wish him well in his new appointment, and asks him to guard against what she calls "the greed for gain".'

'A lady friend, then,' said Bottomley. 'Fourteen years ago. I wonder who she was?' He took the letter from Jackson and examined it.

'It's headed "Friargate, 4 March 1878". Friargate. . . .'

Jackson pointed to one of the scraps of paper laid on the desk.

'There's mention of Friargate in that handwritten receipt. It's dated in June 1890: "One hundred pounds received for consignment brought to Friargate on the railway".'

Sergeant Bottomley had sat down on a stool near the desk. He reached into his pocket for his battered hip-flask and fortified himself with a swig of its contents.

'I'm getting a picture, sir, a fine town centre with buildings from the last century – a prosperous place. Irongate, King Street . . . I went there once on business just before Poppy was born.

Queen Street . . . Friargate. Derby! That's it, sir. It's Derby. That's where Mr Calderdale's Paulina lived.'

'Or was staying, Sergeant. Well done. Now why does Derby ring a bell? Who told us about Derby? Surely—'

Jackson stopped short as Bottomley held up his hand in warning. He was looking intently at the window.

'There was a man looking in just now, sir. I just caught a glimpse of his ugly face flattened against the window! They're dangerous, these dogs, and stupid with it. They're afraid that we're going to find something in here, which means that there's something to find. That cur will run off now to his mates and tell them we're searching through Calderdale's papers.'

Jackson gathered the documents together and returned them to the desk. He softly closed the desk-lid.

'There's a dangerous feeling in the air, Sergeant,' he said. 'I've felt it all day. We'll retreat from here to the mess, and then we'll wait until that poor man Nicholas Stadie gets back. If Mr Tregennis is as efficient as I hope he is, surprising things should be happening in Polwarthan before the day's out. At least,' he added, 'that's what I hope.'

They left the dark office, and Jackson locked the door. The gloomy mess felt more secure than the vulnerable back office, and there was still a fire burning in the grate. They sat down at the table.

After a while Jackson said, 'Derby! I knew it meant something. Calderdale told us that the other partner, Caradyne, was away in Derby. There's a link there, Sergeant. Once we're free of this devil's lair I'll pursue that lead. I worked once on a case with Superintendent Crossway, who's at Derby now. I've no doubt he'll tell us a few interesting things about Friargate and "Paulina" if we choose to ask him.'

Jackson found that he was raising his voice to make himself heard above a series of bangs and rumbles coming from outside the house. He peered through the grimy window and saw a throng of silent figures intent on dragging various heavy burdens over the shale. The mulish intensity of the men somehow seemed to fit in with the general wretchedness of Polwarthan. Although it was only early afternoon the sky was slate-grey and threatening.

The noises outside subsided, and the house fell quiet. The two policemen sat down by the fire, and Jackson lit his pipe. He saw Bottomley's eyes slowly close. The flames leapt up in the mess-room fire. Flames . . . why should that nightmare picture come back now to haunt him? He remembered how he had arrived at his burning cottage to see a vicious column of black smoke shooting vertically from the chimney, almost in mockery. The wave of heat had thrown him back in spite of himself. His clothes had burst alight, but he had not noticed until afterwards. It would never leave him, the stench of burning timbers, the mad chuckle of the flames, the screams. . . .

Jackson sat up in his chair. Enough of the past. There was work to be done. The warm mess-room seemed to be filled with the blue haze of smoke from his pipe. He cleared his throat and knocked the pipe out on the hearth. Sergeant Bottomley opened his eyes, glanced over at Jackson, and then froze as though suddenly turned to stone.

'Sir! Look behind you!'

Jackson spun round, ready to tackle an assailant. Instead, he saw a steady stream of dark smoke pouring under the mess-room door. He sprang to his feet.

'Sergeant! The house is on fire!'

Jackson flung himself at the door and tore it open. A crimson wall of flame leapt at him with what seemed to him like a shout and he sprang back in terror. Bottomley thrust him aside with an oath and slammed the door shut. Already they could hear the shriek of a falling beam at the rear of the house. There was a smell like that of burning oil in the air, and a tightening heat that seared the lungs.

Beside the dresser was another door, leading into the front hall. Bottomley opened it and dragged Jackson out of the mess-room. Dangerous wisps of vapour hung in the dark air. Jackson saw a small triangular space beneath the stairs. A man could hide in that little space. . . .

'Come on, sir, help!'

Bottomley's urgent voice brought Jackson back to the present with a jolt. A noise above them proved to be the cracking of the ceiling plaster, which began to shower down on them in white splinters. Jackson's premonition was coming true. The massive structure of the house above them was starting to shift and collapse.

They threw themselves on to the great front door of the mine-house. Although the key turned in the massive iron lock the door was immovable.

Bottomley sprang to a narrow, barred window beside the door. Piles of beams and machinery had been used to seal off the front entrance to the mine-house. Recalling the earlier noises of activity, Bottomley realized that the rear entrance, too, would have been closed off in the same manner. The murderous men of Polwarthan had prepared a funeral pyre not only for Reuben Calderdale but also for the two detectives. Whatever secrets lay in that house, they would never be revealed.

A ceaseless barrage of stones now came to shatter the windows, and with them a number of tar-primed torches. The hall of the building seemed to have been waiting for these stones as though for a signal. One moment it was a dark, fume-laden space; next, it had exploded into a raging inferno.

. . . At that moment Jackson saw a figure running towards him through the flame, a woman in her late twenties with an oval face framed in curling black hair. He could not hear what she said, but caught the tone of reproach in her words. Charlotte Anne Jackson, housewife, aged twenty-nine. . . .

'Sir! Why don't you move!'

The words brought Jackson back to the real world, but before he could begin to frame a reply to Bottomley's cry, the wall to his left exploded inwards with a demonic roar, flinging him to the floor. He heard a strangled cry and a thud beside him. He smelt burning cloth as the dark orange flames roared around him.

Suddenly strong hands seized him and dragged him across the blazing hall towards an open hatch low in the panelled wall. A man's voice shouted something indistinct, and Jackson found himself crawling through the hatch into a dank, sulphurous passage. The figure hurled itself after him and closed the hatchway door.

It was pitch dark and wet, but the chill atmosphere suggested that there would be a way of escaping the screaming ruin of the burning house. They crouched for a few moments in the dark, listening to the panting of their breaths, and then Jackson heard the whispering voice of Nicholas Stadie.

'Breathe steady, sir. Breathe steady, now. That's right. I did as you told me, master, and the message is sent. I knew they'd try to kill you both, curse them, and me, too, like as not, so I came up into the house through this secret way. I'll lead now, and you follow. We'll come out at a disused entrance near the shore. You'll be safe there.'

Jackson scrambled behind his guide through the dark passage. Beneath their feet was water and loose stone. Their faces were caressed by swathes of cobwebs. But they had escaped the death by fire prepared for them. He and . . . Bottomley?

That thud beside him in the hall, when the wall exploded . . . Jackson struggled to turn himself round in the narrow passage. Bottomley was not with them. Nicholas Stadie read Jackson's thoughts.

'It's no use, master!' There was an almost threatening quality in his shrill voice. 'It's no use! He were dead, or as good as dead when the fire broke through!'

Stadie's powerful hands struggled to subdue the frantic man

144

whose life he had saved. Neither rescuer nor rescued knew what would be the outcome of their desperate wrestling in the narrow muddy confines of the tunnel. They were stopped by the crushing impact of a tremendous cascading crash and shriek of ruin which told them that the whole mine-house had collapsed in a ball of flame, an appalling funeral pyre for Reuben Calderdale.

Before Jackson could frame words to express his desolate shame and anguish a hot, roaring hurricane of heat and debris rushed through the passage from the ruined house, and the arching tunnel roof of stones and clay collapsed down upon them.

8

The Silver Glance

'He's coming to,' said a man's voice. Someone murmured a reply.

Inspector Jackson's consciousness suddenly welled up through an unfocused haze of light to tell him that he was alive. He flung his arms wide to throw aside the choking debris and clogging earth of the mine-tunnel, and was jerked awake by a burning pain. His eyes focused, and he saw above him a whitewashed ceiling. He could glimpse the painted iron pipes of a gas bracket and the reflection of windows elongated across the plaster.

A calm pink face drew near to his, the face of an elderly man with grey hair and steel-rimmed spectacles. He was holding an enamelled dish of some sort. Another, younger, man with a profusion of gingery hair and a fresh complexion, stood beside him.

'Mr Jackson! How are you? You're going to be fine and well very soon. Very soon indeed! You're burnt and bothered, but not badly hurt. How do you feel? My name is Dr Jelk.'

Jackson struggled upright in the bed.

'Where's my sergeant? Where's Sergeant Bottomley?'

'You must not agitate yourself, Mr Jackson. If you gasp and shout like that you'll suffuse the wound with blood and feel unnecessary pain. Lie back – that's right. Try to lie still.'

So that was it. This doctor would not answer his question about Bottomley. The sergeant had died in the flaming inferno of the mine-house because of his panic and cowardice. . . . The doctors were talking together.

'Mr Manners, to which of the six degrees would you assign this burn?'

'To the third, sir. The cuticle, and the uppermost portion of the *cutis vera* are destroyed. There is some encroachment upon the subcutaneous tissue.'

'Excellent! So at all costs we must avoid blood poisoning. Change the gauze in half an hour. Use a solution of picric acid. Two grains to the ounce.'

Jackson's mind drifted away from the hospital ward. Fresh memories were rushing back to him. He and Nicholas Stadie had not been long entombed. Men with shovels had dug them out, men with red coats and white pipe-clayed belts, part of the militia, summoned to Polwarthan by his telegraph message.

They had been half dragged, half carried back through the trees to the village, where what appeared to be a battle was taking place. Soldiers fought with a screaming mob of dangerously armed miners in the driving rain. Some shots had been fired. A detail of blue-uniformed marines had suddenly appeared from the direction of the beach.

He remembered seeing the excise cutter lying off the cove, its deck alive with watching men as the dark secrets of Polwarthan were revealed to the light of day. Then he had fainted with pain, but not before a woman's face floated into his memory, as though willing him to survive. He remembered now with a slight sense of shock that the face had not been that of his dead wife, but of his friend and neighbour, Sarah Brown.

Soon after Dr Jelk's visit, a starched and serious young nurse came with a glass of medicine, and told him to drink it. Jackson obediently swallowed the thin, clear liquid.

'What is this medicine, Nurse?' he had asked.

'It will help you to rest,' she replied. He closed his eyes and almost immediately fell into a deep sleep.

When he awoke he saw that the light was failing. He realized, too, that he had not seen his surroundings clearly until that moment. He was lying in one of six beds in a small ward. None of the other beds was occupied. Where was he? He remembered an endless journey by rumbling horse-van and train, during which he had been scarcely conscious. He closed his eyes again. Soon, no doubt, a nurse or doctor would appear.

Hospitals were curious places. They had their own set of noises, their own punctuation of quiet footfalls, the sudden clink of glass or the clatter of enamel basins. They had their own smells, too – disinfectant, or did he mean antiseptic? And gin.

Gin?

Jackson slowly opened his eyes. Sergeant Bottomley had just lowered his battered silver hip flask from his lips. He was sitting quietly in a white-painted chair near the door of the ward, wiping his mouth with his sleeve. He looked as though nothing whatever untoward had happened to him.

'I thought you were dead,' said Jackson. It was not what he had meant to say, but they were the words that came out.

Sergeant Bottomley smiled apologetically and repositioned his shambling frame on the small chair.

'No, sir.'

He was wearing his usual loud check suit, and clutched his battered bowler hat as though someone was about to steal it from him.

'I don't like these places, sir,' he said, looking around the ward. 'Too prim and proper by half. Little Miss Starchy out there said I could stay for thirty minutes.'

'I thought you were dead,' Jackson repeated. 'I thought you were burned to ashes. Why aren't you? How did you – I suppose it really is you? Or maybe this is a dream and you're not really there at all.'

148

Bottomley looked kindly at Jackson. What was the guv'nor talking about?

'This is the isolation ward in Exeter General Hospital,' he said. 'They put you here because it was empty, and because it's private. There's newspaper reporters on the prowl, sir, after the battle at Polwarthan, but they can't get at you here.'

Bottomley rummaged in a canvas bag that he had brought with him.

'I've brought you a pork pie, and a knife and plate to eat it with. I don't like these places, sir. I don't suppose they've given you anything to eat.'

Jackson felt suddenly much better. Having Bottomley there, miraculously unscathed, was a tonic in its own right. He accepted the pie, first getting his sergeant to cut it in four pieces for him. The sergeant watched him eating for a while, and then launched into speech.

'I'll make short work of all this palaver, sir, and then we can get back to work. When the fire broke out in the mine-house I was thrown to the floor when the wall burst apart. You were dragged away by Nicholas Stadie. I crawled across the floor and curled up in a space under the stairs. A lot of stone and bricks fell down and made a kind of igloo. There I lay, sir, half choked to death, and thinking of Esther and the girls.

'Then the whole house collapsed, and the floor beneath me gave way. I fell into another underground tunnel, which took me out to a cove about a mile north of Polwarthan. These tunnels, so I've been told, were made by smugglers over a hundred years ago. Nicholas Stadie's family had been engaged in that trade at one time. That's why he knew how to rescue us. I escaped without a scratch.'

'I promised to help Nicholas Stadie,' said Jackson. 'We owe our lives to him. I was worried for his wife and child, and what those ruffians would do to them.'

'He'd quietly moved his wife and daughter away from

Polwarthan before he came to our rescue. I told the story of Nicholas Stadie to the Bishop of Pentreathan.'

'The bishop? So you're hob-nobbing with the higher clergy again, are you?'

'Yes, sir. The bishop came into Truro on purpose to find me. He made me tell him how things stood. He seemed a good deal shaken up by the state of things at Polwarthan, and with what was happening to Parson Woodward. He said he blamed himself – "pastoral neglect" were the words he used. I took the opportunity of putting in a word for Stadie.'

'And what did he say? The bishop, I mean.'

'Say? He didn't say much: he was more in the mood for doing things that day. Stadie and his family are now installed in a cottage in the grounds of the bishop's palace. He's been made an assistant gardener.'

'And Parson Woodward? Was anything done about *him*? Or was he sacrificed yet again to save the church embarrassment?'

'Parson Woodward, sir, was carried off by the Captain of Marines while the battle was raging. He was very shocked and confused, so the bishop told me. He was taken to Truro, to the home of a clergyman friend of Bishop Hope Sutherland. And that's where he is now, until the authorities decide what to do about him.'

Both men were silent for a time, counting their blessings and wondering in their different ways about the workings of Providence.

'I telegraphed Esther – the wife, you know – and told her we were all right. And I telegraphed Sarah Brown. She wanted to come down on the train, but I told her to stay put.'

Jackson paused, a morsel of pork pie halfway to his mouth.

'She wanted to come, did she? On the train?'

'Yes, sir, she did. But I see you're blushing, sir, and I mustn't put you at a disadvantage. Show respect to your betters. "God bless the squire and his relations, and keep us in our proper stations".'

Jackson chuckled. 'At this rate, Sergeant, I'll be out of here in a day or two.'

'Yes, sir. Shock and burns, they said downstairs when I arrived. They wouldn't tell me anything at first, not until I'd shown them my warrant and made it clear that I wouldn't stand for any of their lip.'

Jackson had finished his pie. Bottomley took the plate and knife and stowed them safely away in his canvas bag.

'Now, sir, I'll tell you about the battle of Polwarthan. Mr Tregennis at Truro acted quickly on your message, and alerted not only the militia, as you'd requested, but a company of marines as well. Between them they apprehended thirty-two men in Polwarthan. They're lodged for the moment in a military prison near Redruth.'

Jackson sighed with evident satisfaction.

'I sent Stadie all that way to Saltash to make sure the message was sent. I thought he might have been ambushed or worse if I'd sent him direct to Truro. I'd asked Mr Tregennis to arrange for the militia to be on stand-by before ever you and I went to Polwarthan,' he said. 'It's just as well that I did: their commanders must have turned our request into an exercise to have got there so quickly.'

The ward door opened and the prim young nurse appeared. She looked grimly determined.

'That's quite long enough now, Sergeant Bottomley. Please leave.'

Bottomley lurched to his feet and picked up his canvas bag. He bowed clumsily, dropped his hat, retrieved it, and knuckled his forehead.

'Yes, miss,' he mumbled. 'I'll go at once, ma'am. No offence, I'm sure.'

The prim young nurse smiled, and then laughed.

'Oh, go *on*, Mr Bottomley! Poor Mr Jackson's got to rest now.'

Sergeant Bottomley grinned vaguely at Inspector Jackson and ambled out of the ward.

Late the following afternoon Inspector Jackson was helped into his freshly cleaned and sponged suit and led out into a sheltered garden behind the isolation ward. It was warm and quiet, and the young nurse had thawed sufficiently to bring Jackson a book to read. It was an old, tattered copy of Mayne Reid's *The Scalp-Hunters*, which he had read as a boy and long forgotten. He was both surprised and amused to find himself absorbed in the adventurous tale.

After half an hour Jackson looked up to see a lithe, bearded young man striding across the grass towards him. He was carrying a japanned lacquer box under his arm. The face was vaguely familiar, but Jackson could not place it immediately. He put his book down on the wooden bench where he was sitting.

The visitor regarded the inspector through round, gold-rimmed spectacles. A smart, serious young man, Jackson thought, with a private tailor who knows how to work with black broadcloth.

'Detective Inspector Jackson? I'm Lionel Dovercourt.'

'Ah! Sit down, Mr Dovercourt. I've wanted to meet you for some time. What brings you to Exeter?'

Young Dovercourt smiled, and for a fleeting moment Jackson saw the resemblance to his mother. He sat beside Jackson, and put the lacquered box down beside him on the bench.

'I'm here – fleetingly – on business, Mr Jackson. Just for this afternoon, in fact, and then I have to return home. Father and I are building up a particular chemical connection here. Yesterday, Sergeant Bramble – you remember him? Of course you do – came up to Dovercourt House to tell us what had happened to you, and that you'd been brought here. So this is just a brief social visit.'

'Why should Sergeant Bramble want to tell you about me?'

'Eh? Oh, well, you see, the Bramble family used to be in service with us until a few years ago. They'd been with us for well over a hundred years. So it's second nature for Joe Bramble to tell us the latest state of play, if I may put it like that!'

Jackson was attracted to this volatile younger version of James Dovercourt, the chemical merchant. His voice, like his father's, was loud and commanding, but it had not acquired James Dovercourt's rather intimidating tone.

'I was right, wasn't I, Mr Lionel? There was something more than mere lead in that mine?'

'You were indeed, Inspector! My friend Rollo Bateman was highly intrigued to receive your parcel from Cornwall. He was positively entranced when he found your covering note, asking him to give the contents to me! Highly mysterious, he thought, and so it was! Mother has told me that she gave you my address at Old Penfold.'

'And what were they really mining at Polwarthan, sir?'

For answer, Lionel Dovercourt opened the lacquered box and removed from it the heavy stone that Parson Woodward had given to Jackson.

'There it is, Inspector. I have submitted this sample of ore to chemical and physical examination. It's a specimen of the ore of sulphide of silver – "silver glance", as it is sometimes called.'

' "Silver glance",' said Jackson softly. 'So that was what Elmore said! Pray continue, Mr Lionel.'

'Well, Mr Jackson, you said in your letter to me that you suspected the ore was valuable, and asked me to give you a rough idea of its worth. You get sixpence an ounce for lead. Silver will bring you ten shillings an ounce.'

'Twenty times the yield,' said Jackson. 'There, Mr Lionel, was a very strong motive for murder.'

Lionel thoughtfully replaced the specimen of silver glance in its box, and gave it to Jackson. The young man appeared suddenly overcome with sadness. Without looking at Jackson he said, 'When you say "murder", you mean poor Bob Elmore, don't you?'

'Yes, Mr Lionel, the late unfortunate Mr Robert Elmore. Your

153

father told me that you were acquainted with him, and also, I believe, with the late Reverend Samuel Wheeler?'

'How old and haughty you make us all sound! I'll tell you how the three of us came to be connected. After school in Birmingham I went to London University and studied chemistry at King's College. When I graduated I decided to pursue my studies at the School of Mines in Redruth, and it was there that I met Robert Elmore. Although he was a couple of years younger than I, he shared my intense interest in geology. During one vacation we visited some very fruitful sites in Wales and Cornwall. I used to keep a sort of journal at that time, in which I'd record all sorts of facts and fancies. It was in Cornwall that I first met Elmore's half-brother, Samuel Wheeler.'

'I don't suppose that Mr Wheeler was in Holy Orders in those days?'

'No, indeed, though the idea was forming in his mind. At that time, in fact, he had set himself up in business as an assayer and sampler at Redruth. Robert Elmore, too, was living there at that time.'

A clock in a turret over the hospital building chimed the hour of four. Lionel Dovercourt looked anxious.

'I really must go soon, Mr Jackson. But how are you? I've not asked after your health!'

'I'm very much better, sir, thank you. Mr Elmore and Mr Wheeler were half-brothers with different surnames, so I assume they shared the same mother?'

Lionel Dovercourt laughed. 'What a very odd way of putting it! Yes, they shared the same mother, but there was nearly ten years' difference in age between them. Their mother first married a Mr Wheeler, who died when Samuel was a little boy. She then married a Mr Elmore, and after a few years Robert was born. All the parents are dead now. She was a very devout lady who came originally from Derby.'

'Derby! I don't suppose, sir, that you know her maiden name?'

154

'What? Yes, as a matter of fact I do. Benedict-Smith. Miss Paulina Benedict-Smith.'

Jackson sat in silence for a moment, and Lionel hovered impatiently beside him. The inspector seemed to exude a sort of palpable quietness. Finally he spoke.

'Did you ever know a Mr Reuben Calderdale?'

'No, Mr Jackson. But oddly enough, the name is not unknown to me. Robert Elmore's mother, the "Paulina" I just told you about, had taken an interest in Calderdale, and had corresponded with him when he was very young. I really *must* go now. I don't want to miss my train.'

'Perhaps I could talk to you again when I return to Ashgate? Maybe you could consult that journal you kept to refresh your memory of those times. And there are certain other matters that I'd like to discuss with you.'

The young man had already turned away towards the path leading back to the hospital. He paused for a moment and said, ' "Certain matters"? Do you mean of a chemical nature, Mr Jackson?'

The inspector smiled and shook his head.

'Just "certain matters", Mr Lionel. Let's leave their nature until we meet again at Dovercourt House.'

'Polk!'

The single word exploded from Inspector Tregennis's wrathful lips as though it was an expletive.

Jackson had been immediately impressed by Inspector Tregennis, a tall, clean-shaven man with a pale face and piercing blue eyes. His dark blue uniform was well cut, and presented an impressive array of gleaming buttons and buckles.

'Yes, Mr Tregennis,' said Jackson, 'the viper lurking in the bosom of that little Cornish commonwealth was Constable Polk, one of our own kind – the worst sort of villain in the world.'

The two inspectors had been talking in the cramped charge-

155

room of the police station at Truro. Tregennis suddenly felt that somewhere a little more private would be preferable when discussing the treachery of one of their number.

'Come into the back office, Mr Jackson. It's quieter there, and we can talk without too much interruption. I've been wanting to meet you in the flesh, as they say.'

'Likewise, Mr Tregennis, and now I'm discharged from the hospital at Exeter you and I can compare notes.'

For a quiet country town, Truro seemed to have its quota of villains. The three stone cells were all occupied, resulting in muffled curses and shouts sounding down the stone-flagged corridor. Tregennis motioned Jackson into an inner room where a fire burnt in an old-fashioned blackleaded grate. It seemed to Jackson that the room had been arranged around a vast table covered in boxes and folders. Two narrow barred windows let in some weak sunshine, but the gas was lit, throwing pale light on to the whitewashed walls. There was a door leading into a further office, and Jackson could hear the steady clicking of a telegraph.

Tregennis closed the door and motioned towards a chair. Jackson sat down, grateful to rest his arm and so relieve the dull ache in his shoulder. Tregennis sat opposite him across the wide table.

'We can do nothing much, Mr Jackson, until Superintendent Crossway sends a telegraph message. He told me to expect word from him today. The scabrous Polk will walk into our little trap, you'll see!'

'I suspected Polk from the start,' said Jackson. 'Before ever I went to Polwarthan I wondered whether this was a case of a rotten apple in the barrel, someone who could distort the truth, shield the guilty and expose the innocent to danger with impunity. That notion became a little clearer after I'd met Major Giles Redcott.'

Inspector Tregennis nodded in understanding.

'I know just what you mean, Mr Jackson. Major Redcott's very well regarded down here, but because of the state of his health he could easily be imposed upon. I expect you know that he was never a mining engineer? He and his late father were oil merchants originally. It was his father who brought the money into the Polwarthan mining company.'

'I hadn't realized that you knew Major Redcott so well.'

'I'm not an intimate friend of his, Mr Jackson, but I've known him for years. Although he may not sound like it, he's a Cornishman like me. He was born in Redruth. His company still have an office there. But the poor old major's remit would never have stretched as far as Polwarthan.'

'Polwarthan was a dangerous place in which to live,' said Jackson, 'and a dangerous place for visitors, as Sergeant Bottomley and I know to our cost. But Polk was the law in that benighted place, Inspector, so he had power of entry to all parts of the mine, and to any building in the village. He could smooth the path of any rogue who cared to abuse the trust of Major Giles Redcott. I wonder what we're to make of the other partner, Martin Caradyne?'

Tregennis gave Jackson a knowing look.

'Well, he's in Derby at the moment, isn't he? That tells its own tale, perhaps. Maybe we'll hear something about Mr Caradyne soon. From what I hear he's rarely in this part of the world. He seems to travel round the country a lot. He's a lawyer by training, and apparently by preference. That's why the company made such use of expert surveyors. People like Robert Elmore.'

Jackson delicately felt his aching shoulder. His mind conjured up the image of a spider quietly and patiently weaving a vast and tangled web.

'What about Reuben Calderdale?' asked Tregennis. 'Was he accomplice or victim? He seems to have been an enigma.'

'Calderdale was an accomplice, an accessory after the fact of murder, and you're right, Mr Tregennis: there's a mystery about him. Beneath that rugged exterior there was a sensitive man with a conscience. But the villain of the piece was Constable Polk. He was in league not only with Reuben Calderdale but with virtually the entire workforce of the mine. Polk is a clever, subtle man, a man to be feared. The miners shunned him partly to deceive outsiders, but more because of their instinctive fear of him.'

Inspector Tregennis gave vent to a rather bleak sigh. He toyed with a pencil as he spoke, as though his mind was elsewhere.

'The scabrous Polk! It was just our bad luck to harbour that creature in the Force. He's not a local man, you know, though he acquired our way of speaking. He's from somewhere north originally – not that that excuses us for being so remiss. I've heard that he was often away from Polwarthan for months on end. It seems that no one dared break the law when he was away. How did you come to suspect him?'

'I suppose it was that matter of the missing forty minutes. It pointed to connivance and deep corruption, with Polk almost certainly involved. So Sergeant Bottomley took Polk into his confidence, consulted him and commended him. Then he gently led him into a finely sprung trap.'

'What did he do?'

'He pretended to work out in his mind what poor Mr Elmore might have done in his last hours, and how he might have consulted Polk about his suspicions. There was a basis of truth in what he suggested, but to make guesses like that was flying in the face of police practice, as Polk should have realized.'

'But he liked what he heard?'

'He did, and happily agreed with it all. He thought Sergeant Bottomley was a fool. But he's not a fool, as many a subtle villain has found to his cost. Polk's acquiescence in Sergeant Bottomley's theorizing told him that Polk's missing forty minutes meant something. Where had he been? And, more important, where had he been *before* the body was discovered?'

The door from the inner room opened to admit a heavily-bearded elderly constable. The frantic clicking of the telegraph machine could be heard through the open door.

158

'Sir, Superintendent Crossway is transmitting a message. He signals that it will be a very long one, as he's sending it in full speech, not code. There are three sheets through so far, sir.'

The constable handed the sheets of paper to Tregennis, who read them through rapidly. He gave a cry of satisfaction.

'Polk's been arrested in Derby! I'll give you the gist of this message. He was seized earlier this morning as he came out of a house in Friargate. He left Polwarthan under your orders on Saturday, and proceeded to Redruth as arranged. However, he didn't deliver the parcel you'd given to him to the School of Mines. Instead, he caught a train to Derby, and went directly to a house in Friargate belonging to a Mr and Mrs Benedict-Smith. He seems to have lain low there for most of the weekend, and was arrested this morning as he emerged from the premises.'

'I expected him to go to Derby, Mr Tregennis. He thought he was carrying the specimen of silver glance, whereas all the time it was just a common stone I'd picked up near the mine-house. But I knew he'd lead us to his accomplices once he thought he held the damning evidence in his hands.'

A puzzled frown appeared on Tregennis's brow.

'Immediately after his arrest, Mr Jackson, Polk was taken to the main Bridewell at Derby. He refused absolutely to explain his connection with the Benedict-Smiths, but volunteered a full confession about the events at Polwarthan. Why should he do that, Mr Jackson? Why confess so readily to murder?'

'I don't know, Mr Tregennis. I'm beginning to think that Polk's something more than simply a homicidal rustic. As you say, why should he want to confess?'

The telegraph had been working away frantically in the other room. The constable came in with three further sheets, which he handed to his inspector.

'That concludes the message, sir. Superintendent Crossway has closed the wire.'

Tregennis hastily scanned the first sheet.

'Martin Caradyne was also present in the house at Friargate. He was asked to explain his presence in the house, and immediately fell down in a fit. He has been lodged with Polk in the Bridewell. What's this? The house and attached buildings were fitted up with furnaces for smelting. Well, well!'

Tregennis merely glanced at the remaining sheets before handing them across the table to Jackson.

'I think the honours of reading this belong to you, Mr Jackson,' he said. 'These sheets contain the text of Daniel Polk's confession.'

Inspector Jackson took the sheets from his colleague, and read the confession:

For long years we have plundered the Polwarthan Mine of its wealth. When you mine for lead you have to seek it out by tunnelling, and on one occasion the manager, Mr Calderdale, joined the mining party. He and two others stumbled upon a rich vein of silver glance, which is silver ore, and worth big money. He told the active partner, Mr Martin Caradyne, and the two of them arranged for the ore to be moved secretly to Derby, where it was turned to silver without suspicion. I was in on the secret, and the men were paid an extra pittance to keep quiet.

All went well. If Major Redcott sent inspectors or assayers from time to time, they could be scared off. The trouble began when Mr Robert Elmore came. He was a geologist by profession, and a snooper. He knew what he was looking for, and succeeded in penetrating into the hidden gallery of the mine. He knew at once what the ore was, and what was going forward. He filled his pockets with specimens of ore, and came to see me. By doing that, he sealed his own fate.

I arranged to meet him that evening. I told Sergeant Bottomley that the meeting took place in the woods, but, in fact, we met in the church, which is always open, and a safe rendezvous for all kinds of business. Elmore told me of his suspicions, and I advised him to set out at once to Exeter. When he turned away from me I drew my truncheon and stunned him. It was the work of a moment to tip him into the christening-tank. That is how he came to be drowned in fresh water.

At that very moment the manager Reuben Calderdale came into the church. He was as bad as me at that time, and when he saw that Elmore was dead he told me to leave the scene while he lifted the body from the tank and dragged it down to the shore. He was interrupted by the parson, who was out walking, and was obliged to leave the body where it was, with the pockets full of stones. It later transpired that the parson had taken one of these stones, which found its way into the hands of Inspector Jackson.

Calderdale tried to warn Mr Jackson off, but it was no use. Then Calderdale began to fall prey to remorse. I did not trust him, and when he went to the Good Friday service I made sure I was there to keep an eye on him. Eventually he summoned me to the church late at night, and told me that he could no longer bear the burden of conniving at Elmore's death. I saw that he had to go.

We were standing near the baptismal tank while we were talking, and I told him that Elmore had thrown a bag filled with silver glance into the water. Calderdale leaned over to look down into the tank, and I used the truncheon again. I seized Calderdale's ankles and heaved him into the font.

Jackson finished reading, and put the papers down on the desk. Inspector Tregennis made a sound of disgust.

'A rotten apple in the barrel, Mr Jackson. Daniel Polk, Police Constable, aged forty-eight. It makes me sick. He'll hang, of course.'

Jackson sat in silence for a while, staring at the fire. He sighed.

161

'Oh, yes, Mr Tregennis, he'll hang, and rightly so! I suspect there are a few others in Polwarthan would should keep him company by rights. He might have engineered the attempt to murder us by fire, but the idea was probably thought up by the godless gang who ruled Polwarthan.'

Jackson rose to his feet.

'Whatever the truth of the matter, Mr Tregennis, it's only the start for me. We've cleared up the murders down here, but they all link up with my murdered man in Warwickshire. And others, maybe. And more to come, perhaps.'

'It's been a pleasure to work with you, Mr Jackson,' said Tregennis. 'What do you intend to do now?'

'I'm going back to Ashgate St Lawrence, Mr Tregennis, where all this business began. My sergeant's already on his way by train to Derby, and when he's observed the state of things there, he'll join me again. Then we'll go hunting.'

'Hunting?'

'Yes. There's something vile lurking around Ashgate that we've only glimpsed so far. Polk and the corrupt partner Caradyne are in custody, but they're only part of something greater. We think we've done very well in bringing these secret murders to light, but behind it all, Mr Tregennis, I can hear some mocking shrieks of demonic laughter. Sergeant Bottomley and I are going out to hunt for the demon.'

9

Lights in the Darkness

Inspector Jackson looked at the two girls, the young mistress and the even younger servant, and assembled his words carefully before he spoke. Deirdre Dovercourt, he saw, was very pretty, her blonde hair flowing loose over her slender shoulders. Her green silk dress complemented her colouring, as did the ruby drop hanging around her neck on a slender gold chain. Jackson noted how her slim fingers played unconsciously with the jewel as she sat in her fashionable bamboo chair.

What was it, he wondered, that gave her such a haunted look?

'Miss Deirdre,' he began, 'I've come to talk to you today about the Reverend Samuel Wheeler. Your papa and mama have given me permission to do so. You will have heard that Mr Wheeler's body was found hidden in a tomb-chest in the graveyard behind your house.'

'I know nothing about it.' The girl's voice trembled, and she cleared her throat nervously. 'Why should I? He was a bad man, and made me ill. I was only little. I don't remember anything about it.'

The other girl, neatly attired in the black dress and apron of a maid, came across from the window seat where she had been sitting swinging her legs, and sat down at Deirdre's feet. She twined her arms around her mistress's waist and laid her head on

163

her knee. About fourteen, Jackson thought, as dark as Miss Deirdre was fair. Stronger than the 17-year-old, and obviously as much friend as servant.

'Do you remember what he looked like, miss? I promise you that I won't ask you anything that will upset you. But if I were to show you a picture of him, would you recognize him?'

The girl paled visibly.

'A picture? Do you mean . . . a . . . picture of him when they took him out of the . . . the. . . .'

'Indeed no, miss.'

Why had he been so insensitive? Maybe the shock of Polwarthan was clouding his judgement. Bottomley would have been better at this particular questioning.

'I simply mean a picture of him as he was in life, a photograph.'

'Have you got a photograph? Let me see it.'

Jackson took a wallet from his inside pocket, abstracted a small card, and handed it to the girl. He observed her carefully, and saw that the little maid was watching her with equal intensity. A faint smile crossed Deirdre's face as she examined the photograph, and the little maid looked up in warning. The smile disappeared, to be replaced by nervous and clearly assumed indifference. She handed the picture back to Jackson.

'Yes, Mr Jackson, that's Mr Wheeler. I had forgotten all about him, and really, I can't tell you anything at all. You must ask my papa if you want to know about him.'

Annie still clung to her mistress, surveying Jackson with a wisdom beyond her years. For the last minute she had felt the racing of Deirdre's heart, and the trembling that was beginning to seize her. In a few moments, thought Annie, Miss Deirdre would have one of her turns.

'Begging your pardon, sir,' said Annie in a clear, firm voice, 'but Miss Deirdre's had enough of questions now. She's not very strong, and you're not to bother her.'

The dark brown eyes met his in unflinching defiance. It would be prudent, Jackson thought, to accept defeat. Poor child! He already knew what must have been the truth about Deirdre.

'I'm sure I'm sorry if I've upset either of you young ladies. I'll be gone now. Goodbye, Miss Deirdre. Goodbye, Miss—?'

'Annie. It's not "miss". Just Annie.'

When Jackson had left Deirdre's small sitting-room on the third floor of Dovercourt House the two girls sat in silence for a few moments. It was a bright, warm morning, and the front of the house was bathed in the April sunshine.

Deirdre began to cry very quietly. Annie sat motionless, her arms still twined round Deirdre's waist. When she sensed that the elder girl had become once more mistress of herself, she raised her head and asked, 'What's up with you? What are you crying for?'

Deirdre disengaged herself from the younger girl and stood up. She went over to her dressing-table, opened a drawer and brought out something wrapped in tissue paper. She put it in Annie's hand.

'There you are, minx. That's what you've wanted to see all this time. Well, you can see it now. You're a brave, good girl to stand up to these prying men. Go on, look at it.'

Little Annie unwrapped the tissue paper to reveal the ebony-framed photograph of the Reverend Samuel Wheeler, posing dashingly in front of what was supposed to be the Crystal Palace. He looked very romantic, like someone out of one of Miss Deirdre's droopy books. Annie sighed. She turned the frame over, and saw written in a bold flowing style: 'To my dear Lady Friend Deirdre, from Sam Wheeler. Christmas 1887.'

Annie wrapped the picture carefully in its tissue paper and gave it back to Deirdre. She felt proud that her young mistress had shown her this special keepsake. It was a further bond between them.

Deirdre put the picture back in its drawer and went to sit on her favourite window-seat. The book of Keats's poems lay untouched. Annie stood by the table, fiddling with a vase of daffodils.

'Miss?'

'What?'

'I know what you did, you know. There's no need to make such a fuss about it. Your mama knows too. Mr Wheeler ought to have had more sense at his age. He should've known what might've happened. So don't go getting fretful and nervous. He ought to have had more sense.'

Deirdre's voice came cold and low, as though from some far-off chill cavern.

'You know all my secrets now, Annie, and I'm trusting you to keep them to yourself. There he is, all dead and dry, and it was I who killed him. I saw—'

She stopped abruptly and the tears flowed again. Her shoulders sagged in hopeless misery.

'Don't tell them, Annie! You've always tried to help me. Don't tell them!'

Annie resumed her position at Deirdre's feet, and laid her head once more against her knee. The elder girl stroked her hair gently, and the action seemed to allay some of her grief. They were silent once more for a while. Then Annie spoke.

'Sometimes, miss, I think you're as daft as folk say you are!'

Deirdre made no reply, but continued the gentle stroking of Annie's black hair.

Jackson closed the door of Deirdre's room, walked to the end of the passage, and descended a creaking spiral stair which ended in the bare-boarded passage on the works side of Dovercourt House. A door next to that of James Dovercourt's office was flung open and young Lionel Dovercourt appeared.

'Ah! Mr Jackson! You've been talking to Deirdre. Father said that you were coming today. Did she tell you anything interesting? Come into my retreat.'

Lionel's 'retreat' was a working room rather than a study. It was sparsely furnished with a deal table, a bench of chemical apparatus, and a shelf holding half a dozen fat text-books. There were a couple of plain kitchen chairs.

'Sit down, Inspector. How are you? The best thing for a bad burn of that kind is picric acid. We supply it to a number of hospitals. Now, how can I help? Father's away in Didcot this morning, but he sends you his best wishes. What can I do for you?'

Jackson smiled. This younger version of the chemical merchant would have to learn how to listen for answers. Bombarding another man with questions wasn't enough.

'I'm much better, thank you, Mr Lionel. And you can help me by continuing the story of Robert Elmore and Samuel Wheeler. I seem to remember that you spoke to me about a journal that you kept?'

'Yes. The journal. I have it here.'

Lionel Dovercourt reached behind him and brought down a slim notebook from the shelf. He thumbed through its pages for a while until he found what he was seeking.

'Here's the bit I wanted. This section was written in May, 1885. Do you remember that summer? It was very Mediterranean, and the three of us – Wheeler, Elmore and I – enjoyed many long days exploring in Cornwall.'

The young man stopped for a moment and gazed into space. A look of wistful sadness crossed his face.

'It's odd, Mr Jackson, to think that Elmore and Wheeler are both dead, and if what we hear is true, both murdered.'

'It's true enough, Mr Lionel. And I fear the matter is not over yet. But please tell me about this holiday in Cornwall.'

'Sam Wheeler had already paved the way for taking Holy Orders, and had disposed of his little business in Redruth. One day Elmore went off by himself to visit some people he knew, leaving Sam Wheeler and me to laze and talk. We had rented a little cottage for a week or so. It was then that Sam began talking about Polwarthan, and it was a very interesting tale he had to tell me.

'He mentioned Reuben Calderdale and his mother's interest in him, and then said that at one time Calderdale had shown an inclination to read for orders himself. Sam told me that Calderdale had rather too great a love for money to make the life of a clergyman a viable career.'

'Money, yes,' said Jackson, 'money has been the downfall of many a man born with good instincts. There was always an air of desperation about Calderdale. It was as though he committed evil deeds in spite of himself. So Mr Wheeler knew quite a bit about Reuben Calderdale?'

'He did. A year earlier – in 1884 – he had called at Polwarthan with a letter of introduction from his mother. Calderdale, who was the manager of the mine as you know, received him well, and let him explore the mine workings.'

'Ah! I begin to see what must have happened. Presumably Calderdale didn't realize that he was letting a skilled geologist loose in his secret workings.'

'Exactly, Inspector. Sam discovered conclusive evidence that secret mining of something more precious than lead was going on, though he was unable to obtain any specimens of ore on that occasion. He said some very curious words to me, and I wrote them down in this journal:

' "There is devil's work going on there, Dovercourt", Sam said to me, "and one day I'll produce the evidence to prove it. There's one man there to whom I've confided, and no doubt when the time comes he will do his duty. Meanwhile, I've told my brother Robert. Maybe one day he, too, will see his way towards a solution".'

'Devil's work,' said Jackson softly. He stood up and crossed to the narrow window of Lionel's retreat. He looked out at the weak sunlight glinting off something attached to the lintel of a door giving on to the little railed garden at the side of the house. He recognized it for what it was, and remembered the words stamped on it and its fellows: CHRISTE VICTOR OPN.

'Mr Lionel, Samuel Wheeler spoke prophetically. Robert Elmore did indeed follow him into the mining business, a decision which brought him to his death at the age of twenty-five. He took up the investigation of the Polwarthan mine where his half-brother had left off, and was murdered.'

It was very quiet in the small room. Jackson could hear the younger man's quick breathing.

'Mr Jackson, who do you think it was that Sam Wheeler confided in? The man who he said one day would "do his duty"?'

'Oh, Mr Lionel, I fear that it could only have been the murderous constable, Daniel Polk. And to confide in him would be like a sinner confessing to the Devil.'

Lionel closed the journal and looked at Jackson with something approaching horror.

'What? Then do you think that Samuel Wheeler, too, was murdered by that man?'

Jackson turned from the window. His face revealed a kind of vexatious anger and resentment. He made a sound of disgust.

'Samuel Wheeler? I don't know *what* to think. I need more time to examine the facts. Frankly, I can see no way in which Polk could have been involved in Mr Wheeler's death. Polk certainly murdered Robert Elmore, and has confessed as much. But he has made no mention of Mr Wheeler. As far as I know, he had never even—'

With a conscious effort of will Jackson filed the matter of Polk away in his mind and turned to other matters. Polk could wait.

'Mr Lionel, it's been very refreshing speaking to you, because you seem to believe in candour. I wonder whether I can now give you some further opportunity to exercise your candour in talking about your sister, Miss Deirdre?'

'What do you want to know about Deirdre?'

Jackson noted the young man's guarded tones as he mentioned his sister. What was this undefined mystery clinging to the girl?

'I'd like to know when and why Miss Deirdre, accompanied by

her personal maid Annie, went to stay with Mr Loxley Anderson at King's Leyland. I'd also like to know why Mr Robert Elmore was visiting Mr Loxley Anderson at the same time.'

Lionel put the slim journal back on the shelf and stood up.

'Will you come with me, Mr Jackson?'

Once again Inspector Jackson found himself conducted across the passage, through the old linen-fold oak door into the Haunted Room. Dreary, unused, unloved, the chamber had never been allowed to share in the cheerful colour and comfort of the rest of the house. Lionel glanced with distaste at the frowning oval portrait of his ancestor, Amos Dovercourt.

'This is where she likes to come, with her romantic notions. Deirdre, I mean. That man in the picture there really does haunt this family. Father's already told you what Sam Wheeler did to Deirdre when she was only thirteen. She became very reclusive and withdrawn for a while after that business, and took to moping around in here at all hours of the day and night.

'Look out of the window, Mr Jackson. You can see Josiah Anderson's monument quite clearly from here. One night Deirdre saw the spirit of Amos Dovercourt, surrounded by a ghostly light, either getting into, or climbing out of, that tomb. In her mind she regarded it as Amos Dovercourt's tomb, though in fact he's not buried in Ashgate at all. She told Father what she had seen, and he chastized her. I found her sobbing her heart out in her room, and made her tell me all about it.'

'Did you believe what she told you?'

'Yes. I believe that she saw something, possibly the result of a fevered imagination. She tried to describe it to me, but seemed to be confused, as though she was reliving two quite separate incidents. She was only thirteen. Father shouldn't have smacked her. She had been through a lot over Wheeler. The day after he smacked her she became very ill, and only narrowly averted brain fever.'

'And why did she go to visit Mr Loxley Anderson?'

170

'It's all linked together, Mr Jackson. When Deirdre was turned fourteen we engaged a little part-time maid to keep her company and look after her things. Annie Jevons was only eleven at the time, and still at school, but she came in when she could, and became much attached to Deirdre, and she to her. Those rooms up on the third floor front used to be the nursery when Deirdre and I were little, and now she has a sitting-room and bedroom there, and there's a tiny room for Annie. Annie lives out – she's only fourteen – but from time to time she stays here, and has her own little room.

'Well, in 1890 – in early March, I think it was – Deirdre began to see things again, and this time it was clear enough that they were images arising from a morbid imagination. The doctor advised a change of air, and Uncle William was delighted to have her stay with him at King's Leyland. Uncle William – my mother's brother – is an extraordinarily humorous man, and Deirdre benefited greatly from the visit. There was a house party that weekend, with plenty of lively company. Both Deirdre and Jevons enjoyed themselves immensely there. After that, Deirdre stopped seeing things.'

'And Robert Elmore?' Jackson persisted.

'Eh? Yes, he was there. Deirdre always liked him, you know, but on that occasion she complained that he spent most of his time closeted with Uncle William and another gentleman. She asked him what he was doing there, but he wouldn't tell her. But didn't you ask Deirdre herself these questions, Inspector?'

'No, sir. I'm afraid my interview with your sister wasn't very successful. She seemed to be afraid of me. I can't think why. Had my own little girl lived she would have been Miss Deirdre's age by now.'

Lionel Dovercourt glanced quickly at Jackson and ventured a rather nervous smile.

'My mother told me what you revealed to her. It's so difficult to know what to say, isn't it? But I *am* sorry, Mr Jackson. Don't be

THE DRIED-UP MAN

upset by Deirdre. She's such a . . . a *pale*-minded girl, you know, besotted with bamboo furniture and pale wallpaper, and wispy stories about knights and ladies. Father and I laugh about her sometimes. Mother defends her, which is right and proper, but Deirdre's the limit at times!'

Inspector Jackson laughed. The brother's unromantic views of his sister helped to restore a sense of proportion. Perhaps he was making too much of the mystery of Deirdre Dovercourt. He turned to Lionel again.

'Are you still in a candid mood, sir?'

'I might be,' answered Lionel cautiously.

'What, may I ask, are your private feelings about the late Reverend Mr Samuel Wheeler?'

Lionel cast the inspector a shrewd glance.

'You have talked with Mama, I know. You will have guessed that she and I had much sympathy for Sam, perhaps because we are less hasty in our judgements than Father. I deeply mourn for Mr Wheeler, and enjoin you to spare nobody in bringing his murderer to justice. Beyond that, Inspector, I will not say a further word.'

Lionel looked out of the window of the Haunted Room, and let his eye sweep across the hollow of the ancient churchyard.

'Look, Mr Jackson,' he said.

In the distance Jackson could discern two figures walking in the rectory garden. It was impossible not to recognize the stooping figure of old Parson Woodward, walking arm-in-arm with Harry Goodheart.

'He's come back to us, Inspector, much to Mama's disgust. He's acting as a sort of curate here. He preached again the other day, and I must say it was more about Heaven this time and less about Valhalla!'

The young man brought his shrewd glance back to the inspector.

'There's still a mystery in Woodward waiting to be revealed.

There's something brewing over there in the rectory, Inspector, and I've a feeling that whatever it is will come to a head very soon.'

Dr Ambrose Phillips smiled. He parted the tails of his evening coat and sat down on the fender-seat. The many facets of his crystal port glass gleamed in the firelight. Dinner with Harry Goodheart had been an overwhelming affair, with two sorts of soup followed by fish, then roast saddle of mutton, water ices, and a savoury, all preceded and followed by Latin graces. The frail and aged Hezekiah Woodward had not joined them, and they had taken their port and coffee alone in the rector's study.

'Upon my word, Rector,' said Dr Phillips, 'if poor Woodward can recover anywhere, it will be here! I know how eager you are to sweep away clerical cobwebs, given the right broom. I've no doubt that had you been a doctor you'd have sent some welcome fresh winds blowing through the Faculty!'

Harry Goodheart smiled. and poured himself a cup of coffee.

'Well, Phillips, I hope you're right. Won't you have some more coffee? It's Turkish, you know. Very good of its kind. Woodward's very frail – too frail, to my way of thinking. I intend to feed him well while he's here. That should help his recovery! He's keeping to his room for the present, which is why he's not down here for dinner.'

Goodheart recalled how, earlier in the day, he and his elderly guest had walked together in the garden, and he had urged Woodward to drive from his mind the demon of idle fancies. 'Cast off the works of darkness,' he had said, 'and put upon you the armour of light.' It had been a good moment, a moment of grace.

Dr Phillips put his glass down on the mantelpiece and accepted the cup of coffee his host had poured for him.

'By all accounts poor Woodward is well out of it. And Jackson, too, come to that. Out of that Cornish place, I mean – Polwarthan.

173

When I was privileged to assist Dr Venner at the post-mortem I didn't appreciate the sinister side of police work. Inspector Jackson and his sergeant nearly lost their lives.'

The normally ebullient Harry Goodheart relapsed into thought. Jackson had surely come to Ashgate accompanied by an angel of good counsel. His unconsciously righteous questioning had brought hidden truths to light. It was clearly providential that he had been spared to continue his saving work.

'You know, Phillips, Jackson stirred up a hornets' nest here with his probing questions. He certainly made me examine my motives and my conscience, and he seems to have done something similar in Cornwall.'

'What do you mean?'

'Well, I received a letter from a young fellow I know who became chaplain to the Bishop of Pentreathan. A young man called Lander. He said that Jackson's experiences had had a profoundly transforming effect on Bishop Hope Sutherland. Until then he'd made himself a virtual prisoner in his own palace. After Jackson's rescue, though, he seemed to spring into action. He went personally to Polwarthan and – well, let me read you what young Lander wrote.'

Harry Goodheart took a letter from his pocket, and donned his reading glasses.

'Where are we, now? Yes, here it is. Listen to this!

' "The day after the forces of law and order had cleansed Polwarthan of its brood of evildoers, My Lord Bishop left the palace in his private carriage very early in the morning. He took me with him, and three stalwart servants. He refused to be swallowed up in the darkness of that dim, spirit-haunted church, and pitched his cross on a high rise of stones and scree near to the burnt-out mine-house. He cried out for repentance. He preached until he was hoarse, and still the words came!

' "Gradually the few remaining men appeared, and then the women. The bishop told them of the wrath to come and the need

174

for repentance. The sky darkened and the rain came, and still he preached on".'

Harry Goodheart paused for a moment and looked at his guest.

'Remarkable, don't you think, Phillips? Hope Sutherland, you know, seemed to have lost the spark when he was translated to Cornwall. He blamed the diocese, he blamed the surly people, he blamed his clergy – everyone, in fact, except himself! But when he saw Woodward, and heard of the frightful events that had occurred at Polwarthan, he was overcome with the urge to make amends.'

'And in a way Inspector Jackson brought about this change of heart?'

'That's how I see it, Phillips. Just let me finish reading what Lander said about it.

' "The people's hardened hearts were chastened by the bishop's words. There were groans and cries and tears, and something came into that pagan spot to move them. When he had finished preaching they begged him to say some prayers, which he did, standing bare-headed in the pouring rain. Then they dragged our carriage to the road and harnessed the horses. That day, Mr Goodheart, I witnessed the ministry of a true successor to the Apostles, who, in cleansing Polwarthan through the Word, linked himself directly with St Peter and St Paul".'

Both men were quiet for a while, listening to the ticking of the merry clock, and the murmur of the simmering coffee-pot on its trivet over the fire.

'A remarkable story, Rector,' said Phillips. 'I gather that the bishop's renewed ardour included doing something about poor Woodward?'

'Yes. The bishop, too, wrote to me, admitting to pastoral neglect – I think he's being too harsh with himself there, but no matter. He asked me to invite Woodward back here as my honorary curate, which I was delighted to do. He thought that this would be the ideal place for Woodward to confront and defeat his demons.'

175

Dr Phillips joined the tips of his fingers together in a sort of judicial gesture. He looked thoughtfully at his host.

'Demons? Yes, I think that term would satisfy me, Rector. Poor Woodward, to my way of thinking, has fallen victim to morbid suggestion and official indulgence. He's been severed too long from intellectual equals. This obsession with Odin has driven him into a world of legend, where he can no longer distinguish fact from fantasy.'

'And how precisely would you define Woodward's demons?'

'In my book, Rector, they would signify three fatal influences: loneliness, isolation and the embrace of ignorance.'

Harry Goodheart looked earnestly at his guest. Had his words been yet another stricture on the church? Perhaps now was the right time to tell Phillips about the letter that had arrived from Lambeth only that morning. . . .

'Well, Phillips,' he said, 'I'm pleased to tell you that the Archbishop of Canterbury has interested himself directly in the affair of Woodward. I received a letter from him this morning. He thanked me for sheltering Woodward here – that was the word Dr Benson used, "sheltering".'

'And what else did he say?'

'He said that he intends to send a specialist physician down here to probe the secrets of poor Woodward's amnesia. He used a curious word to describe this specialist. An "alienist", he called him.'

'Ah!' Dr Phillips's eyes gleamed with excitement. 'A capital idea! Did the archbishop mention anyone in particular?'

'Yes. The gentleman in question is a Dr Per Cornelis Brant. I see that the name's not unknown to you. The archbishop is hoping that Dr Brant can lodge here in Ashgate—'

'I should be honoured, Rector, to place my house at Dr Brant's disposal. He has a European reputation for this kind of work. He will surely succeed in probing the neuroses underlying Mr Woodward's amnesia.'

'And what exactly *is* an alienist?'

'Well, he's a doctor who specializes in the treatment of mental diseases. He can unlock doors in the mind that have long remained closed. Dr Per Cornelis Brant is perhaps best known for his pioneering work on epileptic insanity.'

Dr Ambrose Phillips looked mightily pleased, and willingly accepted a further glass of old port from his host. Really, this little backwater of a town had proved to be truly exciting – first Dr Venner, and the fascination of police work and now, the great foreign specialist, actually coming to stay in his house!

'I must let Inspector Jackson know about this,' said Goodheart. A speculative look came into his eyes, and he was silent for a few moments.

'I wonder. . . .'

'What is it, Goodheart?'

'I'm just thinking, you know, of Deirdre Dovercourt. There's a curious mystery involving that young lady, and I suspect that the answer to it is lurking somewhere in the inner reaches of her mind. Maybe this Dr Cornelis Brant would help her, as well as Woodward, to remember what needs to be remembered.'

10
Two Exorcisms

It was the time for exorcism. The demons of the past, the destructive phantoms of superstition were to be banished once and for all. Hezekiah Woodward had been fortified by Harry Goodheart's vigorous and careful support. 'Confront them, Woodward,' he had cried, 'confront these demons and drive them out! You have been with me into the caverns beneath the church, and I have shown you that they are mere curiosities of history. The events in Polwarthan have revealed to you the baleful strength of superstition. Now you must begin to remember. There are things of which you are still not sure, and particularly there is a burden upon you arising from our ancient churchyard. Go there tonight, in the dark. Confront the demons of forgetfulness and fear. Drive them out!'

Hezekiah Woodward lingered for a few moments in the dark quiet of the rectory garden and recalled another act of mental rescue performed by his good host. The rector had talked at great length about Cambridge in the forties and fifties, and about the celebrated group of youthful scholars known as 'the Parnassian Band'. He had not thought that a man of Goodheart's background would have known about such long-forgotten things. Had he, perhaps, consulted those who did?

The rector had discoursed about the brilliant books written by

Dr Jouste, Charles Miller, and the other members of the group. Woodward had felt a lost enthusiasm kindled in his heart. It must have shown in his eyes, because Goodheart had then played his trump card.

'I heard the other day, Woodward,' he had said, 'that Mr Gladstone, in his new essay *The Alliance of Church and State*, quoted from your *Celestial City Revisited*, and wondered what had become of you since you first published it.'

Woodward had almost collapsed with pride when he heard this. His book had been virtually dashed off in a month when he was still at Cambridge long years since. Pusey had visited him to read the proofs. It was a link with a world that he thought had been totally lost. And now the greatest living statesman himself had recalled the work and praised it. . . .

It was a warm, still night, and spring perfumes lingered in the dark hollow of the graveyard. The grass was soft and dry underfoot. Carrying a dark lantern, Woodward descended into the hollow from the foot of the rectory garden. A gentle breeze sighed through the leaves of cypress and oak. The larger of the monuments soared up darkly to the moonless sky. Down he went, down into the vale.

He had done this before. Late at night, a dark lantern in his hand. When? And why? He reached the uneven plateau at the centre of the churchyard. Faintly rising above him he could see the bulk of Dovercourt House. There was a dim light burning in one of the rooms which suddenly went out.

How quiet it was! He was standing behind a tall slate gravestone. He stretched out his hand near the top of the stone and felt with his finger for a deeply incised letter P. It was pitch dark but he knew the stone, which marked the grave of a man called Elias Pullinger, his wife Ellen, and their seven infant children.

And now Pullinger's stone felt cold, tingling with the glittering night frost. But that had been in deep winter: there was no frost now, in the quickening spring. . . .

'You could dig a little grave in this wilderness and no-one would ever know.'

The words assailed Woodward's ears as though they had just been uttered, but he knew that he was remembering a previous time when he had stood in hiding near this very stone, and heard a voice say those terrible words.

'You could dig a little grave in this wilderness and no one would ever know.'

The stone was warm again, and the night air flower-scented. Woodward knew that if he ventured a few feet further he would remember everything. It was Providence that had put it into Harry Goodheart's mind to suggest this form of deliverance. He opened the slide of the dark lantern and stepped boldly forward until he stood at the end of Josiah Anderson's tomb.

. . . It had been colder, and the grass had been streaked with frost. February . . . he had stood near Pullinger's tall stone and had seen three men, all strangers to him, grunting and heaving as they dragged the end panel of the tomb back into place. Why had he been there? Think. . . . Yes! He had gone, as he had frequently done at that time, to place talismans in the grass to ward off the demons that waged their constant war against him . . . had he really believed that?

And he had seen the three men in the final throes of some appalling act. He had thought of body-snatchers, but they were clearly something else. And then one had stood up and said those words about a little grave.

They had finally left the spot, closing their dark lantern, and stumbling out the long way into Ashgate Street. He had gone forward, opened his own lantern, and looked at the trampled grass. He did so now, and felt the frost. Was it winter or spring?

He had stood in bewilderment for some minutes before he had sensed another figure standing near in the dark. Yes, it had been the February of 1888. The silent figure had finally stirred, and walked into the circle of yellow light cast by the dark lantern. Matthew Littlechild, metalworker, a steady man, and a staunch confidant. Woodward knew that this man also believed in the power of Odin, and waged his own righteous war against the ancient spirits. They had always been allies, the Cambridge-educated clergyman and the illiterate metalworker, who could not read the letters he stamped on his ban-devils.

'There were three of them, Parson,' he had said, 'all strangers, and they were putting something into that tomb-chest.'

They had spoken no further words. Woodward had stood back while the strong artisan had dragged the end panel up and out of its anchorage. Together they had dragged a body out of the tomb-chest by its feet. It was clad in long cotton combinations, and when they turned it over they saw a great patch of dried blood covering the back. Even in the dim lantern-light they could both see the sawn-off shaft of an arrow.

When the face came in view Woodward had looked on his own curate, the Reverend Samuel Wheeler.

Remember ... what had he and Matthew Littlechild done then? And the voice – the voice that had talked of a little grave. He had not known it then, but he had heard it since: quiet, emotionless, menacing ... where?

Deirdre sighed, and put down the Liberty's catalogue. There was a limit to the number of imaginary rooms one could furnish. One day, she would have her own house, with neat pale rooms full of light, adorned with pastel-coloured curtains. ...

The silk-shaded oil-lamp spread a quiet glow through her little sitting-room. Poor Samuel Wheeler ... no! She would not think of that. Perhaps it was time to join the family in the drawing-room. Papa and Lionel would be talking politics, and Mama would be sewing or reading one of those novels by Mrs Henry Wood. It would be warm and comfortable there. Once Annie had gone home it was dreary on the top floor.

Deirdre was grateful for the glimmering gaslight in the passage, which shed enough of its fitful glow to see her down the creaking spiral stairway to the bare hall below.

She had been wrong about Mama. The tinkling notes of the drawing-room piano came to her faintly from across the house, and as she stood there in the dim hall her mother began to sing. She had a fine contralto voice, well fitted to the song that she had chosen, Thomas Moore's 'The Light of Other Days'. Deirdre listened.

> *'Oft in the stilly night,*
> *Ere slumber's chain has bound me,*
> *Fond Memory brings the light*
> *Of other days around me.*

Between her and the reassuring company of her family lay the Haunted Room. It had always been impossible for her to resist the morbid fascination of that dreary chamber. The sad, romantic words of the song seemed to beckon her to cross the haunted threshold:

> *The eyes that shone,*
> *Now dimm'd and gone,*
> *The cheerful hearts now broken!*

Poor Samuel Wheeler! He was part of her mother's melancholy song. She lifted the latch in the linen-fold panelled door of the Haunted Room and stepped inside.

It was pitch dark, though she could see the crack of light beneath the further door leading into the drawing-room. As she advanced into the room, her mother's song came to its end and the piano fell silent.

Deirdre felt for the small round table she knew to be in the centre of the room, and the rough feel of the embroidered cloth seemed to reassure her. She crossed to the window and peered out into the black expanse of the ancient burial-ground.

When the yellow light flared up at the foot of Josiah Anderson's tomb Deirdre Dovercourt saw for the first time the reality of what she had once believed to be Amos Dovercourt's ghost. What she saw first was the figure of the man she immediately recognized as the Reverend Hezekiah Woodward. She saw him with the outer eye, the lone man bathed in lantern-light, standing sentinel, and even at that distance she could sense his air of puzzlement. He stood still and hushed, as though waiting for some kind of inner illumination. That much was clear enough to the girl's outer eye.

But then the inner eye was opened.

She heard her own voice saying to Annie: 'You impertinent minx! Don't you ever mention that horrid business again. Yes, I *was* frightened. You would have been too. You'd have screamed and screamed if you'd seen old Amos climbing back in his tomb in the ghostly light he shed.' Immediately she felt an enveloping chill, and her mind told her that it was a February long ago.

She stood in the Haunted Room, a young girl of thirteen, looking through the window at a group of men with lanterns in the graveyard below. They had been stooping, but now they straightened up, and she saw a dead body at their feet, a sprawling man clad in some kind of white undergarment. Who was it? Her far sight was always good, and by straining a little she saw that it was Samuel Wheeler.

It had been her fault that he had gone away, and now he was dead. Who were those men with him? Was that Papa and Lionel? No; they would be in the next room. Who was that other man, staring up sightlessly at her? A heavy, settled, brutal man.

Deirdre, aged thirteen, watched as the men opened the tomb and thrust her gallant lover into it. Into the dark. Dark. Dark.

She had stumbled from the window to the chair, and had sat in sick terror for what had seemed hours. She had hoped that the vision would go away, and even at that early moment in her ordeal she had started to deny what she had seen, substituting the face of Amos Dovercourt for that of Samuel Wheeler.

An hour, maybe more, had passed. Numb with cold and sick with terror, even the thick darkness had held no fear for her. She had moved beyond that to something infinitely worse. When she had crept back to the window, Samuel Wheeler was out on the grass again, bathed in lantern-light. Two men this time stood up, and she saw quite clearly now that one of them was the Reverend Hezekiah Woodward. The other man she did not know.

Then came the second burial. Samuel Wheeler was once more placed into the tomb-chest, and the second man hauled a slab of stone into place.

Her far sight had always been good. . . . She must have been wrong about the underclothes. Mr Wheeler was decently clad in suit and shirt, but there had been something hanging near his neck, a rope or cord.

When she ran to tell her father the details had begun to fade, and the story of Amos Dovercourt had begun to reassert itself. It was her fault that the vicar and those other men had killed poor Samuel. They had done it in revenge. Best to forget it. With each slap of her father's hand across her legs the truth of what she had seen had been driven out, and she had truly believed the ghost-story that she substituted for the truth.

But now, in 1892, and aged seventeen, she remembered the truth. Outside, in the spring night air, the Reverend Hezekiah Woodward turned on his heel and became a bobbing light as he strode away towards the distant rectory.

Deirdre paused with one hand on the handle of the door leading to the warmth and reassurance of her family in the drawing-room. Then she recalled her father's anger and her punishment of earlier years. She walked quietly back into the darkened hall, and mounted the spiral stair to her room.

*

'Why, James, how very kind! William has sent us a sort of programme and guest-list for his weekend party at King's Leyland.'

Mrs Dovercourt handed the letter she had just read to her husband, who laid down his knife and fork. Although he much preferred the papers at breakfast, he was prepared to read anything that came from his brother-in-law, William Loxley Anderson.

'Sent it to *us*, has he? A likely tale! He's sent it to tempt Deirdre to come out of her shell. He doesn't mind you and me coming at Christmas time, but it's youngsters he prefers. A crowd of young folk for that boisterous dancing. There'll be a visit to the May Queen, I expect, and goodness knows what else! I take it that Deirdre will want to go? She enjoys it at King's Leyland.'

Dovercourt's large ringed hand hovered vaguely but significantly near his cup. Mrs Dovercourt poured him a second cup of breakfast tea from the silver teapot while he continued to read the letter. It had arrived with the first post prompt at eight o'clock.

'There you are, Grace, I told you! He says he hopes Deirdre will benefit from some youthful company.'

He looked at his wife, the morning light glittering off the lenses of his pince-nez. He suddenly frowned, and tugged at his black beard.

'Did you hear her last night? She was in that damned room while we were in the drawing-room. Lionel says she's taken to loitering in there again. She's been very quiet since Inspector Jackson came to see her. I got that little chit Jevons to tell me what he'd asked her. It was all about Wheeler. It always upsets her to be reminded of that.'

He handed his brother-in-law's letter back to his wife and gulped down his tea.

'There's something else going on in that girl's mind if you ask

185

me,' he said. 'Lionel thinks that she may have been seeing things again. Maybe this visit will cure her like it did last time.'

Before resuming his demolition of bacon and eggs, James Dovercourt slid a bulky packet across the table.

'There you are, Grace. Mr Rattray's plan. I think we should go ahead. Probably in August. I'd certainly like it done before this coming winter.'

Mrs Dovercourt opened the packet and took out a set of architectural drawings. She scanned them appraisingly, sipping her tea as she did so.

'They're very ingenious, James. The Haunted Room would disappear, and the drawing-room gain all that space. He'd block up the window, as we suggested, and open a second window in the long wall where the piano is. I like it.'

Mr Dovercourt wiped his mouth and stood up.

'I must go to the office, Grace. I've a man coming from Ledson's at half past nine. When will Deirdre go?'

'This coming Thursday. They'd stay over till Monday. It'd do her a great deal of good, I'm sure. Mrs Jevons won't mind Annie going with her for company.'

'She won't need much company to judge from William's guest-list there. All those boys and girls!'

Mrs Dovercourt picked up her brother's letter and unfolded it again.

'He says that the Greyson children will be there, and those young boys of the Carews. Oh! And Rupert Selden. *He's* going to be there. I wonder. . . .'

Mrs Dovercourt's eyes lit up with interesting speculations. Mr Dovercourt, who had paused with his hand on the door-knob, came back into the room and sat down. The works side of the house was calling strongly, but he hadn't read that bit. William's handwriting was so peculiar and sloping that it was an effort at times to decipher what he'd written. He smiled.

'The old fox! Rupert Selden's only seventeen. He left Rugby

last year. He's an uncomfortably handsome boy, Grace. You remember that party William gave last Christmas? Deirdre quite forgot Robert Browning's poems when she saw him. And danced with him. Very taken with him, she was!'

'John Keats, James. Not Browning. Yes, I wonder. . . . Is William trying to make a match? It's about time that Deirdre— They're actually from somewhere down south – Salisbury, that's it. Captain Archibald Selden was originally from Salisbury, but came up to this part of the world after he married Miss Mortimer of Lower Sutton. Rupert Selden is his little brother. Well, not little, you know, but younger. Now Deirdre is only just seventeen. . . .'

James Dovercourt gave vent to an indignant snort.

'Oh, really, Grace, don't be too certain about it! Deirdre's only a child, and she's not . . . well, not very robust.'

'Nonsense!' Mrs Dovercourt was warming to the idea of her daughter and Rupert Selden becoming acquainted. For once her husband was not going to have his way. 'Really, James, one of these days you'll start believing yourself! Child, indeed! For goodness' sake, I was only a year older than Deirdre when I married you!'

James Dovercourt did not seem to hear what his wife had said. Evidently Deirdre's romantic future no longer interested him. Neither did the impending arrival of the man from Ledson's. His eyes were riveted to his copy of the *Daily News*.

'Good God, what next?' he said, slapping the paper with the back of his hand and leaning back in his chair.

'What is it, James?' asked Mrs Dovercourt sharply.

'Well, it's about that terrible business in Cornwall. I wonder if Jackson knows? I expect he does.'

'What does it say?'

'I'll read it to you. "Daring Escape at Derby – Monday, 25th April. We learn that during the evening of Monday, 25th April, Daniel Polk, the police constable who confessed so readily to the Cornish murders at Polwarthan, escaped from custody. It is thought that he may make his way back to Cornwall, where undetected accomplices may spirit him away from the reach of the law".'

'How extraordinary, James. How on earth did he manage to escape?'

'Well, I'm trying to tell you, Grace, aren't I? It says here that a respectable fellow visited Polk in the early evening, passing himself off as a member of the Prisoners' Visitation Society. He'd brought tracts and a Bible for the prisoner, and for his alleged accomplice, Martin Caradyne. Caradyne, yes. . . . He was a lawyer, you know, the other partner in the plundered mining venture.

'Anyway, it says here that this bogus prison missioner exchanged clothes with Polk. Polk hurried from the Derby Bridewell unchallenged. Shortly afterwards, his accomplice, dressed in Polk's uniform and wearing a false beard, left the premises by a rear door. Nobody questioned him, apparently, because he was dressed in genuine police uniform.'

'He must have planned it all in advance,' said Mrs Dovercourt.

'He did. I'll just read you this bit: "Since his remand and voluntary confession Polk had been considered a model of co-operation. He had been visited once only by his wife, through whom it is thought this daring escape was effected. No further information is available at the time of going to press".'

A grandfather clock in the corner suddenly banged out the half-hour. Mr Dovercourt jumped with fright.

'I *must* go. The man from Ledson's will be here now. Incredible! I can't imagine what Jackson will do, with Polk rampaging on the loose! We're living in dangerous times.'

11
Rampant Cat and Half Moon

Pale sunlight filtered obliquely through the tall oaks and sturdy beech trees of the vast swathe of woods above the ancient Warwickshire mansion of King's Leyland. A few thrushes and blackbirds were conducting faint rehearsals of spring song.

Inspector Jackson and Sergeant Bottomley walked through the deserted woodland. Bottomley had returned from Derby a couple of hours earlier, and Jackson had brought him out the two-mile walk from Ashgate St Lawrence.

'So Polk's got clean away,' said Jackson.

'He has, sir. The chief constable up there wanted to bring in Scotland Yard, but Superintendent Crossway managed to hold him off. There's no sign of Polk. They think at Derby that he's made for the Continent.'

'Do they, now? Maybe he has, Sergeant. But then again maybe he hasn't. I suspect that Polk's a man with a wide rein. We don't know what further evil he might get up to.'

'You could be right about that, sir. I could feel that man's bane from the moment he loomed up at us out of the rain at Saltash.'

'What's happened to Martin Caradyne, Calderdale's partner-in-crime?'

'Caradyne's locked up still, waiting to be remanded. The Prison-Gate Missioner's been to see him, and he's going to repent, by the

looks of things. They were a strange gang, sir. Weak men for crim-
inals, it seems to me.'

'Weak, yes, Sergeant, but cunning, too. They laid their plans
well. They liked to leave little mysteries lying around. For instance,
there's the accomplice who changed clothes with Polk. Where did
he spring from?'

The two men emerged into an extensive clearing, where several
stunted, ivy-clad ruined arches and the footings of some ancient
buildings remained from a long-vanished abbey or priory.

Jackson sat down on a fallen stone and motioned Bottomley to
do the same.

'The time's come to move forward, Sergeant,' said Jackson. 'It's
over three weeks now since the Dried-Up Man was discovered by
Eves and Bagnall. Let's try to see just where we've got to with this
case, and decide what's still left to do. We need to be clear in our
minds where we're going to concentrate our efforts next.'

Sergeant Bottomley lit a thin, rather battered cigar. His eyes
narrowed as he began to gather a series of recollections.

'Sir,' he said, 'we set out originally to investigate the death of
the Dried-Up Man, the Reverend Samuel Wheeler, MA, aged
thirty-five. He was found in that tomb on the fourth. It's the
twenty-seventh today. So far, we've found out how he was
murdered—'

'Yes, Sergeant: someone fired an arrow into his back as he fled.
But we still don't know *what* he fled from. We still don't know *who*
fired the arrow. We still don't know *where* he was murdered.'

'And for that matter, sir, we still don't know *why*. Until we've
found the answer to that question, we'll be no nearer the solution
of this mystery.'

Sergeant Bottomley stood up and stubbed the butt of his cigar
on the sole of his shoe. He placed the flattened remains carefully
under a stone.

'You say we don't know *why* Wheeler was murdered, Sergeant.
It's a point worth pondering. There's something missing in our

knowledge of Wheeler. Mr Lionel showed me proof that Wheeler had discovered the truth about the frauds at Polwarthan. Mr Wheeler had actually confided in Polk! But where do we go from there? What's the link between a man finding out about chicanery in Cornwall and turning up dead in a remote Warwickshire grave-yard four years later?'

Jackson wandered off towards a ridge of trees from which he found he could look down a wooded slope at the twisted roofs and pointed gables of the ancient mansion of King's Leyland, the seat of Deirdre's maternal uncle, Mr William Loxley Anderson. He could just smell the smoke that drifted lazily upward from the many chimneys. He beckoned to Sergeant Bottomley, who joined him.

'I've brought you out here, Sergeant,' he said, 'because I'm convinced that this is where the answer lies – the answer to the mystery of the Dried-Up Man. Down there, in that old country seat, Mr Robert Elmore was received as a visitor by Mr Loxley Anderson. Elmore was Mr Wheeler's half-brother. Those links are too strong to be merely coincidence.'

'What do you think we should do, sir?'

'I'll tell you what I'm going to do first. I'm going to find out about Miss Deirdre Dovercourt's visions. There's something sinister locked up in that girl's head, and the time's come to find out what it is. She knows something about Wheeler's death.'

'How will you go about it, sir? Are you going to question her again?'

'No. For some reason, she's afraid of me. I'm going to consult the doctor who treated her. I need to have this dressing changed, but I'm not going to our friend Dr Phillips; I'm going to get Miss Deirdre's old doctor to do it.'

Jackson moved thoughtfully back into the quiet woodland clearing.

'And whenever I think of that frightened girl, Sergeant,' he continued, 'with her little fourteen-year-old protector and her fads and fancies, I think too of Parson Woodward! There was a time, I believe, when that haunted man and that frightened girl became linked by whatever lurks in that cursed burial-ground. I've no proof of that, only a feeling. But at times, as you know, feelings can be right.'

'We never did have a little heart-to-heart talk with Parson Woodward,' said Bottomley. 'We had other things to think about down in Cornwall.'

'We did! But now I mean to probe more deeply into this wretched superstition. We've *still* not uncovered the secret of Parson Woodward and his obsessions.'

Some passing memory conjured up in Jackson's mind a sudden vivid image of Ashgate, a thriving, bustling little town, sitting on an ancient pagan shrine, and still clasped secretly in the arms of demon gods. What was it? Of course – the glint of sunlight on winking objects in long grass. . . .

'Sergeant, have you seen those little silver charms or talismans nailed up over some of the doors in Ashgate? The rector told me what they signify, but not where they come from. Somebody must have made them. Who, I wonder?'

' "Ban-devils", they call them, sir. The man who makes them is called Littlechild. Matthew Littlechild. He's a metalworker and tinsmith with a shop in Bridge Rise. He makes them.'

'How did you know that?'

'I was treating a rheumatic old gaffer to some beer the other night, and he nodded him out to me. "That's Matthew Littlechild what makes the ban-devils", he told me. And then he added, "He's a white master". Someone else heard him, and swore at him to keep his mouth shut. And he did. And so did I.'

'Littlechild. Right, Sergeant, I'll make it my business to call on this Matthew Littlechild. A white master? Maybe he knows something that will lead us nearer the truth about Mr Wheeler. Sacrifice? That's what Mrs Dovercourt hinted at. I wonder. . . .'

'And what do you want *me* to do, sir?'

'You, Sergeant Bottomley, must start to unlock the secrets of King's Leyland. Mr Loxley Anderson's holding a great dance there tomorrow night, and the house will be full of guests. I'm sure there'll be room for you, Sergeant, if you know where to find it. You'll use your own methods, I expect, but it would do no harm to nose about below stairs.'

The two men walked down the woodland track and emerged on to the Ashgate road. Some yards to their left Jackson could see the crested gate-pillars at the entrance to the carriage drive of King's Leyland. The wrought-iron gates were open, but there were other tasks to be done in Ashgate St Lawrence before Bottomley could venture along that drive.

They had walked only a short distance in the direction of Ashgate when the sound of a horse's hooves made them seek refuge on the grass verge while a handsome olive-green closed carriage, drawn by a smart chestnut, passed them, throwing up clouds of white dust. As they followed its progress they saw the liveried coachman turn the vehicle through the entrance gates of the old Tudor mansion.

Mr Loxley Anderson's guests were beginning to arrive.

King's Leyland, Mr William Loxley Anderson's Warwickshire seat, nestled in a deeply wooded hollow, where serried ranks of beech and oak rose around, but never overshadowed the long Tudor house. The grounds were romantically wild, a sure sign of careful landscaping and continued attention from a small army of gardeners. There were discreet arbours and alleys nearer to the house, and a range of well-stocked kitchen-gardens.

King's Leyland had been built between 1490 and 1512, so there was much black and white work and imaginative sandstone confections of Tudor architectural fancy. Like many large houses of the period, it was well endowed with spacious windows. Inside, it was always light and cheerful.

The smart olive-green carriage drew up before the house, and a heavily built, rather stooping man in a well-cut suit alighted. He stood on the ancient flagstones before the main entrance, and looked up at the carved inscription above the door. In a land in love with Latin, it always came as a pleasant surprise to visitors when they saw the old national confidence of Tudor England in the power of its native language:

THIS WORK WAS DONE BY ME WM. LOXLEY: COMPLEAT AD 1512.
LONGE LIVE OUR KINGE HENRY 8: THREE YEERES NOW REIGNING.

The visitor pulled the bell, and heard the distant jangle somewhere in the house. The carriage was driven slowly to the stable block behind the mansion.

The door was opened by an elderly butler, who peered at the visitor for a few moments before smiling a welcome.

'Why, Mr Galt! Do come in, sir. It's some while since we saw you.'

Mr Galt stepped into the entrance passage and removed his silk hat, which the butler received. The visitor showed no inclination to take off his heavy, fur-trimmed greatcoat. Nor did he reply at once to the butler's welcome.

The butler opened a door and led the visitor into a very sunny panelled room at the front of the building.

'If you will wait here, sir, Mr Loxley Anderson will be with you directly.'

Mr Galt found his voice. 'Thank you, Craxton, very civil of you.'

It was a flat, defeated kind of voice, which the butler recalled from the previous rare but regular occasions when Mr Galt had visited. It was one of the oddities about this particular guest of his master's: the fashionable clothes, the expensive atmosphere, coupled with a morose, brutal mien. Another oddity was that such a strong-looking man should be, by all accounts, a reclusive invalid.

Mr Galt sat down on the cushions in the window-seat and looked around him. The stone floor of the chamber was covered in costly Turkey carpets, upon which stood many pieces of furniture clearly dating from the time of the mansion's building. There were also newer pieces, valuable and delicate cabinets containing sets of porcelain.

Mr Galt indulged in what could be termed emotionless appreciation. He could remember the time when things at King's Leyland had been more threadbare than this. He would get some things of that kind for his new house in Belgium. He would also get some pictures, expensive paintings to hang on the walls.

What he could not buy would be Loxley Anderson's pedigree. That, he reflected, came with the man, and he was none the worse for that. There was a wide Tudor fireplace, above which was a carving of a round-eyed man and an almond-eyed lady in ruffs, flanked on either side by an array of diminishing wooden children. Every one of those little statues, he mused, represented a Loxley Anderson of ancient times.

In the upper lights of the old windows, were circular armorial bearings in coloured glass. Mr Galt saw them, but could not interpret them. He knew, though, that the owner of the house could read them as though they were words in a book: the rampant cat and half moon of the Loxleys; the same arms quartered with the griffins of the Andersons of Newton Seneschal; the gold discs and axe-heads of the Sherringhams; the lion passant sable of the Mortimers of Lower Sutton; the red diamond chequer-work of the Sands of Sand. . . .

'Why, Mr Galt! I'm so glad you have managed to come. So very pleased. I've told Craxton to prepare your usual quiet rooms in the west wing. You'll not be disturbed should you feel disinclined to join the company.'

Mr Loxley Anderson had charged, speaking, into the room with a characteristic burst of energy. There was no mistaking the genuineness of this particular welcome.

195

Mr Galt surveyed his host with a sort of grudging appreciation. A genial, smiling man with a chuckle in his voice, much the same height and build as himself. A man with a creased face, the result of much geniality. In the main clean-shaven, but with greying whiskers along the line of the jaw. Gold spectacles. Good, regular features. A gentleman.

Mr Loxley Anderson closed the door and eased himself into a rather angular Jacobean chair near the fireplace. He smiled.

'The trouble with these upright carved chairs, Galt, is that one cannot relax in them, but feels obliged to use them. I was telling Craxton just now how lucky he was, not being able to sit down in the state-rooms. Unlike me, his hind quarters have not been worn down to the bone by Jacobean joinery!'

Mr Galt permitted himself a wintry smile. Loxley Anderson was one of the few people who could produce that effect on him. Nevertheless, he did not relax the cautious vigilance that he had shown ever since he had crossed the threshold.

'You are very kind, Mr Loxley Anderson, and I appreciate the quiet rooms. This will be a golden chance for you and me to talk business before I retire with my wife to the Continent. It's been a dark, dangerous affair from the start, and we must secure our gains by what means we can. I have done my part, God knows.'

Mr Loxley Anderson looked thoughtfully at his guest. I wonder, he thought, does he realize the irony of that remark? Probably not. Just as well, maybe.

'And you may trust me to do mine, Galt. I am bound to you by special bonds of gratitude and duty. I know what you have had to endure, year after year, while I have lived spaciously here in health and wealth. The others have their value, but you and I are the secret principals of this particular concern.'

'Do you want to hear how I kept my word to come here today?'

Mr Loxley Anderson raised a deprecating hand.

'Please, please . . . no details. What I don't know, I can't retail to others. We have a list – a mental list, and we need to go through the items one by one. Who is first on *your* list, Mr Galt?'

'Caradyne. And, for that matter, Major Giles Redcott. By this time Redcott will know that he has been swindled out of thousands of pounds through the secret mining of silver glance at Polwarthan, and he's not so frail that he won't raise all hell against us. There's no physical evidence left there, because the minehouse was burnt down, but he'll know now that Caradyne was crooked.'

'Where is Caradyne now?'

'He's in gaol in Derby. There's a very clever man investigating this business. I don't mean Inspector Tregennis, though he's able enough. It's a man from this end of things, Detective Inspector Jackson. He set a beautiful trap and we all fell into it. Jackson had arranged for the house in Friargate to be watched. Caradyne was there, and was taken.'

'Jackson? Yes, I know him by repute. He solved a very unpleasant problem for one of our leading families here in Warwickshire a few years ago. How did he find out about Friargate? The Benedict-Smiths haven't lived in Derby for years. Most people thought the house was shut up.'

Mr Galt made a movement of disgust. There was something reptilian about him, a still watchfulness.

'Reuben Calderdale, our precious manager, was too fond of papers and letters. I suspect Jackson rooted round in the minehouse and found some documents naming the house in Friargate. He may even know that the consignments of ore from Polwarthan were received in Derby by railway, and that the business was completed at the house. I don't know that for certain, but it means the end of our profitable enterprise in Cornwall.'

'What will Caradyne do?'

Mr Galt rose from his seat in the window and crossed to the fire. He pulled his heavy greatcoat around him. He had lived too long in damp, unwholesome places, and the cold had entered his bones. He threw his host an impenetrable glance and then directed his gaze to the fire.

'When Caradyne was in the cells I managed to have a word with him. I told him that he would be struck off the roll of solicitors and forbidden to practise, and that in addition he would be sentenced to a very long term of imprisonment for fraud and forgery. I painted a very colourful picture for him. Quite an effort it was, as I'm not over-fond of words.

'I told him what his future would hold when he finally left Dartmoor. It wasn't all fiction, as he well knew. And when I'd finished I slipped him something done up in a white paper that I'd carried with me ever since Inspector Jackson came on the scene. I told him what to do. Then I told him a bit more about life in a gin-soaked slum. So watch the papers, Mr Loxley Anderson.'

Mr Galt's host shook his head with what seemed like genuine regret. He sighed.

'Dear me, Mr Galt, I'm sorry to hear about Caradyne. He built the legal edifice that houses our projects. It would take a lifetime for the over-curious to untangle what he knotted together. Among countless enterprises he very successfully presented our Newcastle venture as coming from quite a different source. He was brilliant at that kind of thing. It led to people, whom we'd robbed of thousands, thanking us for our care and concern!'

Mr Galt regarded his host moodily. Odd, thought Loxley Anderson, how the well-cut clothes do nothing to disguise the man's brutality. . . .

'I'm making no criticism, you know,' said Loxley Anderson. 'About what you've arranged, I mean. Caradyne was devious and clever, but he was always weak. So was Reuben Calderdale. You look worried. What is it, Galt?'

'I'm beginning to fear the power of coincidence, Mr Loxley Anderson. How much of it can be put down to chance? There's no more God-forsaken spot on earth than Polwarthan. It was a life-sentence for anyone living there. And yet, who should turn up as vicar there but Parson Woodward? Wherever we turn – here, up north, or down in Cornwall, that old crackpot follows us. It's uncanny! So I can feel my ailments coming on already. Woodward's back in Ashgate St Lawrence, so I hear. You've not invited him here, have you?'

Mr Loxley Anderson laughed heartily. Maybe Galt was venturing on the ironic.

'No, no, let me assure you of that. There are a few sober folk from the county assembling here, but it's primarily a horde of boys and girls to lighten the atmosphere. My sister's girl Deirdre's coming, together with her maid.' He chortled merrily. 'I've a little surprise lined up for Miss Deirdre!'

Mr Galt's eyes lit up briefly when Deirdre was mentioned and then regained their usual lack of lustre. He still looked personally affronted.

'And another thing: Robert Elmore. Another link for Jackson to trace back to you. He'll be here asking you questions. To tell you the truth, I'm not so sure that I didn't see him and his poisonous sergeant lurking among the trees as I arrived here. You'd better have your story ready when he asks about Elmore. As for the other—'

'Enough!'

The single word sounded like a whiplash. Mr Galt actually started in alarm, and looked at his host in surprise. The amiable Mr Loxley Anderson had suddenly revealed a hidden depth of command that was not usually exercised so openly.

'If you don't mind, Mr Galt, we'll leave that particular coincidence to lie on the file, as we magistrates say.' His voice resumed its cheery, pleasant tones. 'As the Good Book tells us, Mr Galt: "Sufficient unto the day is the evil thereof".'

'Hold still, Jackson. Hold quite still. That's it!'

Old Dr Churchill Reid skilfully lifted the yellow-stained gauze from Jackson's shoulder with forceps. When he worked, Jackson noted, he tended not to speak, giving his full attention to the task in hand. The only noise in the quiet surgery was the tinkle of metal instruments being placed gently in their enamel dish.

'Now let me see. . . . Yes, beautiful. Lovely scarring. You'll not need splints. Who attended to you at Exeter?'

'A gentleman called Dr Jelk. There was another doctor with him. Manners, I think his name was.'

'Ah, yes, Manners. Ginger-headed young fellow. He's one of a little batch of fledglings from Charing Cross Hospital. Dr Jelk, of course, is a very well-known specialist in burns. Now hold still again while I put this new dressing on. This is soaked in eucalyptus oil, and will see you right in a week or two. There's no sepsis, thank goodness.'

It was half an hour since Jackson had sought out the picturesque house of Dr Churchill Reid. It lay off the narrow main street of Newton Seneschal, a straggling village a mile to the north of Ashgate. The doctor walked with the aid of a stout stick, and his back was bent with advanced years. His eyes, though, were bright, and his manner brisk for his age.

'I got Ambrose Phillips's note, asking me to change your dressing, and talk to you about young Miss Dovercourt. As he's recommended you to me as a discreet sort of person, I'm happy to oblige. I treated Miss Dovercourt during that unhappy time when she was afflicted by visions. I gather that's the period of her life that interests you?'

'Yes, sir.'

'She was a dear little girl, Mr Jackson, but she was subject to what are called hallucinations. She would see things that were not there, you understand.'

'Things that were not there?'

'Yes. She saw a ghostly figure in the churchyard behind her house, and claimed it was that of an ancestor who had committed suicide. She was quite ill, poor child, and spoke in her trance of a man in white trousers lying on the grass. But later she said the man was clad in a suit of black. To that phenomenon we assign the name cerebro-visual aphasia.'

'She saw a man in white trousers?'

'Well . . . not trousers. I say that for form's sake. Combinations. That was the word she used. She would know of such garments, as she had a father and brother living. Still has, for the matter of that.'

'You interest me greatly, Dr Churchill Reid. What did you do for the girl?'

'Deirdre, her name is. I believe it's a Celtic name. I gave her feverfew, and applied ice-packs to the cranium. I had thought of bleeding her, but considered it in the end unnecessary.'

'That was in 1888?'

'It was. In February. That was the month in which Mr Oldacre of Squire's Park developed aggrandisement of the pia mater. We drained his skull through a silver tube, and he died in early March.' He added rather portentously, 'One learns a great deal from the practice of medicine, Mr Jackson.'

The old doctor hauled himself up from his chair and began to fuss about with the basin and instruments on his surgery table. It was time, thought Jackson, to ask some final questions before he was sent on his way.

'I spoke recently to Mr Lionel Dovercourt, who told me that Miss Deirdre started to see things again in March, 1890.'

'Yes, yes indeed. Most unusual. *Most* unusual. I had retired by then, and come to live here, but they sent a carriage for me. Miss Deirdre was certainly very upset, and subject to hysterical spasm. I bled her on that occasion, applied camphor, and rubbed her limbs with Potter's liniment. I advised a change of air, and in fact she went on to make a complete recovery. She enjoyed a bracing holiday with her uncle at King's Leyland.'

Dr Churchill Reid opened a glazed cupboard and peered rather short-sightedly inside.

'What did she see on that occasion?'

'What do you mean? *What* occasion?'

'The occasion in March, 1890.'

'Oh, that.'

The old doctor sat down again. It would be easier to finish the conversation before putting things away where they belonged.

'Well, she saw a solitary man in a long coat, standing in the churchyard looking up at her. It was in full daylight. The man was quite motionless, she said, and his presence made her recall her original vision of two years earlier. It seemed that somehow the same man had stood in the same way at that time, looking steadily up at her. The whole thing, of course, was the product of a fevered imagination.'

He sighed and shook his head.

'These girls, you see, make themselves addle-brained by too much reading of light and giddy literature. A low diet always helps in such cases.'

Jackson left the old doctor to tidy his surgery and walked thoughtfully back along the main street of Newton Seneschal.

'So now we have the Silent Man,' he mused. 'First in 1888, then in 1890. The Silent Man. I wonder. . . .'

Mr Loxley Anderson's butler, Craxton, made his measured way through the labyrinth of ancient, richly furnished rooms of King's Leyland, along winding oak-panelled passages, and into the west wing of the house. Here, in his accustomed suite of rooms, Mr Galt had indicated by pulling the bell that he had finished dining.

Craxton found Mr Galt still sitting at the round table in the dining-room of the suite, thoughtfully sipping a glass of port. The flickering candles caused winking reflections from the cut-glass decanters and silver appointments.

Mr Galt himself looked very fine in his well-cut evening clothes. He had sensibly rung for the valet earlier in the evening. So many gentlemen these days seemed content to dress themselves.

'I trust that dinner was to your satisfaction, sir?'

'Entirely so, thank you, Craxton. Perhaps you'd clear away now? I'll not stir out of here again tonight. See that the fire's well banked up.'

Mr Galt reached into his pocket and brought out a half sovereign.

'There you are, Craxton. It may be that my illness will prevent me leaving these rooms during my stay. I may need to take all my meals here.'

'That is quite in order, sir. Mr Loxley Anderson has already mentioned the matter to me.'

'Where is Mr Loxley Anderson? I thought he might have looked in earlier on.'

Craxton smiled. 'He's in the billiard saloon, sir, playing for pennies with the two young gentlemen who are staying in the house. He's letting them win, of course, and telling them jokes, so it's rather rowdy down there at the moment! He's not much time for grown-up folk, sir, when there are youngsters in the house.'

The ends of Mr Galt's mouth turned downward for a moment, revealing some alarming teeth. He was attempting to smile.

'Your master always had a soft spot for young folk, Craxton. But you have to be fit and well to cope with them, I find. My illness prevents me having much to do with vigorous pastimes.'

Craxton ventured to ask rather delicately whether Mr Galt was much inconvenienced by his affliction.

'It's what it might lead to, Craxton, that worries me. With what I have, you can end up with a severe closure of the wind-pipe. It's always fatal when it reaches that stage. But with due care the patient can survive.'

When Craxton had cleared the table and gone, Mr Galt looked out of the window. There was a thin, not very aggressive rain falling on to a little secluded grass arbour surrounded by privet hedges. It was quiet and private, and dimly illuminated by the light streaming from the uncurtained diamond-paned windows of the main house.

I couldn't ask for better treatment, thought Galt. But is it safe? Due care's what's needed. With that, and a measure of luck, the patient should survive.

12
Spectre at the Feast

The ancient Tudor mansion of King's Leyland blazed with light as dusk drew its dark veil around the trees. Sergeant Bottomley stopped for a while in the drive to survey the scene. The cheering strains of an orchestra came to him from somewhere within the timbered courts of the house. It was a dry, pleasant evening, and there was just sufficient daylight to see the yellow lichens on the old tiles of the soaring roofs. White smoke rose lazily from a dozen chimneys.

The strains of the orchestra began to take on meaning, and resolved themselves into a well-known waltz. The many windows of the entrance-front glowed with the light of candelabra and oil-lamps, and Bottomley could see figures passing and re-passing in every room, men in formal evening dress. and ladies in fashionable gowns. Even at that distance he could hear the sustained murmur of conversation.

He resumed his steady walk along the path until he was within yards of the entrance to King's Leyland, when he turned abruptly to the right and ducked under a low wooden arch into a long enclosed yard at the side of the house. There was a smell of cooking there, mingled with the unmistakable scent of hops.

There was an old, gnarled door studded and strapped with iron, and fixed near it on the wall a metal triangle with a striker hanging

THE DRIED-UP MAN

from it by a chain. Sergeant Bottomley seized the striker and
proceeded to set up a fearful din.

The door was flung open almost immediately, flooding the yard
with light, and sending out a gust of warm air carrying the aroma
of freshly baked bread. Craxton, the butler, peered out at the
visitor.

'Sergeant Bottomley, Warwickshire Constabulary, at your
service. May I come in for a moment? Just for a comfortable chat,
you know. Nothing to worry about.'

Bottomley did not wait to be invited, but stepped over the
threshold into what was revealed as a spacious stone-flagged hall,
warmed by a blazing fire in an enormous grate. The fireplace was
flanked by two upright settles, and there was a scrubbed deal
table, but most of the vast floor space was empty.

Craxton smiled to himself, and waved the visitor to one of the
settles.

'I'm not deaf, you know, Mr Bottomley. You set up a fearful
racket on the triangle: I thought the Day of Judgement had come.'

He disappeared around a corner for a few moments and then
returned with a pewter tankard of ale, which he handed to
Bottomley.

'I don't suppose you drink much, Sergeant, but that'll do you
good. Now, I'll be happy to speak to you for as long as you like,
but you might have noticed that we've got company this week, and
I'll be called away from time to time. Provided you don't mind
that, then we'll have a little chat.'

Craxton sat down on the opposite settle and surveyed his
visitor with growing amusement. Bottomley for his part was
striving to remember something from the remote past, and failing.
It was Craxton who took the initiative.

'You don't know me, do you, Herbert Bottomley?' he said.

'Why, Mr Craxton, I do seem to remember something—'

'You're Joe Bottomley's lad who went into the police. I
remember you when you were a little fellow. I'd never have

thought such a little demon as you were would end up as a policeman!'

Sergeant Bottomley looked rather uncomfortable. but was spared the need to reply by the suddenly grave look that came to the old butler's face.

'Well, Herbert, you won't have come here without a reason, and I expect it's all to do with the mummy they found over at Ashgate. We've been hearing things out here – not very nice things, either, to my way of thinking.'

Sergeant Bottomley sipped his beer and glanced around the large but comfortable chamber in which they sat. The orchestra had struck up again in the depths of the house, and the sound of laughter came to them, mingled with the thudding of energetic feet in some kind of country dance.

'Is this the servants' hall, then, Mr Craxton? It's a huge place. I thought it might have been the kitchen.'

'The kitchens are down there through the arch. I never go in there at this time of day until Cook comes out and tells me they're ready to serve. Dinner's at nine tonight, and there's fifteen sitting down.'

Craxton looked up into the rafters above and pointed.

'Do you see there, Herbert? Those big white letters and figures on the tie-beam? "God Be Thanked For Agin Court: 1415". This hall was the original house before ever the Tudor one was built.'

'And was it Loxley Andersons even then?'

'Loxleys. There have always been Loxleys here, and there always will be. The Andersons married into the Loxleys. The Andersons of Newton Seneschal.'

'I expect you've been here a long time, Mr Craxton.'

The butler sighed. He was old enough to be skilled in hearing what lay beneath spoken words. Bottomley heard the sigh and cast him a shrewd glance.

'What do you want to know?' asked Craxton.

'I want to know about February, 1888. Four years ago. I have only one interest connected with that time, Mr Craxton, and it's concerned with a man called the Reverend Samuel Wheeler, MA, curate of Ashgate St Lawrence. You mentioned the mummy. Well, *he* was the mummy, the Dried-Up Man.'

Bottomley's beer was neglected. He was poised to present a conjecture as a fact, and he needed to convince the other man that it *was* a fact. His kindly, beery face caught the firelight, and showed the fine, shrewd eyes that were normally hidden by half-closed lids. He chose his words very carefully.

'Mr Wheeler came here one day in the February of 1888. It was just after he had been involved in a scandal with a young lady who is a guest in this house. You will know what I am speaking of.'

Bottomley paused for a moment. The butler had not contradicted him. It would be safe to elaborate.

'Mr Wheeler came to this house. He was very agitated and asked to see Mr Loxley Anderson.'

He stopped speaking, and there was silence in the hall. The music in the house had paused for a lull in the dancing. The wood settled and crackled in the fireplace.

'Were you here? Were you watching?' Craxton's voice came fearfully and low. Bottomley's conjecture had proved to be the truth.

'I was not watching exactly, Mr Craxton, but—'

A door let into an old arch further along the wall suddenly opened. There was a renewed surge of effort from the orchestra, and then the door was closed. Herbert Bottomley looked at the young girl who had entered the hall and manfully postponed the business of Mr Wheeler's visit. He rose from the seat and bowed low.

'Miss Annie, by all that's wonderful. My pleasure, miss, I'm sure!'

Annie looked pleased to see him. She smiled and dropped him a little curtsy.

'What's it like in there, Annie?' asked Bottomley. 'It sounds marvellous out here.'

'Oh, mister, it's lovely! Just like last time, only better! Everything's new, and there's big candle-sconces standing round the great hall so you'd think it was the sun shining! I stood at the door and peeped in. Miss Deirdre's wearing her white silk off-the-shoulder dress with the green sash, and the opal pendant Mr Wheeler gave her. She's dancing with Master Rupert Selden, who keeps claiming her for every dance!'

Annie's dark eyes gleamed with various feminine speculations. The orchestra paused for a moment and then launched into a slow and measured Viennese waltz. Bottomley walked gravely across the paved floor to Annie, bowed, and said, 'May I have the pleasure of this dance, miss?'

Annie was delighted. Her station forbade her joining in the dances in the Great Hall, but here was plenty of light and space, and also time in the lull before dinner was served. She allowed Bottomley to take her gently as his partner. He began to dance in step with the music filtering through from the Great Hall. For a large, rather unsteady man, he danced very well indeed.

Round and round they went, carried on by the music. Annie read the physical facts of Bottomley's holding her and confirmed what she knew already: she could trust this grown-up man, and relax in his arms.

Craxton chuckled, reached up to the mantelpiece for a clay pipe, and settled down to watch the dancing couple.

'Annie,' asked Bottomley, 'do you know what an "open secret" is?'

'No, mister.'

'It's something that everybody knows, although it's supposed to be a secret. Well, what really happened between Miss Deirdre and Mr Wheeler was an open secret. Her mama knows, and so does Mr Lionel. And so do you, don't you?'

Annie made no reply. She tried to loosen her hand from

Bottomley's but he held her gently and firmly.

'When Miss Deirdre's papa went into the Haunted Room, Miss Deirdre immediately screamed and fainted. Why, then? Why not when Mr Wheeler first grabbed hold of her? And the answer is, *he never did.* Inspector Jackson went to see Mr Dovercourt this morning. He made him recall exactly what he had seen on that fatal day. Mr Wheeler's arms were not around Miss Deirdre's back; *her arms were around his.* That's why she screamed and fainted. Her father had detected her making an improper advance to poor Mr Wheeler.'

Annie's voice came small and frightened.

'I'm tired now, mister. Thanks for the lovely dance.'

Bottomley released her immediately, and she walked thoughtfully back to the door from which she had emerged. She turned round on the threshold and said, 'I'm going to tell Miss Deirdre what you said. It's not my place to give you yea or nay. Don't leave the house, mister, until my mistress has come to find you.'

Annie threw him one of her old-fashioned, appraising glances.

'I think you're a nice man, and I trust you not to harm a young lady's reputation. When all that happened, my mistress was only thirteen years old.'

The little maid curtsied again and passed through the door into the brilliantly lighted state-rooms of the mansion.

Sergeant Bottomley thoughtfully resumed his place by the fire. Craxton put his pipe on the hearth. He had heard parts of the conversation between the man and the maid, and realized its import.

'You've girls of your own, haven't you, Herbert?'

'I've eight girls, all living. Two are married, two in service, and the other four are still at home. This little one is very like my daughter Poppy, only Poppy's fair and this one's dark.'

Craxton digested this information at leisure. It gave him time to think before he spoke. It sounded as though Miss Deirdre had been one of those precocious little girls, fanciful and romantic.

She'd woven a romantic fantasy around Mr Wheeler, and then clasped him in a crude embrace. No doubt the poor man had struggled, horrified, to release himself, and then Mr Dovercourt had burst in. . . .

'Herbert, I know what you and that little maid were talking about, so I won't beat about the bush. Why didn't Mr Wheeler deny Mr Dovercourt's insinuation?'

'I don't know, Mr Craxton. But I rather think that it was because he was too much of a gentleman to betray the child to her father. I think he would have sought an interview later, to tell the true story, but I'm beginning to think that he never got the chance. For reasons quite unconnected with Miss Deirdre, he disappeared the same month. Folk believed that he'd fled in disgrace to Florence. But he hadn't. He'd been murdered and mummified in the old tomb at Ashgate St Lawrence. A Loxley Anderson tomb.'

Bottomley cast a quizzical glance at the butler, and settled himself to listen to what he had been about to tell him when Annie came into the room. Something in the situation made Craxton address the sergeant in more formal tones than he had done so far.

'Mr Bottomley, it's partly because I knew your father, and partly because I'm becoming afraid and confused, that I'm going to tell you what by rights I should keep to myself.

'It was one day in February, 1888, very soon after word had gone round about the scandal. I'm a man that doesn't sleep much, Mr Bottomley. The doctor says it's insomnia, but I think it's sleeplessness. So most nights I just sit by my bed reading by a rush-light until half-past two or three.'

He leaned forward on the settle, and his voice dropped.

'On that February night, about two o'clock, I heard the sound of talking downstairs. I couldn't fathom who could be about at that late hour. I slipped out of my room on to the servants' landing and looked down over the banisters. My master, Mr Loxley Anderson, was standing in the entrance passage. There was a candle burning on the little malachite table near the front door. He had just admitted the Reverend Mr Wheeler to the house. Mr Wheeler looked gravely troubled and agitated.'

'Had you heard the bell being rung?'

'No, I'd not heard the bell, so I assume Mr Wheeler had thrown gravel up at Mr Loxley Anderson's bedroom window.

' "Loxley Anderson", said Mr Wheeler, "I fear that a great fraud has been perpetrated, and I must seek an interview with you. I am so vilely placed at present that the matter cannot wait".

' "We will talk in the drawing-room, Wheeler", my master replied, "and then you must stay the night. It is already early morning". They passed into the drawing-room and I went back to bed.'

Craxton glanced at a clock above the fireplace.

'Cook will be through in about fifteen minutes,' he said.

Bottomley made no reply. He knew that Craxton had not finished his tale, and he was content to wait.

'The first light of morning had begun to dawn when I suddenly awoke. It must have been around six o'clock. It was a noise that had startled me. I left my bed and went to the window.'

Craxton stopped speaking, and Bottomley saw a subtle change come over the butler's face. His eyes narrowed, and his mouth assumed a thin-lipped petulance that somehow seemed alien to his normal character. The expression passed almost immediately, but not before Bottomley had interpreted its meaning.

Craxton wanted to tell the truth, but was not going to let the truth interfere with his personal comfort and security.

'I think you'll agree, Mr Bottomley, that it's not always easy to see folk clearly very early in the morning? A man's eyes aren't properly focused till he's had something to eat.'

'You're quite right, Mr Craxton. No one expects you to have seen everything clearly. But you'd better tell me what you might have seen.'

'Running across the grass below the front windows of the house was the figure of a man. It may have been Mr Wheeler but I can't be sure. He was running, running along the grass alley towards the butts. I—'

'The butts? What do you mean by that?'

Bottomley's voice was uncharacteristically sharp.

'Why, the archery butts, where the targets and so forth were kept. They're not there now. It's all been grassed over as a tennis court.

'This running man was clad in combinations, despite the cold February weather, as though he had been disturbed from sleep by some great terror.'

Craxton moistened his dry lips and looked covertly at Sergeant Bottomley. The word 'murder' seemed to hang threateningly in the warm air of the servants' hall.

'Clad in combinations,' said Bottomley. He smiled amiably at the butler. 'That's very interesting, Mr Craxton. Try to think back to that scene: I'm sure that the running man must have been Mr Wheeler. What do you think?'

Craxton realized with growing relief that Bottomley was going to play his game. He could afford to be more forthright about this detail, at least.

'Yes, now I come to think about it, I'm certain that it was Mr Wheeler. He'd called unexpectedly, and would have made do without a night-gown at that late hour.

'He ran silently, and then I saw that he was being pursued by . . . three shadows, three assailants, I suppose. It was getting lighter, but there was no one about. Suddenly Mr Wheeler gave a cry and threw up his arms in the air. He fell to the ground, and the three shadows were on him. . . .'

'These three shadows – were you able to see who they were?'

For a moment the defensive petulance returned to the normally amiable face of the old butler. He stroked his chin nervously, and glanced around the hall for a moment before fixing his eyes on Bottomley.

'No, Mr Bottomley. I didn't recognize any of them. A man can't always see too clearly in the morning, as I think you agreed. I went back to bed, and rose at seven, and to cut a long story short there was no sign of any guest having slept in the house other than those already there. There was no sign of any struggle, and the master was his usual genial self. It was a strange mystery, and I've never spoken of it to a soul from that day to this.'

Bottomley stood up. He looked both grim and exultant.

'A strange mystery indeed, Mr Craxton, and one that I'd like you to keep to yourself for the time being. One last question: you say there were other guests present on that occasion. Who were they?'

The danger had passed. Craxton could afford to relax and recollect.

'Let me see: there was a Mr Thirlwood – I don't recall having seen him before – and Mr Galt. Mr Galt is an old friend of the master's, and is staying in the house at the present moment.'

The butler's brow creased in an effort at remembrance.

'No, wait – the other gentleman wasn't called Thirlwood. He came from a place called Thirlwood. Thirlwood Parva, somewhere up north. But I can't now recollect his name. He's not stayed here since.'

A door under the arch at the far end of the room opened and a woman's voice called out, 'Dinner is ready for table, Mr Craxton!'

Craxton drew on a pair of white gloves.

'I must go now to supervise the footmen. There are fifteen sitting down tonight. Perhaps we'll speak later, Herbert.'

The butler dismissed past mysteries with relief and concentrated on his professional duties. Soon Sergeant Bottomley was alone in the spacious hall. He looked up at the beams, with their incised celebration of Agincourt. An old family with a demon lurking in its midst. . . .

He sat down at the fire and was soon absorbed in thought. 'A man can't always see too clearly in the morning'! Craxton had seen clearly, right enough. He'd seen Mr Wheeler admitted to the house and offered a bed for the night. He'd seen his pursuers, and watched him being murdered. He was obviously a decent man, but he clearly knew on which side his bread was buttered. Craxton had known, right enough, who those three 'shadows' were.

'Mr Bottomley!'

Startled, the sergeant sprang to his feet and bowed.

Deirdre Dovercourt looked splendid and triumphant in her ball gown, with the opal on a gold chain glinting at her throat. There was a special look on her face that told the father of eight daughters that this particular girl had suddenly realized that she was a young woman.

So, he thought to himself, there's some fine young lad there in the dance who's just had his heart stolen away!

'Mr Bottomley,' said Deirdre, 'my maid had told me about your speculations. Let me say at once that they were true. Until this moment, I had not dared to face the truth – that it was I who made an assault on Mr Wheeler, not he on me. I was only thirteen, and I am beginning to realize that most grown-up people would not have made such a fuss as Papa did. So there you are. You may do as you please!'

Sergeant Bottomley looked very contrite.

'What's his name?' he asked.

'Rupert Selden. He's – oh! How did you know?'

'It's the look in your eyes, miss. I've seen it many times. So you're not to worry about Mr Wheeler. What happened to him had nothing to do with you. There's one thing I'd like you to do for me though, miss, if you would.'

'What's that, pray?'

'I want you to go away and think about those visions you had. My governor, Inspector Jackson, told me all about them, and how old Dr Churchill Reid covered you with vinegar and brown paper and smeared you with cooking-fat.'

Deirdre laughed, which was what Bottomley had desired.

215

'Those visions were real events, Miss Deirdre, real things that happened in the real world. Go away and think about them, and then come and tell Mr Jackson or me. But first go and have your dinner, and sit next to Master Rupert Selden.'

Deirdre smiled and held out her white-gloved hand to Bottomley, who took it gently. Annie had appeared from the kitchen, looking at her young mistress with open pride. The elder girl moved off towards the door leading into the state-rooms of the house, turned round for a moment and bowed elegantly to Bottomley who clumsily returned the compliment. Then she was gone.

Annie hovered near the fireplace, worrying the unburned end of one of the logs with the toe of her shoe. She glanced obliquely at the amiable, puffed, red face of her friend.

'I heard you say you had eight daughters, mister. How do you manage?'

'Well, Miss Jevons, it could be worse. I might have had nine.'

Annie laughed, came over to Bottomley, and gave him a kiss on his cheek.

'You are funny!' she said, and walked slowly back to the kitchen.

The dancing was taking place in the Great Hall, which had been cleared of its customary clutter of oriental carpets, potted palms and islands of furniture, leaving a great vaulted, panelled space, its walls hung with old portraits and festooned with garlands and swags of flowers for the coming May Feast.

Mr Loxley Anderson mingled with his guests, talking animatedly with various ladies and gentlemen, or gently teasing one or two young ladies who were rushing about excitedly, looking for friends. A great throng of people seemed to fill the house.

'Mr Loxley Anderson,' asked one very young lady in white, 'is it true that you have Anne Boleyn's wedding-dress here?'

'Indeed it is, my dear. And guess what? We've got her head, too! It was chopped off, you know!'

When the squeals of delighted protest had subsided, Mr Loxley Anderson showed the young lady the way to the Tapestry Room. He assured her that only the dress was on show, together with some samplers worked by Henrietta Maria.

Mr Loxley Anderson appeared to be making a leisurely but deliberate progress to one particular part of the house. He passed through two small rooms and then out again into a glittering parlour full of older guests who had left the Great Hall to the boys and girls. The strains of the small orchestra could still be heard here, but they were less insistent. It was a place for conversation.

Mr Loxley Anderson was positively twinkling. He looked very prosperous, and the presence of so many guests clearly pleased him. He chatted with one or two people, smiling all the while, but moving with a definite purpose across the ground floor of the great mansion. Nobody noticed that their ubiquitous host had suddenly become, as it were, mislaid.

Loxley Anderson had paused in front of an old door in a dim corridor, knocked sharply to alert whoever was in the room beyond, and entered a little boudoir, the panelled walls of which were lined with glazed display cabinets. The Chinese Room, as it was called, was a private apartment, where the master of the house displayed his valuable collection of old porcelain.

Mr Galt sat rather massively in an upright chair near to the blazing fire of the comfortable room. He was immersed in consulting a sheaf of papers, which he had spread out on a small table. Loxley Anderson closed the door and turned the key discreetly in the lock. He stood by the fireplace, leaning on the mantelpiece.

'Well, Mr Galt, what do you think? At first glance it looks very similar to that Newcastle scheme. This time it's church land in Nottingham. A large acreage, as you can see. Initial tests have shown that the land is lying on the edge of the Yorkshire, Derby and Nottingham coal field.'

Mr Galt had been wearing little round steel-framed spectacles, which he now removed. He blinked, sat back in his chair, and tapped the documents on the table with a thick, square-nailed finger.

'Mr Loxley Anderson, I hope this project can go forward, despite the uncertainties of the present time for both of us. You'll be visited by a few shrewd folk from Nottingham, I expect, but you'll have to be shrewder than they.'

'They'll want to talk about a price.'

'They will, and you'll have to tell them that prices can vary. In this case the price will depend on the quality of the coal found. That's the first factor. There are hard and soft coal varieties in the area they're talking about, and a lot depends on what the market can take. Work on them, Mr Loxley Anderson. Start to wrap them up in the mysteries of pricing.'

'It could bring us in thousands of pounds a year, Mr Galt. I just need a few more factors to weigh in this particular balance. Charm and pedigree should do the rest.'

A spasm of amusement passed across the basilisk face of Mr Galt.

'Other factors are the depth of the deposit and the depth of the seam. And the working life of the seam. They're the factors, Mr Loxley Anderson. And we'll need some close calculations to arrive at a price. You wouldn't be telling a lie if you let them know that times are difficult and the market's depressed.'

Mr Loxley Anderson continued to stand with his arm resting on the mantelpiece. Mr Galt moved very slightly in his chair. Both men knew that the time had come to talk of other things.

'Well, Mr Galt,' said Loxley Anderson at length, 'I've no doubt that this Inspector Jackson will be calling on me very soon. He will have already found out who's staying here this weekend. I shall tell him all about you: an old business contact of many years' standing, now resident in Belgium.'

'Hmm ... he'll ask you about Robert Elmore. And about Samuel Wheeler. Have you got your stories well rehearsed?'

'I have. Wheeler is now part of history, and I shall merely repeat the old stories. It was an unpleasant business, and I don't want to recall it. He thought he was doing me a favour, having discovered from some imprudent remark made by Reuben Calderdale, that I was the ultimate owner of Polwarthan Mine. Had we given him his head, he would have brought us both into the dock and to Dartmoor. And so we ensured that he did no such thing. Let us say no more about him.'

'And Robert Elmore?' Mr Galt persisted.

'Well, he stayed here two years ago, and was seen and spoken to by my niece and various other people. So, I shall help Mr Jackson all I can. I have a pleasing tale concocted about Elmore – how he had been to tell me of his suspicions concerning Reuben Calderdale, and the local police constable, Daniel Polk. Foolishly I brushed his suspicions aside, et cetera – oh, you can imagine the tale I'll tell!'

Mr Galt gnawed the side of his left thumb while looking speculatively at his ally. Both men wore expensive dress clothes. Mr Loxley Anderson's fitted him like a favourite glove. Mr Galt seemed encased in his, like an apprentice knight of old clad in his first armour.

'How is it that you have proved so staunch, Mr Loxley Anderson? I am what life and inclination have made me, an outcast beyond redemption. But you are a gentleman, destined for gentle ways. You're a mirthful man, God knows, and yet I think you're as ruthless as I am.'

Loxley Anderson treated his stoical friend to the genuine smile of regard that he saved for him alone. Behind the smile Mr Galt suddenly glimpsed the cold ruthlessness of a monomaniac.

'I'm not a titled man, Galt, but I am what is known as a franklin, an untitled aristocrat of very ancient lineage. Our family settled here at King's Leyland before Henry the Fifth was crowned, esquires owing service to great feudal lords, and then free gentleman under the king. We have always been here.

'I have a son – a dissipated, surly man who lives the life of a rake in London. But he is as proud as I am of our ancient family and this equally ancient manor. When I am dead all this will be his. Some years ago it looked likely that I would lose it all: the rents never had covered the costs of the estate. And so I did what I did, both in Cornwall and in the great northern coalfields. And now I am rich. And my son will be rich when he finally settles and returns to his patrimony.'

Loxley Anderson peered through his gold spectacles at an intricate china bowl in one of the cabinets, but he was not really looking at it.

'And all this, Mr Galt,' he continued, 'I owe to your prompting and your support. In return, I give you the sworn loyalty of a gentleman. I will never desert you or betray you. I will do whatever is necessary at all times to preserve what is yours and mine.'

The heavy, brutal face of Mr Galt permitted a mirthless rictus to animate it for a moment. It was another attempt at a smile.

'Thanks for that. I'm not one for words. If I were, you'd hear something similar from me. As you so rightly observed, Mr Loxley Anderson, I shall soon be in Belgium, where I intend to stay. I have my own devious route to Newhaven, where I'll board the steamer for Dieppe. I'm grateful to you for letting me lie low here after freeing myself at Derby. If you don't mind, I'll keep to my rooms for the rest of my stay, and confine my walks to the little enclosed garden on the south side. I believe that one of the footmen is to bring me a meal in my room at nine o'clock, so I'll bid you good evening.'

Deirdre's mind was full of pleasant images as she walked lightly along the dimly lit passage from the Great Hall to the front of the mansion. Her Uncle William had promised her a surprise, but had not told her it was going to be Rupert Selden! The time had come to retire, and she had sent Annie ahead to prepare her bed.

She was so preoccupied with thoughts of the dance and its delights that she hardly noticed the squat figure in evening dress walking towards her until it was level with her. She started in surprise, and her eyes briefly met those of the heavy man before he turned aside and disappeared down a dark corridor.

One of Uncle William's guests, thought Deirdre. Not a pleasant man – perhaps he was too grand to say 'good evening' to a mere girl. She'd seen him before, presumably talking to Uncle William. Never mind him! There were other more interesting things to think about. . . .

It was near to eleven o'clock when Deirdre Dovercourt dismissed her maid and prepared for bed. It had been a wonderful day. Annie and she had sat for half an hour talking about Master Rupert Selden, and weaving plots and plans. Somehow, she seemed to have been exorcised of childish fears and follies since coming to King's Leyland.

She had been apprehensive about talking to Sergeant Bottomley when Annie had told her what he had said in the servants' hall, but on coming face to face with the man she had suddenly felt her guilt fall away, and she had told both him and herself the truth. Rupert Selden's attentions had had something to do with that onset of confidence. . . .

Poor Samuel Wheeler! He must have been amused at a little girl's devotion, and had yielded to her entreaties to give her a portrait of himself as a keepsake. Its inscription, condescending and patronizing, should have told her the truth, but she had been a romantic child. . . .

Poor Sam! He should have known better than to closet himself alone with a giddy girl. He should have laughed at her embrace, and told her loudly to desist. In his exaggerated modesty he had laid himself open to unspeakable insinuations.

She sighed, and put the Dried-Up Man back into the past. Her mind awakened to the music and the dancing, the cheering mirth of her Uncle William, the attentions of the 17-year-old youth who was clearly entranced by her . . . Annie had known all the time that it was 'lads', to use her word, not Keats's poems, that would help her to complete her education.

Now she would give serious and courageous attention to Sergeant Bottomley's plea. She would review her visions as remembrances of real events. There were two distinct memories that insisted on merging. They would not separate to reveal the truth. . . .

Deirdre turned out the lamp and crossed to the window. Should she look out at the little hedged garden below? She paused with her hand on the drawn curtain and then let it drop. No. Sometimes one saw unpleasant things out of windows at night! She slipped into her bed and was soon asleep.

Mr Galt, standing in the garden below, removed his gaze from Deirdre's window when he saw the lamplight disappear. He breathed the April air appreciatively, but then frowned. Curse it! Why had she chosen to walk in that passage, in her fancy ball-dress, just as he was passing? She had shown her alarm when their eyes met. After all these years, she had recognized him. A pretty young thing she'd turned out to be . . . what a pity. . . .

He let his mind recall how he had stood in the sunken church-yard at Ashgate, when he and the others had hidden the body of Samuel Wheeler in the tomb-chest. He had straightened up, and looked across the void in the dark, to where the face of a little girl had been etched on the darkness by the light of a candle she held. Then the light had been extinguished, but not before he had seen and memorized that little face.

He had stood in that same spot in subsequent years, walking over from King's Leyland when business brought him there, looking up at the blind windows of the girl's house, watching and wondering. . . .

He had seen the little face again tonight, the face of the witness to their crime. The face that could still hang them all. Deirdre Dovercourt. And she had seen *him*. Mr Loxley Anderson clearly doted on her, but what he didn't know about he couldn't avenge. The others had all been silenced; she was no exception.

He thought back to his brutalized, cold and wretched existence as Constable Polk of Polwarthan, and inwardly renewed his determination that nothing and no one would be allowed to stand in the way of his new wealth and security.

Yes, a pretty young thing she'd turned out to be. . . what a pity.

13
Twilight of the Gods

Herbert Bottomley, in his wanderings around the town, had found a small alehouse called the Cemetery Arms, a two-room affair with a few tapped barrels, in Ashgate Street, a long, dusty, curving road containing the little-used main entrance to the graveyard. He sat in the empty front bar on a wooden settle against the wall, staring gloomily into a pewter pot.

'I thought I'd find you here,' said Jackson, stooping low as he came in from the quiet sunlight. 'You're on the road to ruin, Sergeant Bottomley. You'll end up with a slice of your liver sandwiched between two bits of glass under a microscope at Surgeons' Hall.'

Sergeant Bottomley sighed, and wiped his mouth on his sleeve.

'Still,' Jackson continued, 'despite the state of your liver, we seem to be making progress. You did brilliantly well at King's Leyland last Thursday. But it's now the merry month of May, Sergeant. We've given them a long weekend to think that all's well. But all's *not* well – at least, not for them, as they'll very soon find out. So remind me again what that butler – Craxton, was it? – told you about Wheeler's visit to Mr Loxley Anderson.'

Bottomley's speech was decidedly slurred, but Jackson noted with satisfaction that his memory remained as clear as ever.

'Well, sir, Craxton obviously witnessed the murder of Mr

Wheeler, though he'd never admit to it in so many words. He saw him pursued across the grounds at first light, fling up his arms and fall dead. There were archery butts there at that time. Someone had picked up a bow and arrow and brought him down.'

Bottomley drank from the pewter tankard and thoughtfully placed it down on the table. Jackson could read his sergeant's speculations in the narrowing of his eyes. He knew from long experience how to break in on Bottomley's train of thought.

'And how many pursuers did Craxton say there were?'

'Three, sir. Three shadows, he called them.'

'So who were they, Sergeant?'

'It's pure supposition on my part, sir, but I'd say one of them was Mr Loxley Anderson. You can't have screaming murder taking place in a house and the master knowing nothing about it. Or the butler, come to that.'

'And the other two?'

'I reckon one of them was this Mr Galt, who, I gather, has been a business crony of Loxley Anderson's for years. He's staying up there now at King's Leyland. And he was staying there then. As for the third man, I don't know. There have always been invisible folk involved in this case, sir. People who were no more than names to us. Martin Caradyne was one of them. Nothing more than a name mentioned by Reuben Calderdale, but you see how important he was. This third man's probably someone we've never heard about.'

'Martin Caradyne is dead,' said Jackson. 'There was a telegraph message brought to me at the Royal William. Found dead in his cell at Derby Bridewell. Cyanide poisoning.'

'Cyanide . . . somebody must have slipped him that, sir, done up in a bit of paper. Maybe it was our person unknown – the man who exchanged clothes with Polk.'

'Maybe. There was also a letter waiting for me at the Royal William. It had been addressed to me "care of Ashgate Police-station", and was brought up by Sergeant Bramble. It was from a man called Michael Croker.'

225

'Who's he, sir?'

'It seems that he was the churchwarden at Thirlwood Parva in Yorkshire in 1876, when Parson Woodward was vicar there. He's read about our exploits in Cornwall, Sergeant, and wants to tell us all about Percy Field.'

Sergeant Bottomley shook himself like a terrier newly emerged from a pond.

'You're losing me, sir. First Michael Croker, now Percy Field.'

'Percy Field, Sergeant, as you'd remember if you were sober, was Mr Woodward's curate. Your friend Bishop Hope Sutherland mentioned him to us. He was found hanged. This Mr Croker wants to tell us all about it.'

Bottomley had thrown off his air of insobriety completely. He looked puzzled.

'This Croker is coming down here? Ashgate's not even on the railway.'

'Very obliging of him, isn't it? He'll be here this afternoon, according to his letter. I look forward to meeting our obliging friend, Sergeant. Meanwhile, I've another appointment to keep – at Bridge Rise.'

Inspector Jackson pushed open the door of the workshop in Bridge Rise where Matthew Littlechild was absorbed in fashioning a harrow for a local farmer. He seemed unwilling to turn away from the heavy spiked frame which occupied one side of the whitewashed room, its black iron looking somehow menacing in the confined space.

Littlechild laid down his heavy hammer and wiped his hands on his oily smock.

'What can I do for you, master? You'll be Inspector Jackson. I've seen you about. And your sergeant, Mr Bottomley.'

There was a strong smell of oil, metal filings and hot ashes in the shop. A small furnace stood in one corner, above which, hanging on hooks against the wall, Jackson saw six black wrought-iron alchemic signs. Perhaps they had been commissioned. It was more likely, though, that they were Littlechild's personal talismans.

'You call me "master", which is very civil of you, Mr Littlechild. I've come here today because I'm told that you also bear that title. I've been told that you are a "White Master".'

Jackson heard Littlechild draw in his breath sharply.

'One of the old fools talking in the William, no doubt. These things are done quiet. They're not to be blabbed out over the ale. Do you know what a white master is, Mr Jackson?'

'I don't. And I'd like to know, Mr Littlechild. So tell me: what is a white master?'

'In the olden days, over a thousand years ago, the air of Britain was inhabited by devils in the guise of gods. I've told this tale before, but rarely. If you've a mind to laugh, I'll ask you to leave the shop.'

'I'm not minded to laugh, Mr Littlechild.'

'These devils came from the lands to the north, and settled in the air, working their evil will on the poor folk of the land. Then Christ came to our shores in the persons of the good saints whose bones lie safe in old cairns and ruins in the Celtic lands. The demons were driven back but not defeated. So God chose two kinds of folk to be dedicated to their destruction.'

Littlechild took up a file from the bench, and began to wipe it with an oily rag. His mind was clearly elsewhere. Jackson urged him back to speech.

'Who were these two kinds of folk?'

'One lot of folk were certain priests, who passed on their book knowledge from age to age. Such a priest was our old rector, Mr Woodward. Those who knew what he was, revered him, and left him to his ways.'

Littlechild threw the file down on to the bench and turned away with an angry frown. He added, 'Those who did not know these things drove him from his parish.'

227

'And who were the other lot of folk?'

'The other lot of folk came from certain humble families. They were always workers in metal, and were known as White Masters. I am such a one. I cannot read or write, but I have endless knowledge of these old gods: Odin, whose seat is here still in Ashgate, Thor or Thunor, and all those demons.'

Littlechild glanced up briefly at the iron symbols hanging on the wall, and Jackson saw his lips move silently before he added aloud, 'I know the special words to drive them back, the talismans to make, and I know when they have reappeared to plague the world. They are back now. There have been sacrifices . . . I will say no more but this.'

Littlechild folded his arms and leaned into the shadows against the wall. Jackson looked at him speculatively. When he finally spoke he chose his words prudently.

'I have followed in the wake of those old gods, Mr Littlechild. I know there are pagan sanctuaries, and that Ashgate is one of them. I, too, am bound up in this fight, not as priest or White Master, but as a policeman. One of my own kind – a policeman – drowned two men in a sacred font at another old pagan sanctuary, and maybe he or an accomplice brought about the death of the Reverend Samuel Wheeler. Do you know how Mr Wheeler died?'

'I do. He was shot with a bow and arrow. Heed the Scriptures: "They shall look on him whom they pierced". It is also written, "He will bring upon them their iniquity and shall cut them off in their own wickedness".'

Jackson was very still. He dared not say what was in his mind in case he lost the man's trust. No one but the police and the doctors knew how Wheeler had been killed, but to say so now would seem like an accusation.

Matthew Littlechild remained leaning against the wall, arms folded. He deliberated for what seemed to be several minutes. Jackson waited.

'I will give you some advice, master. Go to Mr Woodward at the rectory, and ask him to remember what he saw in the graveyard in the February of 1888. He is a guiltless man, and needs only to remember. If he cannot, then come to me again and I will tell you. But it would be better for him to remember.'

'Do you think that what he remembers will help me bring the guilty to justice?'

'I do. Part of the key is locked in Parson Woodward's mind. The other part—'

'The other part,' said Jackson, 'lies in the mind of Miss Deirdre Dovercourt.'

'So you have already sensed that? Yes, I have heard snatches of what she has imagined over the years, and of the things she saw which folk thought were just imagination. She knows without knowing, if you understand me. Have you seen her? Spoken to her, I mean?'

'I have, but I didn't say the right things.'

Matthew Littlechild picked up his hammer and turned towards the great iron harrow that he was fashioning. He gave Jackson a sudden glance which he saw was full of intelligent understanding.

'Bring those three together,' said Littlechild, 'and you might be surprised with the result.'

'Those three?' asked Jackson.

'Aye. Parson Woodward, Miss Deirdre, and Mr Bottomley. Miss Deirdre's afraid of the old parson, but she'd lose her fear if Mr. Bottomley was with her. If she went with her father it would be useless. He'd dry up the wells, because he's a practical man, so he says. But Mr Bottomley's very spiritual.'

Jackson regarded the metalworker with a suddenly enhanced respect. His description, seemingly so ill-suited to the beery, amiable sergeant, showed that he could see through externals to the heart of the man.

Jackson moved to the door of the dim workshop.

'I'll take your advice, Mr Littlechild. I had thought of something along the same lines myself, but your suggestion confirms that I must do it. Thank you for what you told me. I will respect those confidences.'

He turned at the door. He had established a bond of trust, and was entitled to ask one question.

'What of the hangman's nooses? What must I think of those?'

The White Master's answer came firm and with authority.

'In every case, master, the noose will have been placed about the neck by Parson Woodward. There's no disgrace in that. That is part of the ritual. But the parson may not remember having placed the nooses, because when he did so he was almost certainly in a trance. Tell him that you know. Tell him that you know about *me*. There are secrets and secrets. The time has come for some of them to see the light.'

Jackson gave a slight start of surprise when Michael Croker was shown into his room at the Royal William. It seemed for the moment that he was looking in a full-length mirror. He saw how his visitor reacted in much the same way, drawing back on the threshold for a moment before advancing rather hesitantly into the room.

'Mr Michael Croker? Very good of you, sir, to come all this distance. Very public spirited, if I may say so. Please sit down here at the table.'

Michael Croker was of the same build as Jackson, and held himself in the same way. He had the same round, clean-shaven face, but his eyes were grey, and heavily hooded. He seemed to perspire a lot, and made frequent use of a large red handkerchief.

'Not at all, Inspector Jackson. We've read such terrible things in the papers about your experiences in Cornwall, that I felt compelled to help in any way I could. I am not chained to my work, like most men, the Lord having prospered me most abundantly.'

Jackson frowned. His mind was a subtle engine, and something in his visitor's piety rang false. He looked at him more closely.

230

'In what way, Mr Croker, has the Lord prospered you?'

'He prospered me in my trade, Mr. Jackson. I'm a builder. You can see the countless ribbons of cottages I've put up all around Thirlwood Parva and out as far as Harrogate. I've got a big builder's yard just outside Thirlwood.'

'And do you live in Thirlwood Parva? I know from your letter that you've been churchwarden at St Edward's there for over twenty years, now.'

'Oh, no. I've not lived in the village for a number of years. I built myself a fine house on a couple of acres of field out near Spofforth. Not an estate, you understand, but nonetheless a goodly dwelling.'

The perspiring builder shifted his bulk, and threw Jackson a shrewd glance.

'But I think it's my experience as churchwarden that's of interest to you at this juncture? I've read in the papers of your struggles against ungodliness in Polwarthan, and I feel duty bound to tell you of similar wickedness in Yorkshire long ago. It was years ago – oh, fifteen or sixteen years, it must be. Most of the people concerned with that affair are dead now.'

'It was in 1876, Mr Croker,' Jackson said, 'during the incumbency of the Reverend Hezekiah Woodward, that the Reverend Percy Field was found hanging in a grove of birch trees behind the apse of your church, St Edward the Confessor, Thirlwood Parva—'

'It was indeed! Oh, the waste! They brought it in as "suicide attendant upon an emotional failure". He was only a young fellow, Mr Jackson, not more than twenty-five, unmarried and with no family. His parents had perished years earlier when the *Evan Harrington* went down off the Mosquito Shore.'

Michael Croker shuddered, as though a draught of cold air had passed him. But it was warm in the room. Maybe the man was a bit of a ranter, thought Jackson, but he seemed genuinely moved to recollect the death of the young curate.

'And do you remember Mr Woodward?' he asked.

'Indeed I do! He was very learned, and ever so slightly unhinged. I believe he's back again here in Ashgate St Lawrence. I wonder whether it would be in order to call upon him? Perhaps not. My presence could stir unpleasant memories.'

'Why do you say that Mr Woodward was unhinged? I'm most interested in your recollections, Mr Croker.'

'Mr Woodward had discovered that Thirlwood was an ancient seat of devil-worship. It was Odin, or Woden, or one of those awful creatures you read about in the story-books. I take no interest in pagan things of that kind. Anyway, poor young Field was found hanged, and they brought in that verdict.'

The big man shuddered again, and streams of sweat ran down his broad face.

'And the Reverend Mr Woodward left the parish soon after?'

'He did. They'd found charms and medals – a silver fish, or some such childishness – and it seems the vicar had put them there. So he went. And we got the present man, Mr Canmore Ballantyne. We've been lucky with him. Good Bible teaching, you know, and a wonderful tenor voice.'

Jackson searched his pockets for a cigar-case. When he found it he offered it to Croker, who accepted a cigar. Jackson saw how his hands trembled as he lit it. There was, he mused, something tormenting this man, something connected with the long-past tragedy of Percy Field. Or perhaps it was something else? He prepared to delve further into Croker's memory. The trail seemed cold, but instinct and experience told him it was not.

'And *was* it suicide, Mr Croker? Or could it have been something else? Can you remember who found the body?'

Croker hid his face in his hands for a moment. When he spoke his voice trembled.

'It was *I* who found the body, Mr Jackson, and alerted the vicar and the parish constable. The constable cut the poor fellow down. A terrible sight. Terrible. The vicar said it couldn't be true. And then he began to talk about Odin. I remember at the time being shocked that a clergyman could talk about anything so grotesque.'

'And *was* it suicide, Mr Croker?' Jackson persisted.

'Of course it was, Mr Jackson. As a matter of fact, poor young Field had hinted to me that he was perturbed by some emotional entanglement – some girl, I believe. It surprised me, I must admit. Percy Field seemed a level-headed fellow enough.' Croker blew his nose hard on his big red handkerchief. He seemed more in command of himself, and relit his cigar, which had gone out.

'I expect there was a lot of disquiet locally?' said Jackson.

'It was more than disquiet. It was there before ever poor young Field was found dead. Mr Woodward, as I said, discovered that our church had been a sanctuary of Odin in ancient times, and began to preach about it. He frightened people. One lady fainted in church when he spoke about ritual hangings, and some of the children were taken away from the Sunday School. So when Percy Field was found hanged so near the church there was something like panic. Mr Woodward went soon afterwards. The Archdeacon of York moved very quickly to restore sanity.'

Inspector Jackson drew on his cigar. He glanced appraisingly at Croker.

'You have been of very great help to me, Mr Croker. Once again, let me thank you for being so exceptionally public spirited in coming all this very long way to speak to me.'

Michael Croker blushed with evident pleasure. Jackson chose his moment well.

'What did the local people think about the Reverend Percy Field's death?'

'Well, Mr Jackson, you know what country people are like. Nobody believed the coroner's "emotional failure" verdict. Most of the locals had swallowed the parson's fairy-stories about Odin and the Hanging Groves. They believed that Percy Field had been sacrificed.'

*

Harry Goodheart's study seemed to be filled that morning with the rector's six-feet-four frame. He turned from the window as the two policemen entered.

'Mr Jackson! Thank you for your note. And Sergeant Bottomley, isn't it? We've not met before, Sergeant, though your fame has preceded you! Now: there's cake, and plenty of tea, and fresh toast under that china cover on the hearth. If you'll find yourselves seats, I'll go and fetch Mr Woodward.'

Jackson was startled when the former rector came into the room. He had fitted well into the general gloom of Polwarthan, but here in the sunlight of Ashgate St Lawrence he looked painfully frail and fevered. He was more formally dressed than when Jackson had seen him in Cornwall, and he wore the clerical clothes of an earlier generation, a style that since the mid-eighties of the century had started to look rather quaint.

Jackson caught Bottomley's eye and saw that he, too, had grasped the significance of Woodward's dress. It was virtually identical with the time-stained clerical suit that had clung to the mummified remains of the Dried-Up Man.

Hezekiah Woodward spoke.

'So, Mr Jackson, and you, Mr Bottomley, we meet again, but in more cheerful and less threatening surroundings. The rector urged me to agree to your coming this morning. I must confess to being intrigued by your visit!'

Harry Goodheart poured out a glass of port from a decanter, and handed it to his aged colleague.

'I think perhaps this wine will strengthen you, Woodward. I'll leave you to talk to your visitors. You have only to ring that little bell on the mantelpiece to bring me back again!'

Parson Woodward sipped his wine and listened while Jackson recounted his conversation with Michael Croker. From time to time he sighed, and shaded his brow as though half ashamed of the tale that Jackson repeated, but his mind was growing stronger day by day, and he listened with acute interest to what Jackson was saying.

'Mr Woodward, there is one little point that intrigues me. When your churchwarden, Michael Croker, told me how he had shown you the body of Percy Field, he used these words: "The vicar said: 'It can't be true!' " What exactly did you mean by that, sir?'

Woodward looked earnestly into Jackson's eyes. He seemed eager to recollect as much as he could of his strange, grim past.

'Mr Jackson, it *couldn't* have been true. Suicide, indeed! The rope was wrong! My curate was hanged after he was dead! I tried to tell Croker, but he paid no heed to me. Neither did the coroner and his jury. Their attitude was, "What can a mere parson know about hangmen's nooses?" To which I would answer, Mr Jackson, that it's surprising the things some people know!'

Hezekiah Woodward smiled. He's beginning to feel at ease with his own past, Jackson thought. His mind should be strong enough to wrestle with a little problem.

'Let me outline a theory to you, Mr Woodward.'

'A detective theory? All this is very interesting, you know.'

'Yes, sir, a detective theory. A certain Parson Woodward – saving Your Reverence! – causes a superstitious fear in the district through his preaching. Somebody sees this as a good opportunity for a spot of murder—'

'Good heavens, Mr Jackson! Surely you're not suggesting that I have been followed by a murderer to every parish where I've served! The idea is frightful!'

'I don't think you were followed anywhere, sir,' said Jackson. 'I believe that you had the misfortune to be present where different episodes of another drama were being enacted. You were part of the unconscious audience of that drama.'

Parson Woodward sat in silence for a while, toying with the stem of his wine glass. He's searching his memory, thought Jackson, rearranging ideas, judging facts afresh. It was time to jog his memory further.

'Mr Woodward, were there any strangers in Thirlwood Parva at the time of Mr Field's death? I assume that it's a small place, and such things would be noticed. Did anyone have unusual visitors?'

'Visitors? Why, yes, Inspector ... Percy Field was visited the week before his death by a very earnest gentleman who called upon him at the curate's house. Everyone wondered who he was, including me. I saw the visitor walking down the street past the vicarage. A quite distinguished-looking man with side-whiskers, accompanied by a rather rough fellow who seemed more friend than servant. But they could have had nothing to do with the matter, because it turned out they had only been making a social call.'

'How do you know that, sir?'

'Mr Croker told me. The gentleman and his companion had actually called to see Croker, who suggested it would be courteous to call on the curate. Apparently young Field was acquainted with the gentleman.'

Parson Woodward closed his eyes for a moment and shook his head. He put his wine-glass down on the small round table. For the first time in all their weeks of acquaintance, Jackson saw the harassed face of the old clergyman crease with lines of humour as he laughed aloud.

'What is it, sir?'

'It's just a memory, Inspector. I was thinking how little one knows about one's servants! When I was Vicar of Thirlwood Parva I kept a modest house of servants, including a butler called Fisher. He and I were much the same age. I racked my brains for days wondering who poor Percy's two visitors could have been. Eventually I asked Fisher outright, and of course he knew all about it from Percy's housemaid! I hadn't realized that our servants talked about us, and that what we suppose are secrets are usually common knowledge below stairs!'

'And what did your butler tell you, sir?'

'Well, it seemed that this gentleman who came visiting was under some slight obligation to Mr Croker, who at that time needed capital to set up his builder's yard. The gentleman had furnished him with the advance he needed to do so.'

'And who was this gentleman, sir?'

'Well, Inspector, do you know, it was Mr William Loxley Anderson, who has an estate not very far from here. Wasn't that odd? The rough-looking man accompanying him was an associate of his called Galt. Mr Galt.'

The three men sat in silence for a few moments. Woodward had been quick to see the almost gloating look of triumph on Jackson's face, but could not fathom the reason for it. The merry clock ticked away. Jackson hauled up his watch from its depths in his waistcoat, looked at the time, and put it away again.

'Mr Woodward,' he said, 'there is something that I want you to do for me. Earlier today I was speaking to Matthew Littlechild. He said something very interesting to me, and it was this: "Go to Mr Woodward at the rectory, and ask him to remember what he saw in the graveyard in the February of 1888. He is a guiltless man, and needs only to remember".'

The old clergyman sighed. 'February, 1888? I have already remembered in part, Inspector, largely through the urging of my colleague Harry Goodheart. But I see only in part. The whole truth of what happened on that terrible night still eludes me. But you say you wish me to do something for you?'

'I do, sir. I want you to receive Miss Deirdre Dovercourt here at the rectory, and allow her to talk to you.'

'Talk to *me*? Why should she wish to do that?'

'Because, sir, you and she unwittingly shared a strange and terrible experience together. Will you consent to talk to her? I ventured to arrange matters earlier, and the rector has no objection provided that you consent freely to the visit. Miss Dovercourt returned from her visit to King's Leyland yesterday. She has only to walk over here from Dovercourt House.'

237

'Of course, I consent, Inspector. Poor child! I think I see all too clearly how she must have shared in the horror of that graveyard four long years ago. Let her come, and welcome!'

14
Remembrance of Things Past

H arry Goodheart looked appreciatively at the young lady in the grey silk dress who accepted an upright chair near the fireplace. Something had happened to Deirdre Dovercourt. She was no longer the delicate romantic, jealously guarded by her little maid. Even her choice of dress seemed to indicate the end of her love of what he called 'wispiness'. Miss Dovercourt had suddenly grown up.

Deirdre looked around her. In a chair by the fire sat the old rector, Parson Woodward. She had once been afraid of him, because he seemed to commune with spirits, and never even contrived to notice her. She did not fear him now, and was rather intrigued to sense that he seemed to fear *her*.

Her eyes met those of Inspector Jackson briefly and with apprehension, but when she saw the remaining occupant of the rector's cheerful study she smiled an amused greeting. What a heavy, bulky, beery-looking man Sergeant Bottomley was! But he had been rather marvellous on that memorable Thursday evening, with his kindly advice, and his jokes about vinegar and brown paper.

The May Feast at King's Leyland had taken place on the Saturday, and Deirdre had attended the ox-roasting, watched the rural games, and been present at the crowning of the local May Queen by Mr Loxley Anderson himself. There had been two sumptuous dinners, one in the house and the other in the long barn. She had danced until the early hours of the morning.

Although she had returned from King's Leyland with a new sense of poise and confidence, Deirdre was still relieved that it was Bottomley, and not Jackson, who opened the proceedings.

'Good afternoon, Miss Deirdre. It's nice to see you again. May I ask, miss, whether you did what I asked you last Thursday night at King's Leyland?'

'About my visions?' said Deirdre softly. 'Yes, Mr Bottomley. I remembered how you'd described them: "real events, real things that happened in the real world". I have almost seen them as a continuous picture, now – almost, but not quite. What do you want me to do?'

'I want you to listen to something that Mr Woodward here is going to describe. He told us about it while you were crossing the graveyard to come here. Just listen, if you please, Miss Deirdre. When the right moment comes, you will know what to do.'

Bottomley gave her a kindly smile and with a slight inclination of his head he indicated the frail figure of the former rector sitting in the armchair near the fire. Woodward cleared his throat nervously.

'Miss Dovercourt,' he began, 'I hardly thought I would be retailing my own haunted visions in public like this, and to a young lady into the bargain. But I have been told that you are brave and resolute, and that you and I have shared a strange and terrible experience.'

He paused and looked with some agitation at the leaping flames in the fireplace. He continued, almost to himself. 'Had I paid more attention to my duties and less to my obsessions I might have spared you much anguish.'

Harry Goodheart, who was standing near him, placed a reassuring hand on his shoulder. The old clergyman glanced briefly at him and then addressed himself once more to Deirdre.

'What I am now going to describe, Miss Dovercourt, occurred

in February 1888. Absorbed in strange pursuits of my own, I ventured out in the darkness of night into that cemetery yonder. I saw lantern-light, and the shapes of three men, who were closing the end panel of Josiah Anderson's tomb. Before they went, one of them glanced up towards the windows of Dovercourt House, and said: "You could dig a little grave in this wilderness and no one would ever know".'

Deirdre visibly paled. Sergeant Bottomley placed a great beefy hand over both her small gloved ones and said, 'There's your first cue, miss. Be bold: ask Parson Woodward the question you need to ask him.'

'Mr Woodward,' said Deirdre, 'this man, the man who looked up at the house. Can you describe him? I believe that at the very moment that you saw him, I saw him, too!'

'He is a thickset, morose and brutal man. He can comport himself with a dangerous stillness. It was his stance, his intimidating presence, that struck me so forcibly at that time. I did not see his features clearly.'

'Yes! I know that man. I saw him gazing up at the windows from the churchyard, seeing and not seeing. At least – I assume he did not see me. I wonder who he was?'

'I used to wonder, too, Miss Dovercourt. It was that man's voice, rather than his appearance, that stayed to haunt me. I listened to that voice years afterwards in another place, and could not solve the puzzle of it. Only now. . . .'

Parson Woodward turned suddenly pale. For a moment it seemed that he would faint, but with a supreme effort he mastered himself.

'Only now,' Woodward continued, 'talking to you, has the memory of that voice returned to proclaim its identity. I next saw the possessor of that voice in Cornwall. He was a policeman then, at Polwarthan. His name, Miss Dovercourt, is Daniel Polk.'

Sergeant Bottomley held up his hand to silence Woodward for a moment.

'Mr Jackson and I suspected as much, Mr Woodward, but what you've just told us is the proof we needed. Polk was indeed a policeman, a trained constable. But he had been a schemer and intriguer long before that. He became a policeman to further the plans of his associates in great frauds.'

Bottomley returned his attention to Deirdre. He spoke quietly and with authority.

'This man Polk didn't flinch at murder, miss. To our knowledge he has murdered three men. One of them you didn't know, but you knew the others. Robert Elmore was one of them. And the other was the Reverend Samuel Wheeler.'

'Robert Elmore,' said Deirdre softly. 'I met him several times, and thought him so very nice. And poor Mr Wheeler, the Dried-Up Man. . . . Will you tell me how he died, and where?'

'No, miss. At this present moment it wouldn't do for you to know those things. So you saw Daniel Polk looking up at your windows. What else did you see? Tell Mr Woodward.'

'I saw that man, and two others, and at their feet the body of Mr Wheeler. He was clad in undergarments. . . . Yes. He was! I can see it so clearly. And then they thrust him in the tomb-chest.'

Hezekiah Woodward held his head in his hands. He was making a heroic effort to match his impressions to Deirdre's.

'You are right, Miss Dovercourt. When we took him out he was clad in undergarments. When we . . . Matthew Littlechild came to my assistance. He was always staunch and true. He is a White Master, you know. He came and helped me to reopen the tomb and bring poor Samuel out. He was clad in combinations, and in his back—'

'Excuse me, sir,' Bottomley cautioned. 'Best not pursue that line just for the moment. Miss Dovercourt doesn't want to know about things like that.'

'Gentlemen!' Deirdre cried. 'There is something wrong!'

She was surprised by the commanding ring in her own voice.

'This is the point at which my dreams become fantasies. You say

242

that what I saw were real things in the real world, Mr Bottomley. And yet when I cast my mind back to that horrible vision I sometimes see poor Mr Wheeler not in undergarments, but in decent clerical dress.'

Sergeant Bottomley seemed suddenly specially attentive and alert.

'Ah! In clerical dress, you say. Do you mean like Mr Woodward, or like Mr Goodheart?'

'Like Mr Woodward. The old-fashioned style of clergyman's dress, before they began to adopt the Roman collar like Mr Goodheart there. Now isn't that interesting? Why should a young man like Mr Wheeler want to wear old-fashioned clerical dress? He never did when he was alive.'

A long sigh came from Parson Woodward. It was as though he were expelling a demon.

'At last, my dear young lady, our stories converge. You have just told me the facts I need to bring the whole episode to the front of my memory. I will tell all of you what was the end of that business.

'When Littlechild and I retrieved the body of Mr Wheeler from the monument we saw that he was clothed only in undergarments. What profanity! What contempt for his sacred office! I left my companion to guard the body and returned in the dark here to the rectory. I plundered my dressing-room for a complete outer garb – shirt, shoes, everything. As you so astutely observed, Miss Dovercourt, the clothes were those normally worn by an older generation of cleric.'

Inspector Jackson asked a question. He had seated himself unobtrusively near the window.

'And what did you do then, Mr Woodward?'

'We dressed him, Littlechild and I, and reclothed him in some kind of dignity. And then we placed him once more into the monument.'

Nobody spoke for a minute. They were all absorbed by the

243

picture painted for them by Woodward and Deirdre. It was Deirdre who broke the silence.

'That was why I saw Mr Wheeler's body in two types of dress. I remember how I sat in frozen terror for an hour before I dared look out of that window again. . . . In that period, Mr Woodward, you and your helper must have opened the tomb, removed the body, and then reclothed it.'

She turned to Sergeant Bottomley.

'So all my visions were simply the truth, and my silly romancing hid that truth from the light of day. I feel now that I can put the whole business behind me. I was not to blame.'

Something in Deirdre's account seemed to have caught Harry Goodheart's attention. He looked at her with curious interest.

'Indeed no, Miss Dovercourt, you were a victim all along in this business. But tell me: you say that there were three men present at the shocking scene that you have described. You saw the man Polk clearly, and held his appearance in mind. He was standing in the light of a lantern. Why did you not see the other two men?'

'Because they . . . why did I not see them? They were only shadows, Rector. There may have been light on the scene, but they . . . he. . . .'

Deirdre shook her head in bewilderment. Harry Goodheart said nothing, but caught Jackson's understanding glance. He, then, had understood the purpose of his question.

Sergeant Bottomley turned the conversation away from Deirdre and what she had seen.

'Now, Mr Woodward,' he asked in a disarmingly friendly tone, 'I suppose that when you had dressed the body of Mr Wheeler, you placed the noose around his neck?'

The old clergyman blushed, more with embarrassment than shame. He wondered what Miss Dovercourt would think of him.

'I did. I sometimes wonder whether I was not possessed during all those dark years. If I was, then it was by a beneficent spirit, for the placing of that noose is a powerful sign, reversing the efficacy of the Odinic sacrifice.'

Sergeant Bottomley treated Woodward to a dazzling and rather alarming smile.

'But there hadn't been an "Odinic sacrifice", had there, Reverend sir? You'll excuse me if I say that your enthusiasm for those old tales led you to miss what was staring you in the face. Two men drowned in a font to stop their mouths. Mr Wheeler violently murdered and the body hidden in a tomb. Murders, sir, not sacrifices! And so you interfered with evidence by tampering with the victims' bodies, and in the case of Mr Wheeler you connived at the criminal concealment of his body. And so did Matthew Littlechild, aged forty-eight, of Bridge Rise, Ashgate St Lawrence, in the county of Warwick, metalworker. No previous convictions.'

Hezekiah Woodward instinctively understood the purpose behind Bottomley's vehemence.

'Thank you, Mr Bottomley,' he said. 'You have rightly taken me to task with stern but cleansing words. They have recalled me fully to reality. In my confusion and isolation from the bright fires of life, I had confounded myth with truth. I shall not do so again.'

Inspector Jackson watched Deirdre Dovercourt begin her walk back through the haunted graveyard to Dovercourt House. She had taken Sergeant Bottomley's arm, and Jackson could see his colleague's head bent down to listen as Deirdre spoke to him. Strange, how he had failed to gain that young woman's confidence. Even now, she had glanced fearfully at him when she left the room. As he looked at them from the rector's study window, walking together like father and daughter, he felt a slight but definite tinge of professional jealousy.

'What will you do now? About Deirdre Dovercourt, I mean.'

Jackson turned from the window. Harry Goodheart had conducted Woodward to his room upstairs, and had asked his characteristically forthright question as soon as he re-entered the study.

'I'm thinking about that specialist who's staying with Dr Phillips. The one who's been helping Mr Woodward. I wonder whether he could help us in another direction.'

'Dr Per Cornelis Brant. How do you think he can help?'

'I'm thinking of that very shrewd question that you asked Miss Deirdre. She saw Polk in the lantern-light. Why didn't she see the other two men? Well, perhaps your alienist could take an interest in that question, too.'

'An excellent idea! As a matter of fact, Phillips suggested that Brant might be able to help with the mystery of Deirdre Dovercourt. I'll have Brant over here for coffee tomorrow morning. I'll let you know immediately if he comes up with anything interesting.'

Jackson looked around him as though memorizing the contents of the cheerful room. He recalled how he had thought of it longingly in the gloom and danger of Polwarthan.

'Rector, you're obstructing the police! All this warmth and cheer, this toast, this cake – you're stopping me solving my crimes!'

Harry Goodheart did not laugh, as Jackson had expected. He smiled, but there was something questioning and hesitant in his response.

'Mrs Dovercourt has told me something of your tragic family life, Mr Jackson, and I know you'll forgive me for alluding to it. I've sensed how much you like coming here, and you've been all the more welcome for that. I hope that one day soon you'll have a sanctuary of your own again. Something more, you know, than a mere house.'

How kind this man was, Jackson thought. And how much he could suggest behind the words he used! As he walked round the house to the steps down into St Lawrence Square he thought of the special word that Goodheart had used. A sanctuary? Perhaps, one day.

*

'Sergeant Bottomley,' said Jackson, 'the time's come for me to obtain a warrant for the arrest of William Loxley Anderson. We don't need one for Polk, who's a criminal fugitive, but I'll get one just the same in the name of Galt. We'll do that discreetly, so that the birds don't get wind of it and fly the nest. Then we'll make a night visit.'

Bottomley had left Deirdre at the gate into the garden of Dovercourt House, and had returned to wait for Jackson at Josiah Anderson's tomb. The monument had been closed after the recent funeral. A few tributes of marble flowers under glass domes lay at the foot of the tomb.

'Meanwhile,' Jackson concluded, 'I want you to keep a more than benevolent eye on Miss Deirdre Dovercourt.'

'I already intended to do that, sir,' Bottomley replied. 'That girl saw no visions; what she saw was reality. And reality saw *her*. It was Polk. That skulking hulk, that shrinking violet, shy of answering honest questions. Then she saw him again, in March 1890. I don't like to think what he's up to, but whatever it is he's not going to do it while I'm around.'

Bottomley had recourse to his battered flask, and the aroma of gin wafted around the crumbling monument. A movement among some distant gravestones caught his attention. A figure in blue serge was limping towards them, his left arm hugged close to his body. Tired, dusty and dogged, they could both hear the wheezing gasps from his chest as he emerged into the cleared space before Josiah Anderson's tomb.

'Here's Sergeant Bramble, sir,' said Bottomley.

'Sit down on that tomb, Sergeant Bramble,' said Jackson. 'It's a warm day, and you look as though you could do with a rest.'

'Thank you, sir. If you don't mind, sir, I'll have a smoke of this clay pipe. Clay draws cool, as perhaps you know, sir, and the smoke's good for the lungs.'

247

Sergeant Bramble filled his pipe from a pouch. Jackson was content to wait until he had lit it from a box of vestas and was puffing away.

'Now, sir,' said Bramble, 'as regards the man who came to see you at the Royal William, Michael Croker by name, he's left the town. He'd lodged in a house at Cooper's Arch, which is the little hamlet across the river from here, but left soon after he'd seen you. He paid the score without trouble, and left on foot.'

'Thank you very much, Sergeant. I'm much obliged to you. Have you ever seen this Croker before? Here in Ashgate, I mean?'

'No, sir. As a matter of fact, I've never seen him at all. The first I heard of him was when you sent me that note telling me to root him out. There's never been a Croker in Ashgate, to my knowledge.'

Jackson looked at the old sergeant. There was something in his manner, a kind of jauntiness behind the pain, that made him ask a question.

'How are you, Sergeant Bramble? Has anything happened to you?'

Bramble treated the inspector to a wry smile.

'Yes, sir, thanks to you! When you came here the other week you brought a Dr Venner with you. Well, he'd evidently sized me up, because he wrote to Dr Phillips, saying that he didn't think I was fit for work. Dr Phillips examined me, and agreed. I've had the water on the lungs for years, but I didn't know I'd had a stroke!'

'And what's going to happen to you, Sergeant?'

'Well sir, I'm to retire at the end of this month. I've already seen Superintendent Evans over at Copton Vale. There'll be a small pension.'

Bramble suddenly laughed. The sound held a world of relief.

'Do you know, sir, I never even dared to believe that I could stop work and rest! Never dared believe it. I've been in the police since 1857, sir – thirty-five years.'

'And will you manage on the police pension? It's not much, God knows.'

'I'll be all right, thank you, sir. I've told Mr Dovercourt, who'll help me if needed. I'm a widower, and I live with my sister and her husband. We'll make out, you'll see, sir.'

Inspector Jackson watched the old sergeant limp away through the graves towards the town. A life well lived. . . . Men like Bramble were worth hundreds of Polks and Loxley Andersons. They lived largely unknown, and they died unsung.

'You know, Sergeant Bottomley,' said Jackson at last, 'I don't know why Croker came all this way to tell me what he did, unless it was to draw attention to Parson Woodward, and therefore away from Loxley Anderson. He played the innocent when he saw me, but Mr Woodward revealed that friend Croker knew both Loxley Anderson and Galt.'

'Maybe he's the third man in the plot, sir.'

'The third shadow in the murder of Mr Wheeler? Maybe. If so, I think he's near confessing. Another weak link in a chain of crime. Now, Sergeant, I've something else to tell you about Miss Deirdre. Dr Phillips is playing host to what they term an alienist – he's a special kind of doctor who probes into people's minds. He's come to smooth out some of old Parson Woodward's problems, but I think it would do no harm for him to meet Miss Deirdre. Maybe he can probe into her mind. I've asked Mr Goodheart to pursue the matter.'

'What's this doctor's name?'

'It's a curious name, Sergeant, but then, he's a foreigner. Brant. Dr Per Cornelis Brant. He's Flemish.'

'Eh?' Bottomley clutched his chest and gave vent to a moist cough.

'Belgian. Or Dutch. One of those Low Countries. That's where he comes from. He's very clever, and was educated at some university or other in Germany.'

'And he's going to have a go at Miss Deirdre?'

'Mr Goodheart's going to persuade him. And if he succeeds, then I want you and me there on the spot when he questions her. Something might come of it.'

'A little sustenance mid-morning, Dr Cornelis Brant, is very congenial to the English temperament. The almond slices are particularly fine.'

Harry Goodheart poured his guest another cup of coffee, and indicated a flowered china plate heaped with pastries.

Dr Per Cornelis Brant glanced appreciatively around the comfortable sunlit study. He felt immensely cheered. It had been worth the journey from London to probe the layered secrets of Mr Woodward's troubled mind. Two sessions had been held so far, and the patient had responded very well. In addition, the rector's hospitality had proved quite overwhelming

'You are too good, sir. My hospital quarters in London are necessarily Spartan, and the diet sober, to say the least! Bart's is very distinguished, but it is not the Savoy.'

The sun shone on the silver locks and fuzzy beard, and glinted from the gold pince-nez. Dr Cornelis Brant contrived to look very foreign, though his English was perfect and without any notice-able accent.

'And you studied at Heidelberg, I hear? Our bishop's chaplain, the Reverend Dr Bonner, was there in the early eighties.'

'Indeed? I have doctorates from Leyden and Heidelberg, but my best work has been done at Bart's. What one may term the clinical practice of medicine is infinitely more rewarding than mastering the theory.'

'And my reverend colleague Hezekiah Woodward is pro-gressing?'

'He is, sir. An excellent subject. He is enmeshed in an appalling mystery, to which his own fixations have contributed. Further, he is suffering from a form of amnesia that I believe to be self-induced: there are times, so he tells me, when he cannot remember whether he has performed certain actions. But he is more than eager to be cured of his delusions.'

'Do you find it easy to converse with him? He has no scientific or medical training.'

'He and I choose to speak in different accretions of metaphor – what is exorcism to him, for instance, is psychotherapy to me – but we are progressing to the same end. Yes, I have no trouble in communicating with the good pastor.'

Dr Per Cornelis Brant reached for an almond slice. The coffee-pot simmered on a trivet at the side of the hearth. Harry Goodheart judged his time aright.

'Upon my soul, Doctor,' he remarked, 'I wish you'd look at another "patient" we have here in Ashgate St Lawrence. I've been thinking of ways of approaching the topic, and have just decided to ask you outright. Both myself and the senior police detective working on the case – the case in which Woodward is involved – agree that you could probably help our young "patient" to see things clearly.'

Very succinctly Harry Goodheart told the alienist about Deirdre Dovercourt's visions, and of her curious inability to see the companions of Polk in her initial experience of 1888.

Dr Cornelis Brant was absorbed by the tale. He removed his pince-nez and polished them on a voluminous white handkerchief. He seemed to hold his breath until his face was quite alarmingly red, then gave vent to a long and luxurious sigh. He put the pince-nez back into position and joined his fingertips in an apparent attitude of prayer.

'It is a classic case, as you recount it, of the subliminal self blocking the recurrence of an inconvenient or insupportable memory. You see it in the selectivity involved. The man she sees frightens her, but is unknown to her. Of the two remaining figures – well. . . .'

'Yes, Doctor, what of them?'

'One or both of them *was* known to her, but – and this is the

251

important part – the prospect of acknowledging that identity was too terrible to sustain. And so the memory was blocked out. There are learned terms we use for it, both Latin and German, but to use them here would simply demonstrate my own professional vanity. Your coffee, Rector, is quite superb.'

Harry Goodheart poured the doctor a third cup of the reviving fluid. He took none himself, and thoughtfully returned the pot to the trivet.

' "Blocked", you say. And is there any way in which your special knowledge could be used to unblock that hidden memory?'

'There is. But were I to use it, this young lady's father would brand me as a charlatan. So would her lady mother. So would you, probably.'

'A charlatan? Whatever do you mean?'

'The little closed door of memory in Miss Dovercourt's mind could be unlocked by the use of mesmerism, or hypnotism, as they are calling it now. If this young lady were to prove a suitable subject, I could place her in a mesmeric trance, and question her in such a way as to reveal the hidden images to the light of day. There, I'm speaking in yet another set of metaphors.'

Harry Goodheart sighed.

'I see what you mean, Doctor. The young lady is not actually ill, and the secret of the two figures in the churchyard belongs properly to the criminal mystery that Inspector Jackson and his colleagues are striving to solve. So it would be quite wrong to expose the young lady to mesmerism for any reason other than the restoration of her health.'

'Quite so.'

The two men sat in silence. The merry clock on the mantelpiece ticked away. The coal settled in the grate. They could both hear the coffee-pot gently simmering.

'And yet—' ventured Dr Cornelis Brant.

'Indeed! I'm sure you're right!' cried Harry Goodheart, springing up from his seat. 'We must set the matter in train as soon as possible. I'll send over to Dovercourt House and ask her brother for permission to see Miss Deirdre.'

'Her brother?'

'Yes. The Dovercourts tend to move about like chess-pieces at this time of year. Straight after what they call the May Feast, Miss Deirdre's parents leave for a visit to her Uncle Barnabas. So her brother Lionel is in charge at Dovercourt House.'

'So there are two uncles?'

'Yes, indeed. Mr Loxley Anderson lives at his seat of King's Leyland. He's Mrs Dovercourt's brother. Barnabas, the other uncle, is Mr Dovercourt's brother. He lives in Worcester.'

Goodheart tactfully omitted to mention that Barnabas was a glover by trade, living in a tall, limpet-like house built into an angle of his factory at Worcester. He had abbreviated his name for trade purposes, so that the sign painted in big red letters across the front of his busy factory read: 'Dover's Glove Works'. Deirdre only rarely ventured into her Uncle Barnabas's territory.

'If her brother gives his sanction, Mr Goodheart, I should prefer to carry out the experiment in the room from which Miss Deirdre saw the episode in 1888. The milieu, if I may use that word, will greatly assist the possibility of a successful outcome. The Haunted Room, I think you called it.'

On hearing about what was going to happen in the Haunted Room, Annie had eagerly volunteered to hold her young mistress's hand while the mesmerism took place. Lionel Dovercourt, however, was a judicious young man. He thanked her for the suggestion, but firmly sent her home for the rest of the day.

The Haunted Room emanated its usual chilly air of neglect and decay. It looked like a repository for old, unwanted furniture. There was nothing on the small round table, and no fire in the iron fireplace. The old dark portrait of Amos Dovercourt lowered from the dark panelled wall. The fateful window, though clean, was uncurtained.

Deirdre sat calmly in the straight-backed chair near the table, seemingly unaffected by the room's usual thrall. There was a faintly amused smile on her face.

Jackson, Bottomley and the rector stood behind her out of sight. Lionel, who was intensely interested in the proceedings, stood on his sister's left near the fireplace. Dr Cornelis Brant had brought a chair in from the drawing-room next door. He sat down facing his subject.

'Here we are, then, Miss Deirdre, in the Haunted Room! There is no need to be afraid. Outside, the sun is shining, and all the tombs and monuments are glowing quietly in the sun. Your brother and other gentlemen known to you are here in the room. Are you content that I should place you in a mesmeric trance?'

'Certainly. I'm not in the least afraid. What do you wish me to do?'

'I see that you are wearing an opal pendant, Miss Dovercourt. I should like to borrow it, if I may.'

Deirdre looked surprised, but without replying she took the pendant from her neck and handed it to the Belgian specialist. It was the opal that the Reverend Samuel Wheeler had given to her when she was thirteen years old.

Dr Cornelis Brant held it up to the light, suspended from its thin gold chain.

'Look at it, Miss Deirdre! Look how it glows! Just like the old tombs basking in the sun. Look at it! See how it glows. See how it grows in size. Weight . . . heaviness . . . look at it. Look at the opal. Sleep . . . sleep will come and your eyes will close. Close. Close.'

It was very quiet. Deirdre's eyes had indeed closed, and she seemed to be asleep. As Dr Cornelis Brant leaned forward towards her, the other men in the room drew further away from Deirdre, as though instinctively leaving the area free for the conduct of the experiment.

The doctor drew his hand upwards in front of Deirdre's eyes and they immediately opened. Someone gasped in awe. The opal was placed carefully and quietly on the table.

'Deirdre! Deirdre! Can you hear my voice?' The doctor's tone had become high and flute-like. It rang uncannily in the gloomy chamber.

'Yes.'

'You will hear no voice but mine, Deirdre. What voice will you hear?'

'No voice but yours.'

As the other men listened, Dr Cornelis Brant took Deirdre back to the age of thirteen. Her eyes remained open, fixed on him, and she betrayed no fear. He talked her through her experience until the point where Daniel Polk had looked up at the windows of Dovercourt House.

'There are three men beside the monument, Deirdre. One of them has paused and looked up at the window. What is his name?'

'Polk. I do not know his name.'

It came as a shock to the three men when the doctor turned to them and said in loud tones, 'By that, gentlemen, she means that although she knows his name now, she did not know it then. That is called asynchronization.'

He turned once more to Deirdre, and resumed the high, urgent tone.

'Can you see the two men who are with Polk?'

'No.'

'You can! I tell you that it is not night but day! The sun is shining and you can see the three men. Who are the other two?'

'It is not night but day. Yes. I see the other man. I know him. His name is Inspector Jackson.'

There came a strangled oath from Bottomley which he immediately suppressed. Dr Cornelis Brant held up his hand for silence.

'That cannot be his name. You do not know Inspector Jackson yet. It is 1888. You are thirteen years old. Look. Describe the man to me.'

THE DRIED-UP MAN

'He is a stout man, forty, he has a double chin. He walks like the man I do not yet know. He is one of the three. They have killed my lover and hidden him in the tomb. They have killed him. Polk, and the man I do not know.'

The doctor turned to his audience.

'What does she mean? Who is this man?'

Inspector Jackson said quietly, 'The man she sees has a general resemblance to me. I have met him, and can vouch for that.'

Jackson looked at the mesmerized girl with a sudden special understanding. That was why she had been so afraid of him! To her, Jackson seemed to be the double of the second man she had seen long ago in the churchyard, and then blotted out of her conscious memory. He was one of the 'shadows' that Craxton had seen at King's Leyland – Michael Croker.

Dr Cornelis Brant had turned again to Deirdre.

'And the third man? It is daylight. You can see him. Who is he?'

For the first time Deirdre began to show distress. She moaned and shifted her position slightly on the chair. Lionel stepped forward to bring the experiment to a close just as the flute-like voice repeated the question.

'Who is he?'

Deirdre's eyes turned from the doctor's face towards the window.

'It is my uncle, William Loxley Anderson.'

The picture of Old Amos Dovercourt fell to the floor with a crash.

For one tense moment the group was seized with a superstitious fear. The coincidence of Deirdre's terrible answer with the falling of the picture was almost too much to bear. The moment did not last long. Before Harry Goodheart could cheer the company with some sane and sober words that he had prepared, the doctor had preceded him. The high voice disappeared, to be replaced by his usual tones.

256

'Inspector Jackson,' he asked, 'does that answer make sense to you?'

'It does, sir. It confirms what Sergeant Bottomley and I already know to be the truth.'

'Is Miss Deirdre fond of this uncle?' asked Dr Cornelis Brant.

Lionel replied to the question.

'My sister likes her uncle very much. I have never cared for him, I'm afraid. There was always something still and serpent-like about him, despite his jollity.'

'Then I shall tell Miss Deirdre to forget what she has just seen. I shall restore her memory to what it was before, with the sole exception that she will now be able to visualize the second man, the man you say is called Michael Croker. Could you please draw apart once more?'

Dr Cornelis Brant drew his hand down from Deirdre's forehead to her chin, and her eyes immediately closed. He leaned very close to her and whispered for some time into her ear. He straightened up and clapped his hands. Deirdre's eyes opened.

'Certainly,' she said. 'I'm not in the least afraid. What do you wish me to do?'

The doctor placed a kindly hand on hers.

'You have already done it, my dear.'

Lionel opened the door and Deirdre passed through into the light and cheerful drawing-room. The others followed her. Some ghosts, at least, had been laid that day in Dovercourt House.

15

'And So the Ghosts Are Laid'

After dinner on the following Thursday evening, Mr Loxley Anderson indulged a fancy to stroll through the brilliantly lighted rooms of his ancient house. There was no one about.

In the front parlour the round-eyed man and the almond-eyed lady in ruffs stared as always in surprise from their carving above the mantelpiece. William Loxley and his wife Alison with their children . . . his ancestors. You couldn't see the armorial bearings properly when it was dark outside, the rampant cat and half moon of the Loxleys, the griffins of the Andersons of Newton Seneschal. . . .

Loxley Anderson sat down carefully in one of the uncomfortable upright chairs near the fireplace. It was very quiet, and the flames of the candles burnt steadily. He was deeply troubled. Whisperings had been coming to him like the noise of rats behind the wainscot. The whole operation in Cornwall had been destroyed by this Inspector Jackson. Years of careful harvesting brought to nothing. . . .

Caradyne was dead. Polk had told him to watch the papers. His prediction of Caradyne's suicide had come true. There lay the chief danger, because once Caradyne's elaborate schemes were unravelled all would be seen to point to King's Leyland. Presumably the powers that be still believed that Major Giles Redcott was the sole owner of Polwarthan. Poor old fool! He probably believed that himself.

The master of King's Leyland moved uneasily. The silence and stillness of the house were causing him to remember things best forgotten. Michael Croker. . . .

The last time he had seen Croker he had become a heavy, stuffy churchwarden. God alone knew how he could reconcile holding that office with the heinous crimes he had committed all those years ago.

Croker had been his original accomplice, a near-bankrupt builder who had joined him in a desperate gamble to exploit a little-known mine near Derby. That had been in 1875, when it had seemed that King's Leyland would fall into the hands of Loxley Anderson's many creditors. Croker and he had prospered. With what he had made from that venture he had begun the process of secret purchase that had brought the Polwarthan Mine under his control.

Loxley Anderson almost fancied that he could smell danger in the air. He was giving shelter to a man accused of two murders, a fact which made him an accessory. Very soon now Inspector Jackson would trace the killing of Samuel Wheeler back to King's Leyland. He had already sent his crafty sergeant to make Craxton say more than he should. He wondered very much what his butler had told the police. He dared not ask.

The Reverend Samuel Wheeler . . . it was best not to think about him, but on this strange memory-haunted night he could not banish him from his mind. They had hastily determined to smother him silently in his bed, but he had leapt up and ran out into the grounds. What else could Loxley Anderson have done? The lives of all of them lay in Wheeler's hands, and there had been bows and arrows lying on the grass near the butts. . . .

William Loxley Anderson was suddenly conscious of eyes

fixed on him, although he had heard no sound of anyone entering the room. He half turned in his chair and saw the black-clad figure of Daniel Polk or Mr Galt as he was called there, standing in the doorway

'You're worried, Mr Loxley Anderson. Maybe the time has come to decamp.'

Loxley Anderson stirred restlessly. He had sat too long weaving fantasies in his ancestral chambers. Mr Galt, with a different background, saw through dreams to the chill truth.

'You may be right, Galt. Our luck no longer holds. I wrote to Croker at Thirlwood Parva some days ago, warning him to look out for police activity. I've had no reply, so perhaps he's taken the hint and moved on.'

'Croker? I'd almost forgotten him. It's long days ago. It was kind of you to warn him, but I'd be wary of Croker if I were you.'

It was shrewd advice, thought Loxley Anderson. Croker had left incriminating letters lying open in his house in Yorkshire, where a young curate, Percy Field, had seen and read them while on a pastoral visit. He had urged Croker to repent. Croker had contrived to poison him, and had then hanged his lifeless body on a tree . . . that man was now a pillar of the church.

'I take your warning kindly, Mr Galt. I have no liking for Croker, but I dare say he's harmless enough these days.'

Mr Galt threw out one of his brief, basilisk glances in Loxley Anderson's direction and said, 'People are strange, Mr Loxley Anderson. You'd be surprised if you could read folk's minds.'

There was something profoundly unpleasant about Mr Galt's tone that made Loxley Anderson shiver. He got up from his chair and walked out into the corridor. Galt followed him.

Their steps took them into the Great Hall, still garlanded and festooned from the past weekend feast, but empty now and echoing.

'The Great Hall,' said Loxley Anderson. 'The panelling above the gallery came from Scone Palace. This man Inspector Jackson will find out all about Croker and his abominations. He'll find out all, and delve into everything, and trace it all back here to King's Leyland. Where is he, Galt? I have my tales ready for him, but he never comes. The third portrait from the left in the gallery is by Holbein. Is Jackson playing cat and mouse with me?'

Mr Galt glanced briefly upwards to the portrait and then made an observation.

'He could be. Perhaps he's delved deeper into Caradyne's paper mazes than we know.'

Mr Galt laid a firm heavy hand on his companion's arm.

'Keep your courage firm, Mr Loxley Anderson, and don't give way to fear. Gather your assets about you, and put as great a distance as possible between yourself and Jackson.'

Polk moved towards the door that would take him to his private apartments. He ventured a few parting words.

'I shall leave in the dark hours of this coming morning, before you are up, and make my way to Newhaven. From there I'll slip aboard the Dieppe steamer. Once I'm in Belgium this country will never see me again. Goodbye, Mr Loxley Anderson. I'm going away on foot, so I make you a present of my carriage, which is in your coach-house. Realize your assets quickly, and decamp. Otherwise it's the gallows for us all. Goodnight.'

Ever soft-footed, Mr Galt had gone before Loxley Anderson had raised his eyes to the door.

The conversation with Polk had helped Loxley Anderson to renew his sense of determination. The time had come to leave England, and the means of achieving that aim lay in the iron safe in his study, a private retreat that occupied the ground floor of a small, separate two-storey building looking on to a paved court. It had at one time been the steward's offices, and above the lintel of the door was carved:

Gyve Account Thereof in ye Day of Judgement: AD 1536

Loxley Anderson worked steadily at his papers until just after the stable clock had struck eleven, when he heard a low knock at the door. Who could it be at this late hour? For a moment he could not recognize the portly figure standing on the threshold. When he did so, he drew back, and motioned to the man to enter.

'Come in, Croker,' said Loxley Anderson. 'I'm glad you received my warning. As you see, the time for flight has come. You and I must follow Mr Galt and disappear to the Continent.'

The old panelled study was warm and secret, lit discreetly by shaded oil-lamps. There was a blazing fire in the grate. On the desk he had spread out a number of bundled papers and stout wads of Bank of England notes. An iron safe set in the wall near the fireplace stood open.

'Negotiable bonds, Croker, which my contacts in Amsterdam will sell without trouble. Sixty thousand pounds' worth.'

Michael Croker deposited his ample bulk on an upright chair. His double-chinned face was unshaven, and his brown suit seemed to hang on him as though he had suddenly lost weight. His eyes were wild and restless.

Loxley Anderson suddenly sensed danger. This man, his early partner in iniquity, was not listening to his words. What was it about him that sounded such an urgent alarm?

'Take courage, man! "The good old times are dead", as Tennyson says, and we must make our escape while we can. I'll be very sad to leave this patrimony of mine, but no blame attaches to my son. He will be furnished with money, and in the fullness of time he will succeed me here. You, I'm sure, will have made your own plans.'

Loxley Anderson began to fill a Gladstone bag with the notes and bonds. He planned to walk to a nearby town where there was a station, and make his way discreetly across the country to Harwich. Like Mr Galt, he had long ago mapped out his way of escape.

Croker still seemed not to hear him. He began to speak in a

262

lisping, canting bleat from which Loxley Anderson physically recoiled.

'My mind is sorely troubled by the remembrance of my sins, Mr Loxley Anderson. I'm compelled to rehearse my wicked deeds, when for so many years I've been able to thrust them from me. I think of the death of poor Mr Percy Field, and of the terrible fate of the Reverend Samuel Wheeler. Where can I hide from the Wrath to come?'

What could have taken possession of this seedy poisoner turned master-builder? What did it mean? What lay behind it?

Croker's flaccid features had broken out in a sweat, and his eyes roamed around the study, fixing themselves anywhere but upon his host's face.

Loxley Anderson snapped shut the Gladstone bag and looked at Croker with burning contempt. A craven fellow after all, a canting hypocrite. How distant he felt from the likes of him!

'You fool, Croker! The time for repentance has long gone, so you can cease preaching this vile sermon. You're becoming unhinged through fear. Take thought for the future. The time has come for flight.'

Croker's next words chilled him to the marrow.

'Put aside your thoughts of flight, Mr Loxley Anderson! Such words are folly. Can you not see that the time of our punishment has come? I knew that all was lost when I received your letter. They may already have sent the police to Thirlwood Parva. As for me, I will hide the truth no more. I intend to go straight away and confess the truth. Who knows? I may not hang. They may judge me insane, and so spare my life.'

In a bitter moment of truth, as Croker's eyes finally met his, Loxley Anderson saw the cunning smile of self-regard flash across the heavy, sweating features. This traitor had almost certainly approached the police already to take soundings. The hypocrite knew the game was up, and had seen a path away from the gallows where his betrayed confederates would hang.

How could he bear the shame of breathing the same air as this base creature? Had he parted from the true and loyal Polk only to be yoked to this cringing Judas? Was this leering, nodding viper *laughing* beneath that loathsome smirk? Well, he could go the way of the others.

Loxley Anderson lunged in fury at Croker. The two men struggled for mastery, blundering against the furniture until a glowing oil-lamp was knocked over and smashed to pieces on the blazing hearth.

At twenty minutes past eleven, Inspector Jackson and Sergeant Bottomley, accompanied by a uniformed constable, drove in a pony and trap through the proud entrance gates of King's Leyland. In Jackson's pocket were the warrants for the arrest of William Loxley Anderson, and one Galt, thought to be a fugitive from justice.

The house was in darkness except for one detached portion where the dim glow of oil-lamps could be seen. It was a deceptively serene view, an old black-and-white timbered wing of two storeys with diamond-paned windows and twisted brick chimneys, separate from the main house.

'It might be as well to call at that lighted building first, Sergeant,' said Jackson. 'I take no great pleasure in these late-night arrests, but in this case I think we're more than justified. Tomorrow would be too late—'

His words were lost in the sudden mind-numbing explosion of the building that they were approaching. Later, Sergeant Bottomley would say that he had seen the quick brightening of the light within, betokening the bursting of an oil-lamp. The windows of the detached building exploded with a deafening crash, and in a moment the whole edifice seemed to rise into the air on a huge ball of fire, flinging timbers and stones and ruin in all directions. The horse reared in terror and bolted, hurling the policemen out on to the grass. It thundered off into the trees, smashing the trap to pieces in its frantic instinct to escape.

By some miracle the rest of the house escaped burning. The fire-engines arrived in time to keep the flames away from the adjacent Agincourt hall, but they could make no impression on the white-hot inferno of Loxley Anderson's study, engendered from ancient dry timbers and the demon of fire.

Almost in mockery it rained lightly throughout the night, and soon after dawn the firemen pushed their way through the mess of fine ash and charred timbers to bring out the calcined remains of Michael Croker, Master Builder, and William Loxley Anderson, Esquire, Gentleman.

Inspector Jackson filled his lungs with the fresh May morning air. The sun was already strong, and the night's rain had soon dried. Earlier, a shocked and silent woman from the kitchen had given him a mug of strong tea. He had stood sipping it in the great Agincourt hall of King's Leyland, where a white-faced Craxton, seated at a scrubbed table, had dictated a long statement to Sergeant Bramble. Jackson had deliberately chosen to send for the old sergeant to share his triumph in solving the riddle of the Dried-Up Man.

'I saw my master seize a bow and arrow from the grass, draw to the shoulder, and fire. The arrow entered Mr Wheeler's back, and with a cry he fell to the ground. . . .'

Jackson had wandered out of the hall into the open air. There were others there now to supervise the winding-up of the case, uniformed officers from Copton Vale, and a man from the coroner's office. He stood before the swollen, blackened timbers that had once been Loxley Anderson's study. It was a familiar sight to him: heaps of soaked ash, marked with runnels of water, bulbous wood, charred brick. But the tormenting images of his own tragedy seemed somehow to have receded.

He turned over one piece of charred wood with the toe of his boot. He saw that it had once carried some kind of inscription, and the raised white letters seemed to speak aloud with special significance:

Gyve Account Thereof in ye Day of Judgement

Jackson turned away from the great Tudor mansion and began to walk down the carriage drive to the Ashgate road.

And so the ghosts are laid, he reflected, and the innocent dead avenged. Robert Elmore. The Reverend Samuel Wheeler. Percy Field.

It had been a complex and dangerous case, the stark facts of murder for gain obscured by a fantastic overlay of superstition and fanciful legend. But now the truth was known, and some kind of justice had been done.

He reached the gate pillars of King's Leyland. He could glimpse a handsome open carriage beyond the paling, with a young man in capes on the box. There was a lady sitting upright in the carriage.

He passed through the gates, and saw that it was Sarah Brown. She swung open the carriage door and stepped down into the road.

'You don't mind, do you, Saul?' she said timidly. 'Me coming, I mean, and you so busy?'

'Mind? No, I don't mind. How did you get here, Sarah?'

He was able for the first time to look at her properly, and to realize how young she looked, and how her dark-green dress complemented her fair skin and her rich brown hair. No, he didn't mind her coming like this. Sarah Brown was his next-door neighbour, a widow of thirty-eight. He was a widower of forty-six. Why shouldn't she come?

'I had to come, Saul. We've all read about it in the paper – about what happened to you in Cornwall. Mr Bottomley

arranged it with the rector at Ashgate after I telegraphed him . . .
I . . . you don't mind? This is the rector's carriage. He hopes that
you'll avail yourself of it to return to Ashgate. That's what he
said: "avail yourself".'

Jackson smiled. He remembered Bottomley's impertinent
question: 'Why don't you like her?' and the teasing bit he'd
added after that: 'She likes *you*'. Well, he did like her. Very much.

'So Bottomley arranged it, did he? I'll have a few words to say
to him next time I see him.'

'Is he not here with you?'

'No, Sarah. He's otherwise occupied. I'll tell you all about it
when we get home. Suffice it to say that there were three
shadows. Two of them perished back there last night. The other
shadow's still at large.'

Jackson glanced briefly back in the direction of King's
Leyland and then set his face towards the Ashgate road. He
helped his companion up into Harry Goodheart's carriage, got in
beside her, and closed the door.

'Come on, Sarah Brown,' said Jackson. 'Let's avail ourselves!'

Annie Jevons sat in the chair beside her bed in the tiny bedroom.
She had moved in to Dovercourt House at Mr Lionel's request,
in case Miss Deirdre became upset at her uncle's death. Mr and
Mrs Dovercourt would be returning from Worcester the next
day.

It was nice to be resident again, particularly as Miss Deirdre
did not seem very upset at all. She knew all about the horrible
murder, and her heart had hardened against her wicked uncle
who had shot her lover with an arrow. It was like a fairytale, but
not droopy.

It was quiet up on the third floor. The little room had a
cheerful wallpaper, white, with little red flowers. You could join
the flowers up in your mind and see faces.

Mr Lionel had gone over to Newton Seneschal for the day.

Miss Deirdre was lying down for an hour. Someone was running a bath.

You could hear the bath being filled up on the third floor, because there was a great big tank in the attic, and the water rushed down pipes hidden in the walls. The bath was a huge enamel thing, with mahogany sides and big brass taps. There was a lever, and when you pulled it the water began to pour down the drain. Gungle, gungle. Annie laughed.

Who could be taking a bath at this time of day? Three o'clock on a quiet May afternoon?

Annie ventured out into the passage, and tiptoed down the little staircase to the floor below. Maybe Mr Lionel had come back after all. She could see the half-open door of the bathroom, and hear the water thundering into the bath. The shadows moved behind the door.

Annie's hand flew to her mouth to stifle the scream that rose unbidden. A man was standing beside the bath, watching the water filling it up. A heavy, cruel-looking man with an unmoving face, looking thoughtfully down at the water.

The little maid felt sick and faint. Who was this bad man? Why did he want to take a bath in another gentleman's house? She crept lightly back to the staircase and up to the third floor. Once in her room, she lay on the bed and listened.

After what seemed an age the flow of water stopped. There was silence for a while, and then she heard heavy, slow footsteps mounting the stairs. Someone was coming up for her. Or for Miss Deirdre? Heavy steps. They passed her door, sounding like thunder. She heard the door of Miss Deirdre's bedroom open.

A quick, high scream. Silence.

The footsteps, heavier now and slower, thundered past her door. Annie lay in the grip of total fear. She was a brave girl, and wanted to venture out of her room, but her body would not let her.

More hideous silence, and then, from the floor below, a vile scuffling and dragging and grunting, followed by an echoing plunge of something heavy into water.

Annie began to cry.

Heavy footsteps came again, up the stairs at the end of the passage, and thundering again past her door. She could hear a panting, grunting sound. The footsteps turned and came back. They stopped at her door.

When Annie saw the handle turning she sprang from the bed and flattened herself against the wall near the window. There was still a chance of escape. She could fling herself from the open window into the cobbled yard below.

As the door swung open her eyes widened in terror.

'It's all right, little chick!'

She was just able to register that it was her friend Sergeant Bottomley before she fainted in a little heap beneath the open window.

Deirdre Dovercourt opened her eyes in fright. Some horrible image lurked at the edge of her memory, a thick-featured, dead-eyed man stretching out his hands towards her. . . . She had screamed and fainted. Where was she now? Someone took her hand, and a rough but gentle voice enquired, 'How are you now, Deirdre?'

She was lying on her own bed, and beside her sat Sergeant Bottomley. It was his hand that enclosed hers. She looked at him.

'You've hurt your head.' There was a cut above his left eyebrow, where the blood had already clotted. His face was bruised.

'Yes. Everything's all right now, my dear. You don't mind me calling you that, do you? I'll stop it and be very respectful once you're better. You've had an awful shock, poor girl.'

Deirdre smiled. 'You are funny,' she said. 'Annie told me you said funny things. What happened? Was it that man Polk who came in here? The man I used to see in the churchyard – my silent, staring ghost?'

'It was indeed Daniel Polk, my dear. He was the man who helped to murder the Reverend Mr Wheeler. He also murdered Mr Robert Elmore, and another man called Calderdale.'

'Where is he now?'

'He's dead. Drowned, but not in the sea.'

'Drowned? How could he be drowned? He was here only minutes ago.'

'You're seventeen now, aren't you, Deirdre? The same age as my Rachel Elizabeth. So you're old enough not to have any more secrets kept from you. There have been too many secrets.'

He released Deirdre's hand and she sat up on the bed, looking enquiringly at him.

'That man, as you say, was the man you saw in 1888, looking up at you from the graveyard. You saw him again, in 1890. He was always curious, because he knew you'd seen him. He used to come back from time to time, and look. He wouldn't hurt you because he genuinely liked your late uncle. But then your uncle died in the fire, and that man felt free to cover his tracks for good. He came here today to murder you.'

Deirdre paled. The kind, appraising eyes of Sergeant Bottomley looked out from the flushed, boozy face with admiration and concern. It encouraged her to remember a chance encounter. . . .

'Mr Bottomley, I've just realized . . . I passed one of Uncle William's guests in the corridor at King's Leyland on the night of the dance. I fancied I'd seen him before, but he was dressed as a gentleman. I'm sure now that it was Polk.'

'So it was! He probably thought that you had recognized him, and that's why he came here today. But I have hardly let you out of my sight since I knew what was going on. I was in the house, waiting. He came, and he filled the bath on the floor below with water. Then he went to fetch you. He would have hit you to make you unconscious, but you fainted instead.

270

'He took you down to the bathroom, where he was going to drown you. He liked drowning people. Very good at it, he was. But I was waiting for him. He dropped you on the floor like a rag doll and went for me. He and I never liked each other. Anyway, the upshot of it was that I knocked him out and he fell into the bath. He drowned almost immediately.'

Deirdre was quiet for a while. She suddenly realized how much she loved her own uncomplicated father and mother, and the unfussy, bustling household of a town merchant. Her mother, she knew, would not grieve long for wicked Uncle William: she was of too practical a nature. The next thing to concentrate upon was the matter of Master Rupert Selden, aged seventeen.

Deirdre rose from the bed and looked out of the window. A little crowd had gathered in front of the house, and one or two motherly women were busy gaining entrance. A burly figure in a brown suit joined them, firmly pushing his way through the crowd.

'Look, Mr Bottomley! Here's Inspector Jackson. I'm sorry I behaved so boorishly to him. Perhaps you'd tell him so? I expect he's come to fetch you away.'

'I expect he has, miss,' said Bottomley, ruefully scratching his head. 'I've a feeling I'm in for a telling-off, which I must bear like a man!'

Deirdre laughed and kissed Bottomley on the cheek.

'I think you're the most wonderful man I've ever met. None of the things they say about you in the town are true. I must go and find Annie. When I'm married, I shall bribe her to be my personal maid. I don't know what I'd do without her.'

Deirdre Dovercourt slipped lightly through the doorway and was gone.

Herbert Bottomley turned away from the window. He stopped for a moment, a puzzled expression crossing his flushed face.

'What did she mean by that? "None of the things they say about you are true"? What am I supposed to have done?'

271

Shaking his head ruefully, he went out into the passage, and carefully closed the door of Deirdre's room.

In his workshop at Bridge Rise, Matthew Littlechild, metal-worker, tied a piece of string around the box of tin ban-devils and put it away at the back of a cupboard. They would not be wanted now.

Not until the next time.

me